ROYAL REBEL

By the Author

A Royal Romance

Heart of the Pack

Courting the Countess

Royal Rebel

ROYAL REBEL

by

Jenny Frame

2017

ROYAL REBEL

ISBN 13: 978-1-62639-893-1

This Trade Paperback Original Is Published By
Bold Strokes Books, Inc.
P.O. Box 249
Valley Falls, NY 12185

First Edition: May 2017

CREDITS
EDITOR: RUTH STERNGLANTZ
PRODUCTION DESIGN: STACIA SEAMAN
COVER DESIGN BY SHERI (GRAPHICARTIST2020@HOTMAIL.COM)

Acknowledgments

As always, thank you to Radclyffe and the whole BSB family for fostering such a great supportive community for us writers to be a part of. Also, thank you to all the Bold Strokes staff who work tirelessly behind the scenes to make sure every little thing is done to bring our books to fruition.

A huge thank you to my editor, Ruth Sternglantz. A lot of writers dread editing, but I always look forward to it with excitement, as every time Ruth helps build my writing skills and I learn something new.

Thank you to my friends Amy and Christine, who always support me and my writing and give me a friendly ear.

A big shout of thanks to all those readers who have bought a book and contacted me with lovely emails and messages. I appreciate every one and your support.

Thanks to my family, and especially my mum and dad, who help me on almost a daily basis.

Lou, you are my inspiration, my strength, and my one true love. Twelve years might have passed since we first became a couple, but I know in my heart that you love me more and more each day, and just like Lex and Roza, I will always be your princess. Thank you for everything you do for me and our crazy Barney boy. I love you, darling.

For Lou
ego dilecto meo et dilectus meus
I am my beloved's and my beloved is mine

CHAPTER ONE

The ticking of an antique clock mirrored the nervous beat of Princess Rozala's heart as she waited outside her father's study. She had been in this ornate waiting area inside Ximeno Palace in Denbourg's capital too many times over the years, awaiting the wrath of her father the King, but none of her past indiscretions could compare with the situation she was in now.

Rozala's eyes were drawn to the muted twenty-four-hour rolling news channel playing across from her on the wall. It showed footage of her at various glitzy social events, laughing, dancing, and generally not behaving like the princess she was supposed to be—and that's why she was sitting here, why she *always* found herself here, because she wasn't the princess her father wanted her to be.

The footage changed to her clasping the arm of her now ex-girlfriend, Thea Brandt. It struck her now that she had been letting herself be led around like a lamb by the much older and impeccably dressed businesswoman. She had been introduced to Thea at a party six months earlier. At twenty-seven years her senior, Thea had seemed so strong, so powerful, and Rozala quickly fell under her spell.

Tears welled up in her eyes as she remembered their burgeoning relationship. The first few months, she enjoyed Thea's controlling personality. She felt safe, protected, and looked after, but it soon began to become suffocating, as Thea told her what to wear, where to be seen, and when to see her family. As much as she began to feel their relationship was wrong, she couldn't seem to leave and felt panicked about life without her, to the point she had begged Thea to stay with her in their many arguments.

Thea had conditioned her to believe that she couldn't exist without her, and it was only the recent revelations about Thea's business dealings splashed all over the media that prompted Rozala to leave. Even now she felt scared about being apart from her.

King Christian's private secretary, Lord Dahl, came out of her father's office and bowed to her. "The King will see you now, Your Royal Highness."

The only time he ever wanted to see her was when she'd done something wrong.

She stood, pausing to follow the private secretary's gaze to the TV news. It had changed from images of Rozala to footage of UN troops engaged in artillery and bomb strikes in the Middle East, and shame simmered within her. She wondered how things had turned out so badly.

With a sigh she walked into her father's office, and found him writing on some documents. The King was an old-fashioned man in all ways and didn't like to rely on computers when he didn't have to.

She stood silently in front of his desk waiting for him to speak first. King Christian's office was hung with many paintings of the past kings and queens of Denbourg on the walls, and Rozala felt their eyes stare at her accusingly.

After an age of silence, King Christian said without looking up, "Sit down, Rozala."

Determined to be defiant as always, she replied, "I prefer to stand, Father."

He snapped his head up from his papers and gave her a frosty look that matched the atmosphere in the room.

"As you wish." King Christian put his pen to the side and clasped his hands. "Where do I even start with you, Rozala? You have no idea of the scandal and trouble you have brought to the country and your family. The prime minister has informed me that the media speculation about Thea Brandt is true. She is an arms and drug dealer who is part of a global crime syndicate. She has been selling arms to unfriendly countries and terrorists that have been using them against our own UN troops. Regiments of our troops that—may I remind you—have your cousins and extended family serving in them."

The House of Ximeno-Bogdana-de Albert, of which she was part, had close and distant relations spread throughout every European royal house, and many of them served as part of their countries' armed forces. It made Roza feel sick to think that someone she thought she'd loved had put them in danger.

"I swear I had no idea, Father. If I did, I would never—"

❖

"Of course you didn't know. You were too busy partying with your glamorous, unconventional, and criminal friends. Rozala, when will you realize you are not a celebrity? You're a member of the royal family with many duties to perform. I thank God your brother Augustus was born to be my heir."

Each sentence from her father's mouth was like a sword stabbing her in the stomach. It had always been like this. As a little child she had tried to gain her father's attention and acceptance, but she could never do anything to please him, so she'd started doing the wrong thing just to anger him.

"I don't need to remind you that your brother's wedding is in six months' time, and I will not have this cloud of scandal hanging over my heir. The prime minister believes that with careful diplomacy we can clean up this mess with the country and our allies, but you need to keep a low profile. You're going to stay with your aunt and cousins in London."

"You're sending me away?" Rozala said with surprise.

"George will be a good influence on you, and it will allow this situation to calm down. You will be assigned new bodyguards. The last protection officers obviously failed in their task if they didn't keep you away from these types of people."

Rozala was so hurt, and so very angry. "You can't just send me away like a child, away from my friends, my life—everything is here, in Denbourg."

"That is exactly why you need to go."

She folded her arms defiantly. "I won't go. I'm not leaving."

King Christian jumped up and leaned across the desk. "You will go and do exactly as you are told, even if I have to carry you onto the plane myself. I will not have the House of Ximeno-Bogdana-de Albert brought down by a girl who doesn't know how to behave as her station demands."

The anger and disgust in her father's eyes shocked Rozala. He had been angry before many times but not like this. Tears started to roll down her cheeks, and she wiped them away quickly.

"I've never been good enough for you, have I?"

King Christian sat back down, his anger now under control. "Go back to your apartments and start to make your preparations. You leave tomorrow."

Rozala walked to the office door, but just before she opened it she turned and looked at the painting of her mother on the wall. "I took her away from you, didn't I? Every time you look at me, you are reminded of what you lost. I think you wish I had never been born. You wish it had been just you, Augustus, and Mama."

He held her gaze for a few moments before he simply said, "Go, Rozala."

She slammed the door and with shaking fingers tapped the mobile phone on her wrist to call her best friend and lady in waiting, Cressida. "Get to my apartment and start packing, Cressie. We're going on an extended trip to the United States, and we are going to party like we never have before."

Rozala didn't stop to meet up with her new secret service bodyguards, but as she sped out the palace gates, she saw their black armoured vehicles pull in behind her sports car seamlessly. Her grip on her steering wheel tightened just as surely as the royal shackles were tightening on her life.

"I've got to get out of here."

Some of the media who were encamped outside Ximeno Palace took to their cars and high-speed bikes to follow her. She tried to switch routes but just couldn't shake them off her tail.

Since this story about her girlfriend—ex-girlfriend—had broken, the media had gone wild, and they had besieged her. In a way Rozala believed she deserved what she was getting. At least the scales had finally dropped from her eyes and she'd ended the relationship.

Rozala felt a bump to the side of her car as a photographer's bike got too close, and she swerved dangerously across the lane of traffic, shooting headlong into a pole by the side of the road.

❖

Queen Georgina watched with awe as Bea threw her head back and moaned low and long, as the waves of pleasure surged through her body. She straddled George, grinding her hips and sex on the fingers buried deeply inside her, coaxing every last bit of pleasure from her body.

George gazed at her with a mixture of lust and wonderment. "You are so beautiful like that."

Bea let George's fingers slip from her body but held her position astride her partner. She grinned and said, "The things you do with your fingers are beautiful."

"Well, Mrs. Buckingham"—George used the nickname they had coined on their honeymoon. Bea had remarked that she craved the time when they were alone, when she wasn't the Queen Consort, but just simply George's wife. In an instant, George had christened her this sweet term of endearment, and Bea loved it—"I have to keep you satisfied, since half the world would like to steal you away from me." George joked, but there was truth to it.

The world had fallen in love with their new Queen Consort, and just as George had predicted, Bea's irreverent and approachable style won the people's hearts and minds.

After a short honeymoon together on the royal yacht, they'd returned to duty and a six-month world tour. Everywhere they went, people wanted to meet the fairy-tale girl who had become a Queen Consort, and no one was disappointed when they met her.

The tour promoting Britain's business and trade was a roaring success, and when they returned, Bea had thrown herself into her charity work and had become a style icon the world over, helping UK designers make their name across the globe. Yes, George knew she was one lucky monarch.

Bea chuckled and slipped back into bed and into George's arms. "I think I'm the lucky one, Georgie."

They lay in silence for a few moments, drinking in the warmth of the afterglow. It was five thirty on a Monday morning at the start of a busy week at Buckingham Palace. George was always up well before Bea, so she had time to work out with her personal dresser and close protection officer, Captain Cameron, in the gym before starting her workday. This morning she'd returned from the gym and was going to dress when Bea enticed her back to bed.

"What inspired your accosting me and taking advantage of me?" George asked with a smile.

Bea ran her fingers from George's cheekbone down her shoulders and arms. "The way you looked, fresh from the shower earlier. Your muscles were pumped from your exercise and your hair was wet and sexy, and that made *me* feel wet and sexy."

George kissed her head. "You're always sexy."

"I love this. Just lying with you," Bea said, burrowing her head further into George's neck. "I can almost make believe we aren't in a palace, and the whole world isn't waiting for us outside those bedroom doors."

"You do feel at home here, don't you? You would tell me if you weren't happy here." George recognised what a huge change it had been for Bea to go from her small family home with her mum and dad to a big impersonal palace.

Bea said, "Of course I'm happy, but this isn't home. Windsor is home. It's where we go every weekend to be together, where Mum and Dad live, where we fell in love, and where I can be just your wife, just Mrs. Buckingham, not the Consort. Buckingham Palace is our office."

"You're right, of course," George said.

She remembered the joy on Bea's face the day she took her and Bea's parents to see the large Primrose Cottage on the Windsor estate. Bea's mum and dad hadn't said anything, but she could tell they—and Bea—were worried about Bea becoming distanced from them, as Bea's new duties took her away to all corners of the globe.

With her parents at Windsor, Bea was happy in the knowledge that her family was close, plus George wanted them to be well taken care of. She had become very fond of both Reg and Sarah, and the media intrusion and security concerns made it impossible for them to live at their former home.

"How much time do we have? Can we have breakfast together? I don't have any engagements until lunchtime," Bea asked.

"Yes, I have a surprisingly light day for a Monday. I need to finish my boxes by eleven, then take the helicopter to Newcastle. I'm touring a new factory, and then we have the premiere theatre performance tonight."

Bea rolled on top of her again and held George's wrists above her head. "Excellent, I'm sure your breakfast can wait for ten minutes." Bea gave her one of those teasing looks that made her heart and her sex beat in anticipation.

George could have easily removed herself from Bea's grasp, but she was quite happy to be under her wife's control for whatever she had in mind.

"Let me wash you, Your Majesty."

George groaned out loud. That one sentence flashed an image of Bea on her knees in the large shower, making her come with her mouth. Bea was a strong, confident woman, and that made these little moments of apparent submission all the more exciting.

"Yes, yes—now, let's go."

❖

Bea poured George's coffee just as her partner walked into the breakfast room. Bea looked to the young footman waiting by the door and said, "You can serve now, thank you, Sam."

Their food was served and they ate in quiet companionship as the news played on the wall, and they both read morning newspaper websites.

An item came on the news about the upcoming state visit to Britain by President Loka of Vospya. Crowds of protestors were gathered outside both the embassy and the Houses of Parliament every day, creating as much noise and disruption as possible.

Bea felt more and more angry the closer the state visit got. "I don't know why we're having him here, Georgie. It'll make me sick to have him stay and give him hospitality."

The small but oil- and gas-rich Eastern European country of Vospya had quickly earned the reputation of one of the world's worst human rights records since President Loka led a coup against the democratically elected government there.

George took a sip of water and patted her lips dry with the cloth napkin. "We've already been through this, Bea. We have no choice. We are servants of the government and the prime minister, and we must welcome whomever they wish to offer the hand of friendship to. It's not always pleasant, but service comes before self."

"Bodicea Dixon makes a huge thing about Britain being a liberal democracy, but when there's a trade agreement at stake, she's willing to shut her eyes to their appalling human rights record." Bea was barely restraining her temper. President Loka's military coup had set his country back a hundred years. Gay people, women, and generally anyone not agreeing with him were brutally oppressed.

"It's the way it has to be. We are servants of the democratically elected government," George said firmly.

To make matters worse the news channel reported next on a royal exclusive. Bea hated the speculation she got in the press.

"I'll put it off," George said.

Bea sighed. "No, I want to know what imaginary story they've got about us now."

The pictures showed the royal couple on a visit to a whisky factory in Scotland, as the voice-over described: *At the end of the tour, Their Majesties were given a sample of the finest casked whisky, but the Queen Consort passed on the offer. Our sources tell us this could be due to a royal baby on the way. We expect an announcement any day now."*

"Bloody idiots," Bea shouted and threw her napkin onto her plate. "There's a new story about me being pregnant every bloody week. We have to put out so many denials to the press, I've lost count. I feel like a baby-making machine not a person."

"I thought you wanted lots of children with me," George said with disappointment.

Now Bea felt bad. Children were a touchy subject between them. George had wanted to start a family as soon as they came home from the world tour, and had in fact given her doctors at their clinic all the stem cell samples needed to create their child as soon as they were married. Bea could become pregnant at the private London clinic anytime, but she was reluctant.

"You know I do, so don't pout. I just need time to settle into this life first. If I'm not settled, how can I bring a child into the world who will be glared at by the media from the first day of their life? I know you want an heir—"

"If that's what you think, then I obviously haven't explained myself properly. I don't just want an heir. I want a child with you, Bea. A child brought about by our love. A little piece of us, to love, protect, and care for. I don't see what's so wrong with that."

When George put it like that, she couldn't see anything wrong with that—in fact, everything seemed right with it. In her mind she saw an image of George, so big and strong, holding their baby in her arms, and Bea's heart fluttered.

They ate on in silence for a few minutes before George said, "Gussy called me about Roza. She'll travel tomorrow. Are you sure you don't mind her staying indefinitely?"

"Of course not. She's family."

George took her hand and tenderly caressed it with her fingers. "I really feel badly for her. Brought up without her mother, and Uncle Christian is a very old-fashioned father. It seems to me she has just been crying out for love, attention, and affection. That scoundrel Thea Brandt knew exactly which buttons to press with her."

"I was thinking, Georgie. She needs an occupation while she's here. Something to give her a new perspective. Why don't we send her to work at Timmy's?"

Bea had given up her job at the hospice charity when she became the consort. But Timmy's was still very close to her heart, and she had now become its royal patron.

"That's an excellent idea, my darling. There's nothing better to make you appreciate your responsibilities than trying to help others."

"My thoughts exactly. I'll make a call and organize it."

"Do you think your new director can handle Roza? She's quite a handful," George said.

Bea smiled smugly. "Lennox King? Oh, I think she'll handle her very well."

Just then a breaking news story on TV caught their attention.

"We are just getting reports that Princess Rozala of Denbourg has been involved in a high-speed car crash, not far from Ximeno Palace."

"Oh God, Georgie." Bea gasped.

George immediately called her private secretary. "Bastien, Princess Rozala's been involved in an accident. I need you to find out everything you can."

CHAPTER TWO

Lennox King pounded her feet on the treadmill below her, trying to strain every last bit of energy from her body. Sweat dripped down her forehead and she quickly wiped it away with her hand. The high tempo music in her ears and the adrenaline shooting through her body were taking her towards that special place that gave her the best natural high she could get.

She glanced down at the timer and saw she had just over a minute left to go. The treadmill was already set on a steep incline, but she wanted more, wanted to push her body further.

"Computer? Incline up two."

Immediately the running track moved upward so Lennox was running at breakneck speed virtually uphill.

Lennox felt the increased acidic pain in her legs straight away, and that slight moment of panic when her body told her that she couldn't do it, but she shook that off and closed her eyes.

Push, push, she told herself.

Her lungs burned intensely as if they couldn't get enough oxygen into them, and then it happened. She got past her body's point of no return, the point where her body stopped resisting, and she was hit with the most intense burst of pure pleasure.

Lennox let out a groan and finally the timer beeped and the treadmill started to slow and lower to the ground. She fell forward and leaned her upper body over the front of the machine. "Jesus." She was gasping, desperately trying to get her breath back.

As hard as it was, and as hard as her body was screaming in rebellion at what she had just put it through, the aftershocks of pleasure still spread all over her body. "Better than sex."

She grabbed her towel hanging on the side and wiped her face and ran it through her sweaty short brown hair. Only then when she came out of her own personal bubble did she notice the other gym patrons.

They were spread over different cardio machines that faced a wall projecting a bank of TV channels. Rolling news and sports, and the music to which her earbuds were currently hooked up. The gym wasn't too busy, seeing as it was lunchtime, and that's how Lennox liked it. She hated the gym in the evening when all the people came to be seen, and not to truly work out.

Lennox took a big swig from her water bottle when something on the news channel caught her eye. The breaking news banner flashed across the screen, and she quickly told the computer to switch to the news channel.

She saw footage of a white sports car with its front end crushed into a pole, and then the reporter started to say, *"Denbourg's under-fire royal, Princess Rozala, is in the midst of more drama today after she sped away from Ximeno Palace and her protection team this afternoon, and became involved in an apparent car accident with members of the press. At the moment we haven't been able to ascertain her condition. A five-mile exclusion zone has been implemented around the palace and the accident, to ensure the princess's security and for police investigations. This comes on the back of a troubled few days for the princess the media dub the Royal Rebel..."*

Lennox watched intently as the footage switched from the scene of the accident to that of the princess attending glamorous parties and hanging on the arm of a much older woman. The princess was a beautiful young woman, Lennox thought, but if the press were to be believed, quite a handful. As she got wrapped up in the story, a woman's voice interrupted her. "You really push yourself hard. I wish I had your stamina."

Lennox looked down to her side and saw a blond woman leaning against her machine. She smiled, stepped down beside her, and wrapped her towel around her neck. "I like to keep in good shape."

Lennox felt the woman's eyes caress her shoulder muscles and arms, while the woman stroked her fingernails seductively down Lennox's neck.

"I can see that. My name is Gill, by the way."

Lennox could tell she was being hit on, and it wasn't a rare occurrence in the gym. She wasn't arrogant but knew that her tall, solid body and confident demeanour were attractive to women, and it was something that she had exploited in the past—but not any more.

She took Gill's hand and noticed the wedding band and large engagement ring on her finger. "Lennox King."

Gill took a step towards her and gently caressed her biceps. "I've seen you a few times in here, Lennox. You work harder than anyone I've seen and leave without saying a word to anyone. I just had to come up and introduce myself. Would you like to get some coffee after you've finished?"

A few years ago, she wouldn't have thought twice about it. They would be having sex in the changing room by now, regardless of the rings on Gill's finger. The shame that her memories brought her were her constant companion. She looked down to the Roman numerals tattooed on her wrist and tried to gulp away the sick feeling inside.

"I'm sorry, Gill. I have to get back to work."

"Maybe next time? I'm at the gym quite often during the week." Gill took another step into her personal space and whispered, "It doesn't have to be anything serious. I appreciate discretion."

Lennox lifted her water bottle from the holder on the machine and said, "I'm sorry. I don't do casual." She took a long swig of water. *I don't do anything any more.* Before Gill had the chance to push it any further, she ended the conversation. "Excuse me, I need to get started on my weights or I'll never make it back to the office in time. Nice meeting you, Gill."

Lennox walked off and brought the conversation to an end. As she walked away she heard Gill say, "You should learn to relax and have some fun when it's offered, Lennox. You know where I am."

That's the problem, Lennox sighed to herself. She'd had more *fun* than any one person should ever have.

❖

"There's nothing wrong with me, Doctor." Princess Rozala lay on a private hospital bed while the doctor ran a handheld body scanner over her body.

"If you'll permit me, Your Royal Highness. I have to check for internal injuries."

All Roza had wanted was to get out of the palace without her new security entourage following, meet her lady-in-waiting, and get out of the country and away from her father. That idea had fallen apart when she had swerved off the road into a pole. Luckily she had been shaken up more than anything. When her new security team had gotten her out of the wrecked car, she knew she had lost her chance to get away.

She heard a knock on the door of the hospital room and a familiar voice say, "How is she, Doctor?"

Her brother, Crown Prince Augustus, marched into the room. Dr. Vann bowed to him and said, "Just a few minor injuries, cuts and abrasions mostly, Your Royal Highness. Princess Rozala has been very lucky indeed."

Prince Augustus shook his hand. "Thank you. Could you give us some privacy?"

"Of course, sir." He bowed again and left brother and sister alone.

"Did Father send you to reprimand me?" Roza said with heaps of attitude.

A look of anger flashed across the Crown Prince's face. He strode right up beside the bed and said, "I sent myself because my little sister was in an accident, or do you not think I care if you hurt yourself?"

Her brother's righteous anger broke through all the emotions she had stubbornly kept locked up inside for the past few days, and tears tumbled unrestrained down her cheeks.

"I'm sorry, Gussy."

Augustus took her into his arms and held her tight. "It's all right, Roza. I'm here. You mustn't drive yourself around—if you'd been with your security people in your armoured state car, this wouldn't have happened. You scared me. I couldn't take losing you. We've already lost so much in this family."

Roza felt her usual stab of guilt at his reference to their mother and held on to him even tighter. He was the only one in the world who would show her affection now, the only one she could be herself with, and she was being sent away from him. "Gussy, please don't let Father send me away. You're the only one who understands."

He pulled back from her slightly and took a handkerchief from his suit pocket. "Here. Dry those eyes."

Roza dabbed her eyes and tried to pull herself together. Perhaps if she could persuade her brother she should stay, then he might have a word with her father.

"Gussy, I didn't know what Thea did. She never would tell me. I would never have been with someone who made arms to hurt our people...or ruin your wedding preparations. I loved her—*thought* I loved her."

Augustus picked up a seat and brought it over to the bed. "I know that, Roza, and I know exactly why you were drawn to her. I realized over the last couple of days that I've let you down."

"How could you ever let me down, Gussy? You're my big brother."

Augustus took her hand and looked accusingly at the ring Thea had given her, the ring whose meaning was speculated on in the press for a few months, while Roza had delighted in the discomfort that had caused their father.

"Big brothers are supposed to protect their sisters. I was so busy, caught up in my royal wedding hysteria, that I left you unprotected from a shark like Thea Brandt."

Roza's natural defiance surfaced in a second. "I don't need protecting and I can choose my own partners, Gussy," she snapped.

"Ah, my feisty sister's back. Yes, you do need protecting. Father's been cold to you, and you're always seeking acceptance from someone strong and someone to annoy him. Ms. Brandt gave you that in spades. I should have nipped it in the bud."

Roza pulled her hand back from her brother and twisted the ring around her finger. She should have taken it off as soon as she walked out on Thea, but quite frankly the thought frightened her. "I wouldn't have let you. My romantic choices are my own," Roza said angrily.

Now apparently confident that his sister was safe, Augustus sat back in his chair and became all business. "I can't persuade Father not to send you to Britain—one, because he is immovable on the subject, and two, I think it's a good idea. It'll get you away from your champagne swilling set of friends and give you some distance from the Denbourg press. Anyway, you love Aunt Sofia's family, especially George and Theo."

That was true. Two of the most stable times in her life had come when she stayed with her aunt and cousins, when she'd attended school and her last year of university in Britain. But as she had been then, she would now be under a more watchful eye than she was used to at home.

"Of course I love them, and Bea is a lovely woman too, but the British court is so much more *domestic*."

Gussy laughed softly. "You say domestic as if it was a bad word."

"It is."

"Perhaps domestic is what you need, Roza. Without a mother—"

"You and Father would have been much better off without me. Then Father would have had Mama and you just like he always wanted."

"Don't you ever say that, Roza," Gussy said angrily. "Our mama gave her life for you. She wanted you to have a full and happy life, but that you should do your duty like we all have to."

Her brother got up and started to pace angrily. "I've treaded softly with you for too long. I need to step in and take over from Father because he just continues to alienate you. You're twenty-three, Roza. Time to grow up."

"What do you mean?"

"I mean I asked Father to hand responsibility for your future to me."

"Excuse me? I'm not five years old, Gussy. I don't need a guardian," Roza said angrily.

"Clearly you do. You might not like it, but I must try and help you, Roza. You have an important role to fulfil in this family."

Roza got up from the bed and started to gather her things. She felt absolutely furious. "What important role? Being spare to the heir? It's like having a pair of old shoes in the wardrobe that you know you'll never need, that just sit there getting dusty. I have no role, Gussy."

"That's the sort of attitude that's got you into trouble. You have countless engagements you should be taking on to help the family, but you're too busy partying. You have great privilege, Roza, and you need to pay for that with service to your people."

Roza couldn't quite believe the change in her brother. He had never spoken to her this harshly. She picked up her bag and said, "You're turning into Father, Gussy."

"I'll ignore you said that. The royal plane will take you to London tomorrow."

"Tomorrow? Why so quickly? I won't have time to say goodbye to my friends."

"So you don't do one of your disappearing acts."

That was exactly what she had planned. Maybe she could get out of the country tonight if she and Cressie could sneak away.

"I've appointed you a new five-man security team."

"Five? I've only ever had two before."

"And you had them wrapped around your little finger. I chose this team with advice from the head of Denbourg secret service. Your chief of security is the woman who rescued you from the car."

Roza recalled the striking woman who'd pulled her from the car wreck. "The tall, silent, Amazon-looking woman?"

Augustus nodded. "Major Ravn."

Yes, she'll be putty in my hands. Maybe I can get out, thought Roza. If there was one thing Roza was confident about, it was using her feminine wiles to charm both men and women.

Augustus must have seen the glint of mischief in her eyes. "Don't even think about trying to use your many charms on her. She was picked for specific reasons. Major Ravn has served in the army and intelligence services for twenty-five exemplary years, has been happily married to her wife for fifteen years, and has two little children. Apart from the fact that she is the consummate professional, I know even you wouldn't disrespect someone's marriage just to get your own way. You're too good a girl for that."

She didn't answer but he was right. Infuriatingly right. Just then a message came through on her phone from her lady-in-waiting. When she read it, she became more enraged. "Cressie says she's been removed from her post."

"Yes, she was a bad influence on you, Roza."

"She was my choice!"

"Keep your voice down, please." Augustus walked to her and tried to take her hand, but she pulled it away.

Augustus sighed and approached her more softly. "Roza, please. I'm trying to help you. One day Father will be gone, and it'll be down to you and me to carry this family. You have to face your responsibilities."

Roza was not only angry, she was hurt. She put on her coat and picked up her handbag. "I want to go back to my apartment now."

"I've appointed Lady Linton as your new lady-in-waiting. She was Mama's best friend from school and her lady-in-waiting until her death. I think you need to be around someone who knew Mama well."

Roza slowly walked toward the door and held it ajar. Everything that had happened to her was now truly hitting her, and when she saw Major Ravn and her team of guards waiting for her in the hospital corridor, claustrophobia threatened to suffocate her.

She turned to her brother and said sadly, "You were the only one, *the only one* who understood me, and who was on my side. I'm truly alone now."

Then she walked sombrely out the door.

"Roza, wait—"

❖

Lennox looked into the mirrored interior of the lift, and checked her grey suit and tie were sitting just right. As always they were perfect, and she waited for the lift to arrive at the fifth floor where her office was located. She exited onto her floor of Timmy's new London headquarters. Lennox thoroughly enjoyed her work at Timmy's and making a difference. She'd come to Timmy's with a reputation for making money, having worked in the high-powered London financial district. Lennox had made a lot of money for herself and a lot of companies but now she was determined to make money for those most deserving.

Lennox loved this part of the day—coming back from an intense workout, ready to work hard for the rest of the afternoon. When Danny Simpson, Bea's old boss, medically retired from work, she applied for and was given the directorship.

Lennox strode purposely to her office, and when her PA Conrad saw her, he quickly got up from his desk outside her office.

"Everything under control, Conrad?"

Conrad was in his early twenties, exceptionally well organized and immaculately dressed. He needed to be, to keep up with Lennox's pace of work. She was a highly driven individual and expected no less from her staff. But he appeared to be in a state, both nervous and excited.

"Lex, the Queen Consort's private secretary Lali Ramesh called. The Consort would like an urgent word with you."

Lex smiled at him. Conrad became awed and star-struck whenever Beatrice called or visited the charity, but he wasn't the only one. Beatrice had a kind of star quality that endeared her to everyone she met. In the first year of her marriage to the Queen, Beatrice had charmed not only the country, but the world, and the staff at Timmy's couldn't have been prouder that she had worked for them. The media had named her the Consort of the People, and they were not wrong. Lennox couldn't remember a time when the monarchy was as popular as it was now, and all because an anti-monarchist joined their ranks.

"Give me a few minutes and put me through to the palace."

"Will do, and I ordered your lunch. It should be here anytime."

Lennox shut her office door and slung her gym bag on the couch, before taking a seat at her desk. The Queen Consort often called her to keep in touch with how things were going at Timmy's. She had in fact been one of the people that conducted Lennox's interview for the directorship job. Timmy's was Beatrice's baby. She had helped build the charity from a tiny regional charity to a national, and now international, charity, with healthcare centres now being built in some of the poorest countries of the world.

Luckily Lennox and Beatrice had hit it off straight away and enjoyed a good working relationship.

The computer beeped with an incoming call. Lennox straightened her tie one last time and said, "Answer."

The Queen Consort's smiling face appeared. "Hi, Lex. How are you today?"

Lennox bowed her head quickly. "I'm fine, Your Majesty. It's nice to speak to you again. How can I help?"

Bea pushed a strand of dark blond hair behind her ear. She was a beautiful woman and Lennox could easily see why Queen Georgina fell in love with her. She was both beautiful and totally without guile.

"I, or I should say the Queen and I, have a favour to ask you."

"Of course, ma'am. What can I do?"

"It's a delicate situation, and we would need your complete discretion, but you're the only one I would trust to do it."

"Thank you for your trust. You know you have my word that I will be discreet."

Bea sighed. "The Queen's cousin Princess Rozala is coming to stay with us for a while. You've probably seen she has been in the media a lot recently."

That was an understatement. The Denbourg princess's private life was constantly being splashed all over the news and celebrity websites.

"Yes, I understand she was in an accident this morning. I hope she wasn't injured too badly."

"No, thank you for asking. Only a few bumps and bruises. Her father, King Christian, wants her to have some time away from the Denbourg court, until things calm down a bit. The Queen would like her to be useful while she is here, and I suggested that she come and work with you at Timmy's."

Lex groaned internally and tried to hide her horror at the thought of babysitting a spoilt princess.

"You know I'm completely at your service, ma'am, but…"

Bea smiled, obviously reading her less-than-enthusiastic response. "But?"

"May I speak frankly?"

"Of course."

"Is it really the best place for her? I'm sure she would get bored with the day-to-day grind of business meetings and endless emails and telephone calls."

She watched a smile creep over Bea's face. "That's exactly what we want. She needs to experience the real world, a different world from the closeted court of Denbourg and her privileged friends. I want you to show her the business from the bottom up—think of her as a second PA. I'm sure Conrad won't mind sharing you."

Sharing her? That was a joke. Conrad would happily give her over completely if it meant working with a princess.

"I don't doubt that." Lex could foresee falling behind with months of work because of this. She had no choice but to ask this direct question. "Ma'am? I'm sorry if this is a bit disrespectful, but I must ask. Is this just a PR exercise for the benefit of the Denbourg royal family and world media after the arms scandal Princess Rozala was involved in?"

"It's not disrespectful, Lex, and I appreciate your honesty. No, it's not a PR exercise. We want her working hard eight hours a day, and being useful to you. Believe me, I know what you're feeling. You're thinking what a waste of your time this will be. I remember when my boss, Danny, told me I was working with Queen Georgina and I point-blank refused. I could only imagine how much it would disrupt my important work. But it didn't work out too badly in the end, did it?" Bea joked.

Lex laughed out loud and said, "I'm in a slightly different situation, ma'am. I can't exactly refuse."

"Maybe not, but then I couldn't either. Danny told me in no uncertain terms that I was doing it. I want you to treat her as you would any other new start."

"Will I have your full backing if she doesn't follow instructions? For this to work I can't have her running to the Queen with complaints."

Bea leaned forward towards the screen and said seriously, "You have my word, Lex. We want her to experience the real world, and I'm certain you are the one to do it."

Lex puffed out her cheeks and let out a long sigh. "I'll do it."

This had disaster written all over it.

CHAPTER THREE

Roza had to admit, her new security chief was efficient and single-minded. Despite all the media that had swarmed all over the hospital, she had an easy escape thanks to Major Ravn. Roza had been taken from the building in an armoured car without the press even knowing she had gone.

Her previous team would have followed meekly as Thea led Roza through the clamouring crowds. Thea'd enjoyed the attention Roza's position gave her. Before she had met Thea, Roza already had her security eating out of her hand, but then Thea stepped in and they followed her lead. They had been seduced by the glamorous lifestyle alongside Thea's hired bodyguards. But as Roza looked across the state car to the upright and professional Major Ravn, she knew that would never happen with her.

Major Ravn had a strong, steady gaze that appeared incorruptible, and a physique that looked as if she could rip your arm off and beat you with it—and of course that thick gold wedding band on her ring finger.

Gussy had been right. As much as she liked to use her looks to gain an advantage, and as flirtatious as she was, she would never try it with someone who was married. She wasn't that sort of a person.

Roza sighed. What a shame—she would have had such fun with Major Ravn. She was just her type, an experienced older woman. Just like Thea.

She looked down at the ring Thea had given her, which she still hadn't taken off. In some deep part of her soul, Thea still had a hold on her, and she wasn't strong enough to let go, yet. "Ravn? How long till we get back to my apartment?"

"About fifteen minutes, ma'am."

Roza felt the need to talk, and despite the fact that conversation probably wasn't her strong suit, Major Ravn would have to do. "Major Ravn—you're married?"

"Yes, ma'am."

One-word answers. Great.

"My brother says you have two little children too."

Ravn looked at her with a hint of suspicion. Prince Augustus had obviously briefed the major on Roza's penchant for gaining leverage through personal friendships with her staff.

"Don't worry, Major. I know what my brother probably told you about me, but believe me, I'm only interested to get to know you since we're going to be together a great deal."

Ravn hesitated, then said, "Yes, they are ten and five."

"That's nice. Are they going to visit you a lot when we go to the UK?"

"My wife and children are coming with me. I've rented a house in London for them. I couldn't be without my family."

"Wow. Your wife's very lucky to have you."

Major Ravn took off her sunglasses and put them in her top suit pocket, before making her position clear in the nicest possible way. "I'm the lucky one. My wife and children are everything to me and there's nothing in this world that could change that, ma'am."

Roza's heart sank. Everyone had such a low opinion of her, and that made her feel sad. No one really knew who she was, not even her brother any more.

She plastered on a smile and said, "That's nice. You sound like a really loyal person, Major."

"I am, both personally and professionally. I can assure you that you will be well protected. No one will get through me."

"Great." Roza sighed, leaned her head against the car window, and stared out at the passing scenery. Denbourg's ancient capital of Battendorf was alive with people going to and from work, laughing and having fun, or shopping together. Tears started to roll down her cheeks. *They are free.*

Freedom was something she would never have, especially after her recent transgressions. This state car might as well be a prison van taking her to her punishment.

Cressida being replaced as lady-in-waiting was the last straw.

They might be keeping me under lock and key, but I'm going to make as much noise as I can, and you're going to hear it, Father.

❖

Timmy's was a hive of activity after Lex's earlier call from the Consort. She had passed responsibility for the preparations over to her PA Conrad so that she could continue with real work.

When Lex had first told Conrad that the princess would be joining them, he literally let out a squeal and then jumped into action, organizing teams of cleaners to scour the building with a fine-tooth comb and make every conceivable preparation. Since then word and gossip had spread like wildfire and the whole staff was buzzing with excitement.

They didn't have to babysit her though, did they. Lex pushed up from her desk with a sense of resignation, walked over to her office fridge, and pulled out one of her protein and vitamin drinks.

As she took a sip, her computer signalled a call.

"Answer."

"Lex, it's Mel from PR. I think we need a meeting about Princess Rozala."

Bloody hell. I'm sick of the girl and she's not even here yet.

"Why would that concern PR? The palace wishes this to be a useful exercise, not a publicity stunt."

"Oh, come on, Lex. Bea knows this is going to be huge in the press, no matter what happens, and we have to handle it."

Lex strode back to her desk and glowered at Mel on the screen. "That would be the Queen Consort to you, Mel."

She always tried to discourage any sense of overfamiliarity between the Timmy's staff and Beatrice. She might have once been their colleague, but now their positions had changed and despite the fact that Bea herself was very easy-going about it, the staff had to remember that they were dealing with Queen Georgina's wife, not their colleague.

Mel looked annoyed. Lex had noticed that her head of PR wasn't as pleased as the rest of the staff were about Bea's advantageous marriage. She had been told the two had been like chalk and cheese when they worked together, and it showed.

"Of course. The *Consort* would be well aware of the press interest and would expect us to use it for Timmy's benefit."

"I don't want it used or hyped up any more than it needs to be, Mel. Prepare a report for me on the likely media intrusion and any recommendations you have. That's all."

"But—"

Lex ended the call before she could say anything else. "This place is going nuts."

She immediately got back to work on the budgets for the overseas Timmy's medical centres. Only there in the numbers would she find calm in this sea of royal excitement.

A knock on the door was followed by Conrad popping his head in her office. "Lex?"

"Yes?" She was beginning to lose patience with all the interruptions she had been having ever since Bea had called.

"The tech people are here."

Conrad said it as if she would automatically know what he was talking about.

"What for?"

"To install Princess Rozala's desk and computer facilities." He opened the office doors wide and a large group of technicians came in carrying a desk and other equipment.

This was just too much for Lex. She leapt up and said in a menacing voice, "Oh no, her desk is not coming in here. There are plenty of desk cubicles out in the open office."

Conrad gulped audibly. Lex was a popular boss and well liked, but everyone knew that she had little tolerance for anything that disrupted or slowed down productivity.

"I got orders from Denbourg security, Lex. I emailed you the instructions they sent. They insist that she is situated in a closed office, and in close proximity to you."

Lex could feel the stress and pressure building up inside her. She was losing control of her surroundings and her job and she didn't like it. The banging of the tech guys fitting the desk together didn't help. She took a few deep breaths and tried to calm herself.

Just as her stress started to calm, another call came through—this time from security.

"What?" Lex snapped.

"Lex, we need to have a meeting about the security arrangements for the princess's arrival. A Major Ravn has been in touch and—"

She was going to blow if she didn't get away from what was rapidly turning into a circus. "Conrad will give you a time this afternoon."

Lex shut off her computer and marched out of her office, which now seemed to have an open door policy, and growled in Conrad's direction, "I'm going upstairs for a while. Make an appointment for me with security for later in the afternoon." Conrad knew when she said she was going upstairs, that she needed some time alone.

"Yes, Lex."

Lex got on the lift and pressed the button for the top service floor. The lift doors opened and she walked through a pair of fire doors out into a hidden oasis on the top floor of the office building, the roof garden.

The little garden featured a small variety of well-landscaped shrubs, plants, and flowers, plus benches and the calming sound of running water from the water feature. The roof was her sanctuary when she needed to breathe, and get out of the high-pressured office environment.

Lex walked over to the steel and Perspex railing that surrounded the roof area and looked out over the London skyline, and let out a long breath.

She closed her eyes and concentrated on the sounds around her and her breathing. Serenity wasn't Lex's natural state. She was impulsive and didn't deal with stress well, but these flaws in her character were something she was well-practised in attempting to keep under control.

Lex looked down at the tattooed date on her wrist under her watch and felt the fear of losing that control. Losing control had taken her down a dark road before and she never, ever wanted to go there again. She couldn't shake the feeling she was on the verge of a storm that was brewing, but Lex promised herself that she would use every tool she had to ride out whatever was coming her way.

❖

The Denbourg royal plane was coming in to land at Heathrow. Roza caught her new lady-in-waiting, Lady Linton, gazing at her and said, "Is there something I can help you with? You keep gawking at me like I'm some exotic animal at the zoo."

Despite the sharpness of her tone, Lady Linton—Perri, as she had instructed everyone to call her—smiled and said, "Forgive me, ma'am, but you look so much like your mother. She was my best friend and I haven't seen you since you were a baby. It's a surprise to see so much of her in you."

Roza shifted uncomfortably in her seat. There it was again, that feeling of inadequacy. Everyone who had known her mother saw a facsimile of Queen Maria, but were then disappointed in Roza's character.

She had felt her new lady-in-waiting's eyes on her quite a few times since they had met last night, and it was beginning to annoy her. Lady Linton was an elegantly put together older lady, who had fashionably let her hair go silvery grey but looked remarkably young for her age.

The flight from Denbourg's capital to London was fast, but Roza's anger and resentment seemed to grow with every second of the journey. She was being sent into exile by her family, the ones who were supposed to love her the most, and stripped of all her friends.

Her bad mood wasn't helped by Perri. They had already come into conflict that morning when she had laid out a rather sober looking outfit for traveling in. Roza completely ignored her advice and wore the shortest minidress she had, short enough that eyes, as well as the flashes of photographers, followed her all the way through Battendorf airport.

At the time, she had gotten satisfaction from the thought of her father seeing the pictures on the newspaper sites he read over breakfast, but now she just felt empty and a little silly in a dress more suitable for clubbing than meeting with her cousins.

Major Ravn and her team started to take their places by the exit as the plane taxied into the royal terminal.

Roza stood up and got her handbag from the overhead locker, her resentment growing arms and legs. She looked down at Perri and said, "I'm sure I'm a great disappointment to you, Perri. No one can compare to the perfect Queen Maria, can they?"

She walked towards the plane doors without looking back, and felt shame at what she'd just said. Shame that she resented the woman who'd given her life to give Roza hers. As usual she gulped down the bad feelings and put a fake smile on her face as she walked down the stairs. Ravn and her second in command, Johann, waited at the bottom while the others lined the red carpet up to the terminal.

Years of training kicked in, and Roza politely shook hands with the airport reception committee.

As she walked up the red carpet she spotted Prince Theo waiting for her. Roza hurried the last few steps and threw her arms around one of her favourite cousins.

"Theo! I'm so happy to see you."

Prince Theo spun her round in a circle and gave her a kiss. "Roza, did you forget to put on part of your dress?"

Roza laughed. "Oh, this is just to annoy Father. How are you, big cousin?"

"I'm very well. All the better, now you're here."

She placed her hands on his cheeks and was serious for a moment. "Are you really okay? All recovered?"

A little under a year ago there had been an assassination attempt on Theo and his sister, and Theo got the worst of it.

Theo smiled and took hold of her arms. "I'm quite well. I get enough fussing over me by Georgie, Bea, and Mama, without you as well. Come on, let's get going."

Roza and Theo were escorted to their waiting car. Major Ravn held the door open and closed it once they were in.

"Your Major Ravn looks quite scary, Roza. I don't think anyone would dare try to go through her to you," Theo joked.

"Yes, she is a little serious. I think she saves up her smiles for her private life. So? Where to first?"

"We're going for tea with Bea, Granny, and Mama at Buck house—Georgie has a full day of engagements unfortunately."

"I'll need to go and get changed first, Theo. I can't meet them dressed like this." Roza could almost feel Perri say, *I told you so*, and it aggravated her.

"Don't worry. We've got time. I'm to take you to your apartments first. Georgie has organized for you to stay next to me in St James's Palace."

"Wonderful! We can get up to all sorts of mischief."

Roza laid her head against his shoulder. Maybe it wouldn't be so bad to see out her exile here in Britain. It would be nice to be back with the Buckingham side of the family. They were a real family, unlike her own, and she instantly started to relax. "What club are you taking me to tonight then?" George, Bea, and her aunt might be domestic, but cousin Theo was a kindred spirit and could always be relied upon to organize a wild night out.

Theo sighed. "Unfortunately I can't take you out tonight. I have a full day of engagements tomorrow."

Roza sat up and looked at him pointedly. "Since when do you take on so many royal engagements, and when do you not want to go out to a club?"

"Since I realized it was time to grow up," Theo said seriously.

"Theo, you can still have fun—"

"Roza, I nearly died last year, and even worse, someone tried to kill my sister, all because Julian…"

Roza saw the haunted look in his eyes when he mentioned his treacherous cousin's name. She took his hand in support.

He continued. "All because someone in my family didn't know their place, and their responsibilities to the head of our family. When I was lying in hospital, I promised myself that if I recovered, I would throw myself into royal responsibilities and support George and Bea as best I could."

Roza smiled and gave him a kiss on his cheek. "I can't fault you for that, Theo."

Somewhere deep inside, Theo's heartfelt declaration chimed with her. Was that what she should be doing? Then she pictured the disappointment on her father's face yesterday, and her defiant anger returned.

"Don't worry, big cousin." Roza grinned gleefully. "I'll have enough fun for both of us."

"I don't doubt it." Theo laughed.

CHAPTER FOUR

Bea sat at the ornate dressing table in her bedroom while her friend and dresser-stylist Holly Weaver added the finishing touches to her hair.

Holly rested her chin lightly on Bea's shoulder. "What do you think?"

"Perfect as always, Holls. Just like the outfit you picked out for me. I don't know what I'd do without you," Bea said, smiling.

When George, Bea, and their advisors had made plans for her new staff as Queen Consort, the post of dresser had been the one position that had irked her natural socialist tendencies the most. The thought of having someone whose whole job was to dress her every day…well, she just couldn't comprehend that. Bea had dressed and looked after herself her whole life, and she didn't want to change now, but she wasn't naive.

She knew that logistically she couldn't shop personally for the constant stream of outfits and accessories she would need, far less take care of them. Her best friend and new private secretary, Lali, had suggested offering Holly the role and combining it with being Bea's hair and make-up person. Both she and George had thought it a wonderful idea. It meant the people at the heart of Bea's team were those she trusted without question, and they would never talk to the press.

Holly spent her time planning Bea's wardrobe, purchasing and ordering from designers, and taking care of the Queen Consort personally. Bea felt so lucky to have her friends around her as she took on this enormous role. The only friend not around her every day was Greta, who had her own family to take care of, but the friends made sure they had a girls' night every month, Bea's schedule permitting, to keep their bond tight.

"You would be gorgeous as you always have been, Your Majesty," Holly said.

Bea sprayed on some perfume and said jokingly, "Holls, if you call me Your Majesty one more time, I'm going to get Georgie to send you to the Tower of London."

Holly rubbed her hands in excitement. "Oh, all those Beefeaters all to myself? Yes, please, Your Maj."

Their laughter was interrupted by a brief knock and Lali walking into the room. "Princess Rozala and Prince Theo's car has arrived, Bea." She checked her computer pad. "You have ninety minutes to meet with them, and then we need to leave for your afternoon appointment at the city farm and then on to St. Wilfred's care home."

Bea nudged Holly. "You see what a slave driver she is, and this is a reasonably quiet day."

Holly crossed her arms and raised a quizzical eyebrow. "Yeah, Lali, are you this strict with your dashing officer, Captain Cameron?"

"No, I am not, Holls. Well…not much, and if I didn't keep you on schedule, Bea, you'd never, ever be on time for anything."

Bea chuckled. That was true. She did have a reputation in her new family for taking the longest to work her way through a crowd, meeting and talking to people. She just couldn't walk away thinking she had missed a child or an adult who had waited all day to see her.

"You're right as always, Lali."

"So what's this princess like, Bea?" Holly asked. "Is she as wild as the press say she is?"

Bea stood up and smoothed down her dress. "No, I don't think so. She was lovely when I met her at the wedding. Georgie says she's had a difficult childhood and just needs to be around family. I better go, Holls. Lali has me on the clock. See you later."

She looked over to the bed where Rex, her faithful Labrador, lay sleeping with his teddy bear toy. The rest of George's dogs, Shadow and Baxter, were out being walked by one of the staff, but Rex wanted to stay by her side.

He had taken a shine to Bea since they'd first met and now was basically hers. "Rexie, are you coming too, or do you want to go out walkies?"

Rex was up like a shot and by Bea's side in a second.

"I think that's his answer, Bea. That dog adores you." Lali laughed.

Bea stroked his soft head. "That's because his mummy loves him, don't I, Rexie?"

Rex licked her hand in return, and Holly said, "Seriously, you're getting soft or maybe broody."

Bea rolled her eyes. "Don't even mention that word. The country and George think of nothing else. Come on, Rexie."

They left Holly and walked briskly down the long ornate corridors of Buckingham Palace, Rex following behind. Footmen and footwomen and cleaning staff bowed and curtsied as they passed. Royal protocol calling for the deference of others was something she thought she'd never totally get used to, or wrap her mind around.

Since becoming George's wife, she'd had to do a lot of wrapping her mind around new things. Her life had changed overnight. She had expected it to, but nothing quite prepared you for the reality. No matter how much her life had changed, her freedom restricted, she would do it again gladly just to be by George's side.

There had never been someone like her in the role of Queen Consort. So she had to find a way to make the role her own. To justify her position to herself and the people, she had to treat this as a real job, and Lali had been instrumental in helping her to do that.

In a certain sense her role was similar to what she had done her whole working life, working for charities. Only now it was on a much larger scale, shining a light on lots of different causes and raising money. As sceptical as she had been, Bea had seen the evidence for herself. Just by her endorsing a charity and making an official visit, donations increased by at least fifty per cent.

Bea looked at her friend beside her, walking while working on her computer pad furiously. Lali was as much the reason for her success as Queen Consort as she was, and she didn't know where she'd be without her. Sometimes though, she felt guilty at taking Lali away from her own important charity directorship.

"Lali?"

"Uh-huh?" Lali said, only half listening while she worked.

"Do you ever regret coming to work with me?" Bea asked.

Lali slowed and gave her a questioning look. "Regret it? It's the best thing I've ever done. This job we're doing…we're earning more money for all the causes we care about than we could ever have done before. This is important work. Added to that, I'm working for my best friend, travelling the world, and getting time to spend with Cammy."

"I'm so glad you've found happiness with Cammy, Lali. You deserve someone to love you the way she will."

The doors to the drawing room were just up ahead, and two footmen, one male and one female, flanked either side of the doors.

Lali slowed and stopped before they were in earshot of the staff, and said, "But I'm taking it slowly, Bea. She's never had one woman in her life before and when the honeymoon period ends, she might feel differently about me."

Bea could understand Lali's fear, but Cammy had loyalty embedded deeply inside her. She would die for George, and someone capable of such loyalty didn't take love for granted.

"Lali, she might have been a ladies' woman but she didn't make any promises to them—and I believe she has made promises to you. Am I right?"

Lali blushed and nodded. "And she's not pressurizing me about going slowly. She's happy taking things at my pace, which is a change from other people I've gone out with."

"That's because she knows how lucky she is. She's a keeper, Lali. Don't let her go."

"I won't. Anyway, Mum and Dad like her too much."

Lali's parents were old-fashioned only in the sense that they demanded a lot from their daughter's potential suitors, so if they liked Captain Cameron, Lali had a winner.

They arrived at the drawing room and Lali went off to meet Princess Rozala and Prince Theo downstairs and conduct them to the Queen Consort.

The doors were opened and Bea strode into the room. She smiled when she saw the Dowager Queen Adrianna and Sofia, the Queen Mother. The two royal matriarchs couldn't have been more welcoming of her into the family. Bea didn't come from a big family, so to have those two ladies and Theo to love her was a wonderful feeling.

Queen Adrianna and Queen Sofia even went so far as having afternoon tea with her mother Sarah every week, to make her feel part of the family, and that meant the world to Bea.

Adrianna and Sofia rose as she entered the room, and Bea had to stop her instinct to curtsy to the older matriarchs. Both women had gently chastised her for it so many times that she was finally getting the message. To them, she was not only George's wife but the Queen Consort, now second only to George in order of royal precedence.

Bea kissed them each on the cheek. "Good morning, Granny, Mama. Thank you for coming."

"You look beautiful as always, Bea," Queen Adrianna said.

"Thank you."

Rex bounded up to Sofia when he saw her and gave her a kiss. He had been her husband's most trusted friend and a big part of her life.

Queen Sofia ruffled his ears and said, "Hello, Rex. Are you behaving yourself?"

"He is perfectly behaved, and getting more confident by the day. George is really pleased with him." As soon as he acknowledged Sofia he ran to join the Dowager Queen's dogs on the other side of the room.

"George mentioned you had a plan for Roza, Bea," Sofia said.

"Yes, I'm new to this world of royal duty, but to me the best way to show her what duty means and to show her how important her role is would be to work for charity. Not just a visit and unveiling a plaque, but a proper nine-to-five job."

"That sounds excellent. A bit of hard work will do her good, less time to go to parties with her friends," Adrianna said.

"At your old charity Timmy's?" Sofia asked.

Bea nodded and smiled. "I think the director there, Lennox King, will be a great help to her. She's driven, professional, and unlikely to be affected by Roza's royal position."

"It's certainly worth a try. She could lose her way even more if we don't get through to her. She's a hurt little girl, and my brother-in-law Christian has made it worse over the years. I need to see her succeed and find happiness, for the sake of my sister Maria. Not to mention how hard this arms scandal has hit Denbourg itself."

Bea pressed a discreet button on a side table to signal Lali to bring in their guest. "If nothing else we can show her a warm, loving family."

❖

Prince Theo and Princess Rozala followed Lali up a grand palace staircase to be taken to meet with the rest of the family.

"How's Gussy, Roza? Getting ready for his big day?" Theo asked.

Roza rolled her eyes. "You could say that. The country has gone crazy over it. I'm glad to see him so happy."

Theo turned his head to her and said, "I feel a *but* coming."

Roza sighed. "Not really, you know we've always been close but lately we've drifted apart. He's been so busy."

"I know how hard it is to keep up your family when they have commitments and travelling all over the world. George and I always make an effort to call each other each week, wherever we are."

They reached the top of the staircase. "When I met Thea and began to see her, Gussy and I argued a lot and it became easier just to not call him back. Now, I don't know if that closeness will ever return."

As they were nearing the private drawing room, Theo placed his hand on the small of her back and rubbed it soothingly. "I'm sure it will. You just need some time to regroup, and we'll help and look after you," Theo said with a smile.

Lali was waiting for them. "Your Royal Highnesses, I'll just introduce you before you go in."

"Thanks, Lali," Theo said.

Lali walked into the room and announced, "Your Majesty, His Royal Highness, Prince Theodore and Her Royal Highness, Princess Rozala."

Theo hurried to Bea, gave her a bow, and took her into his arms for a big hug.

"Theo, how are you today? George wants a report tonight."

"Do you two ever stop fussing?" he said in mockingly annoyed fashion.

Bea stood on tiptoe to kiss him. "No, because we love you."

"And what about you, Bea?" he said with a smile. "Any baby Georges on the way? The media seemed convinced we're to expect the patter of royal feet anytime soon."

Bea play-hit him on the arm. "Suddenly everyone has an opinion on my fertility. And for your information, Theo, you'll just have to stay as second in line to the throne for the time being."

"Woe is me!" Theo said dramatically.

"Where's my kiss, boy?" Queen Adrianna said, stamping her stick on the floor.

"Sorry, Granny, Mama."

❖

A few paces back, Roza stood awkwardly watching the intimate family scene. The ease with which this side of her family interacted was foreign to her, and she envied it.

"Roza?"

Her thoughts were interrupted by Bea calling to her. Roza walked forward and curtsied. "It's nice to see you again, Your Majesty."

Bea was not stiff or formal. She smiled at her and opened her arms to pull her in to a hug. Roza was stiff at first, but relaxed when Bea squeezed her tightly and said, "It's great to see you again."

She then was equally welcomed by Aunt Sofia and Great-Aunt Adrianna, as she had always called her.

They had tea, cakes and some chit chat, before Sofia said, "I hear Perri is your lady-in-waiting now, an excellent choice."

"She wasn't *my* choice," Roza said sharply.

Sofia gave her a serious look. "She is one of your godmothers, Roza, so I can't think of anyone better to look after you."

Roza felt like she'd been sucker-punched in the stomach. "She's my godmother? I thought—I thought I only had a royal godmother, Princess Eloise of the Netherlands?"

"No, Roza. Perri was my sister's best friend and was first choice. She only chose Princess Eloise out of convention. Surely you must have seen still photographs and footage of your christening."

She hadn't seen much, apart from the times it was shown on TV and she wasn't quick enough to change the channel. Roza never wanted to see the ceremony without her mother there. Besides, her christening was more reminiscent of a funeral than welcoming a baby into the world.

"I haven't seen much. I thought she was there just as Mother's friend."

"No, she was there to vow to help in your care both spiritually and physically," Sophia said.

And she left me too.

❖

Princess Roza's car arrived back at St James's Palace. When Major Ravn opened the door, Roza got out quickly and stormed up the steps, fury building inside. She burst into the apartment and shouted, "Perri! Where are you?"

"In the bedroom, ma'am," Perri replied.

Roza stalked into the bedroom to find clothes spread across the bed as Perri was putting all her luggage away neatly.

"Are you all right, ma'am? Did you have a good meeting at the palace?"

She ignored the question. "You're my godmother, my mother's first choice."

Perri stopped hanging up the clothes. "Yes, I am. Your mother and I were the best of friends. She named you after me too. Didn't you know?"

There was just one revelation after another lately, and the fury in Roza was rising. "What is your full name?"

"I was Rosa Percy until I married Lord Linton."

"Why didn't you stay with me after she died? You were my godmother—you should have stayed in contact at least."

Perri looked down in sadness and perhaps guilt. "My best friend had just died. I had known her since I was five years old, all through school and university. We were like sisters, and I was grief-stricken like everyone else, but I thought it best—"

"You left me on my own." Tears tumbled down Roza's cheeks. "A little girl that nobody wanted around because she reminded them of what they'd lost. You should have been there for me."

Perri appeared shocked at Roza's outburst. Somewhere inside Roza knew she wasn't just angry at Perri, she was angry at her mother for leaving her.

"I thought it was best to leave—I thought your father would marry again and I would be in the way..."

"No, you were just like everyone else, you blamed me for Mother's death."

"No, Roza, that's not true." Perri came closer and tried to take her hand, but she pulled away.

Roza grabbed one of her most revealing dresses off the bed and said with coldness in her voice, "I'm going out. Don't wait up, *Godmother.*"

"What about your appointment tomorrow at the Queen Consort's charity?"

"Oh? You know about that too? Is everyone conspiring against me?" Roza sneered.

When Bea told her about working at Timmy's, she had put on her very best false smile, but inside she was frustrated and annoyed. Not that she minded helping a charity—she had taken part in raising money for charity all of her life, auctions, parties, polo, and racing events. It was the idea she was being sent to work a nine-to-five job to keep her out of trouble.

Well if that's what everyone thinks, they are sadly mistaken.

"Nobody's conspiring against you, Roza. The Queen Consort's private secretary simply called me with all the information you would need. That's all."

"I'll get there when I get there." Roza left the room full of anger and frustration. Why did everyone leave her? Why was she never good enough for people to want to be with her and love her?

She was going to get some attention and make some noise.

CHAPTER FIVE

A t seven thirty a.m., Lex stood in front of a projected screen in the Timmy's conference room, going over her plans with all the heads of department in preparation for the princess's arrival at nine. "Okay, even though Princess Rozala will be based in my office, it is my intention to show her some of the work we do from every department. So to that effect I have drawn up a program of tasks and duties for her to get a taste of the business." She indicated to the screen behind her. On it was a timetable of tasks and events for every department.

"As you can see, she will be taking part in the organization of front-line staff collecting money on the streets, to the marketing, financial, and corporate fundraising departments. Now—"

"Excuse me, Lex," Mel the PR executive interrupted, "this is a golden opportunity to get publicity, raise our profile even higher, and make more money. We could have the press cameras out on the streets following the princess as she collects money in amongst the ordinary people. The public and media would lap it up."

Lex was furious. Since they had already discussed this privately, she could only conclude Mel was trying to gain support among the other department heads to exert pressure on her.

She fixed Mel with a penetrating stare. "I think I've made my position clear on this matter, Mel. This is not a PR exercise—it is something the Queen Consort has asked us to do with discretion. I'm not naive enough to think there will not be media interest in Princess Rozala's work here, but we will not help them by cooperating. Besides, security would make it impossible to have her out on the streets. Need I remind you what happened to Prince Theo last year?"

Mel held her gaze defiantly for a few seconds before looking down.

"Which brings me to security. The Denbourg secret service agents will be in charge while the princess is here, and if you receive an instruction from the protection unit, you must comply. Let me remind you the importance of wearing your staff passes. Anyone found without will be taken to the security office, plus this floor and my office will be on special alert. You will need prior clearance or an appointment to gain access to this floor."

She heard a few sighs and mutterings from the department heads around the table, and she couldn't blame them. Having the princess here would be restrictive and a nightmare in terms of everyday work, but there was nothing she could do about it.

"I know this will be difficult and may hold up our work, but remember this is a request from Queen Beatrice. Timmy's would be nowhere without her. We would not have expanded as we have if it wasn't for her patronage, and in fact a lot of you wouldn't have jobs if it hadn't been for the money she has generated, so we owe her. Any questions?"

When none were forthcoming, she looked at her watch and said, "Okay, it's half-past eight. Let's go downstairs and get the welcoming committee organized."

It took some time to get the staff ready in Timmy's reception area, mostly because of people thinking they should be nearer the head of the line than others. Egos were clearly on show today, but finally they were ready.

As nine o'clock came and went, and no Princess Rozala arrived, Lex's frustration started to build. After an hour and a half she finally got through to Major Ravn, head of the princess's protection team, and was informed the princess wouldn't be leaving St James's palace anytime soon. In Major Ravn's words, *The princess was indisposed.* Clearly her party reputation was well earned.

Lex was furious, and ordered everyone back to work. There was disappointment throughout all the staff. Everyone had been so excited about Princess Rozala arriving. Lex walked into her office and slammed the door shut.

She had been prepared to give the princess a chance despite her rebellious reputation, but she had failed her one simple task: arrive on time.

What a waste of time and energy.

❖

Morning had come too quickly for Roza. Despite repeated attempts by Perri to wake her for her first day at Timmy's, she didn't leave St James's Palace until half-past twelve after many black coffees to get her feeling somewhat alive again. Roza had met up with some old friends from school the previous night, and the get-together had turned into a night of clubbing at one of London's most exclusive venues, spilling out at five a.m. to the flashes of the paparazzi cameras.

Finally Perri had managed to get Roza organized and into the car to take her to Timmy's. Roza hid behind a pair of dark sunglasses and burrowed her way further into the side of the car.

She felt terrible. Her head pounded, she felt nauseous, and all she wanted to do was sleep, but even she knew she would have to put in some sort of an appearance at this charity Bea had insisted she go to. Hopefully after a few handshakes and smiles she could get home and sleep for a while longer.

She opened the drinks fridge in the state car and took out a bottle of water. Her body was demanding water after the excess of last night. Roza caught Major Ravn looking at her with what she could only describe as a parental look of disappointment.

"I suppose you're quite disappointed in me, Major Ravn."

"It's not my place to be disappointed in you, Your Royal Highness. I'm simply here to protect you."

Maybe she was projecting her feelings of shame from last night, but she was sure she had seen that emotion in Ravn's eyes as she was carried out of the club after getting too drunk, and the club patrons getting too close and personal with her.

Her late night antics also meant the major hadn't been able to go home to her family, and for that she was sorry. Why did she do this to herself?

What was the point in partying last night and drinking cocktails till she couldn't remember anything? Her so-called old friends were more interested in the attention of being with a VIP and the special treatment that came with it. It used to give her pleasure to know she was causing her father and his many courtiers who looked down upon her as much discomfort as possible. Now it didn't feel good. She thought of the many Denbourg military forces, many much younger than her, away from home, risking their lives, combating people using Thea's weapons, while she was drinking cocktails and dancing.

"I'm sorry I kept you out last night, Ravn. I promise I'll be tucked up early in bed tonight, and you can go home early."

Ravn's face softened. "Ma'am, I don't need to go home early. My job is to protect you, and I will be here wherever you need me and however long you need me. My wife understands. It's my duty and an honour."

Roza was quite touched by Ravn's words. As much as she didn't deserve such loyalty and reverence, the major and her team would willingly serve her without thought for themselves.

"Thank you, Major. I appreciate that, and I promise to think of others the next time I go out."

They pulled up outside Timmy's headquarters, and Ravn said, "Wait till I open your door, ma'am."

Roza smiled and saluted. "You're in charge, Major."

❖

As soon as Lennox rounded the corner from her gym onto the street where Timmy's headquarters was situated, she knew the princess had arrived. On either side of the entrance were two agents checking the credentials of everyone who went in.

She let out a long breath. Lex had thought the princess just wouldn't turn up at all, and that might have been better for everyone involved. She had been so angry before she left to have her lunchtime workout, but thankfully the exercise had calmed her emotions as it always did.

She showed her security pass at the door and entered the lift to take her up to her office. She tried to think out how she would approach this first meeting, as her attitude would colour their entire working relationship. For this to work she had to show Princess Rozala who was boss but temper that with the due courtesy and respect her position demanded. It wouldn't be easy, and she just had to hope the Consort was true to her word and would support her.

The lift doors opened and two more agents checked her pass before Conrad came hurrying over from his desk.

"Lex, Princess Rozala has been here for an hour in your office and she is not happy."

"I'm sure. Let's go and take her wrath then."

Conrad led her over to her office doors where a tall, solid woman dressed in a black suit took a few steps towards her.

"Lennox King?" she said.

"Yes, that's me."

"I'm Major Ravn, head of Princess Rozala's protection team, and this is Johann, my deputy." She indicated the silent man in a dark suit to her left.

Lex shook her hand. "Pleased to meet you, Major."

"Likewise. Both myself and Johann will be stationed outside your office while the princess is here. I would appreciate it if you keep me apprised of any proposed changes to the princess's movements."

"Of course, Major. I will."

Lex walked through the door with her gym bag over her shoulder. She saw the princess by the glass windows, looking out over the London skyline. The princess turned around when she heard the door close, and in that split second before she opened her mouth, Lex was struck by the gentle beauty of Rozala. Her soft, wavy chestnut hair, rosy skin, and beautiful figure all made Princess Rozala breathtaking.

Lex's few milliseconds of admiration were rudely interrupted by the rage that erupted from Rozala.

"Do you know what time it is? I've been waiting for you for over an hour and a half."

Lex quickly set her bag down and bowed as protocol dictated. "Your Royal Highness, we had a welcoming committee waiting for you at nine o'clock this morning."

"Ah, well I was out with some friends last night and we didn't get in till later, but I'm here now."

Lex had seen the pictures all over the net this morning with the headline *Royal Rebel hits London.*

She knew she would have to set the rules here and now or this would never have a chance of working. Lex took Bea at her word that she would have both her and the Queen's backing, and said firmly, "Go home and come back when you're ready to do a full day's work."

"Excuse me?" Roza said in a shocked and surprised voice. "Do you know who you are talking to?"

Lennox sat at her desk calmly and began to work on her computer. "Yes, I'm quite aware I'm talking to Princess Rozala of Denbourg, who is also my PA. As such you need to turn up on time for work and follow my instructions, ma'am."

Roza stormed over to her desk. "How dare you speak to me like that. You are very lucky I'm here at your silly little charity in the first place."

There were a few moments of silence during which Roza probably was waiting for her to give in and apologize, but she didn't react to her anger, and kept her head down.

"Look at me when I'm talking to you," Roza demanded.

"Sounds more like screaming at me, ma'am."

Roza exclaimed a frustrated and angry shout, like a toddler in a tantrum. "You are the most disrespectful, infuriating person I've ever met. You can be sure the Queen will hear about this."

She stormed off out the office doors and slammed them shut.

"That went well."

This was the first test. If she truly had the Queen's and Queen Consort's backing, Roza would be back, and if not maybe she would be getting a nice cosy room in the Tower of London.

❖

George and Bea began their day with a joint engagement to open a new hospital in Manchester. George stood by the state car and watched Bea with pride, as she interacted with the crowds gathered around them. After touring the facility and speaking with both patients and staff, they were due to leave for their next appointment.

George had said her goodbyes, and efficiently worked her way down the crowds waiting for them outside, receiving small gifts, shaking hands, and taking pictures with the people, thanking them for coming along, but as usual, Bea lagged well behind her.

At the moment a long line of little children were lining up to give her flowers. The public loved her, and George was delighted to let her have the limelight.

Cammy walked to her side and whispered, "She's a natural, isn't she?"

George felt like her chest might burst with pride as she watched Bea bend down to the children's level, and engulf them in hugs, making sure she gave each one her time.

"I always knew she would be, although Lali looks as if she's getting increasingly agitated." Lali looked at her watch constantly as she passed the flowers Bea received to Major Fairfax and the aides behind them.

"We are running twenty minutes behind, ma'am," Cammy said.

"It's worth it, Captain. We'll just take a shorter lunch before the next appointment. It's the children who are important."

"Princess Rozala called you by the way. She asked if you could call her back at your earliest convenience. She sounded a bit upset."

George let out a sigh, and watched Bea say goodbye to the last child and Lali gently manoeuvred her towards the car. She had been planning to call Roza later about the press pictures of her out late last night, and maybe now was as good as ever.

"This was her first day at Timmy's. Why do I get the feeling she's going to give me a list of complaints?" George gave the crowd one last wave before Cammy opened the car door and she got in.

Lali did the same at the other side and Bea slipped into the car beside George. "Those kids were so cute, Georgie. I didn't keep us back too much, did I?"

George leaned over and kissed her on the cheek, making the crowds outside cheer at the tender moment. "Don't worry about it."

"That means I did. Lali was prodding me the whole time, trying to get back to the car, but I'm sorry, I just can't walk away when there are people who want to talk to me."

"I wouldn't want you ever to change, my darling. We can make up the time."

They both waved to the crowds until they got out of sight, and then Bea kicked off her heels, and sighed, "Ah, that's better."

George leaned forward and asked Cammy to get Roza on the phone. "Roza called. I'm expecting her first day hasn't gone well."

"Give her the benefit of the doubt, Georgie," Bea said as she took a bottle of water from the fridge in the car.

"You saw the pictures in the press this morning—she was out partying and drinking as if she hadn't a care in the world. How does that look to our UN partners who are being shelled by her ex-girlfriend's weapons?"

"I take your point, but when I met with her, she seemed hurt and… lonely. Yes, I'd say lonely," Bea said sadly.

George shut her eyes for a second, just to think before she spoke. "Bea, I know, and that's why she's here, to be part of our family. I want to help her, but she doesn't make it easy for me after events like last night. I already had to fight the prime minister for her to be allowed in the country."

"Bo Dixon? Why? It's your family. Why shouldn't she come?"

"We aren't just a family, Bea. We are both servants of the government and representatives of the people. The PM is concerned lest any part of the arms scandal attaches itself to Britain. She felt Denbourg were passing off their problem to us."

Bea took a swig of her water and said, "Oh, tell her to go and mind her own bloody business."

George laughed softly. "I should ignore my prime minister? This coming from the anti-monarchist I met over a year ago?"

"Oh, shut up." Bea stuck out her tongue at her. "That was before you enticed me with your blue eyes and good looks."

George leaned into Bea and whispered softly, "Oh, really?"

Bea trailed her fingers teasingly along her jaw, and George's heart began to pound. It didn't take much for her to get lost in Bea, but just as they began to breathe each other in, Cammy said, "Princess Rozala on the line, ma'am."

Roza's voice filled the back of the state car. *"Your Majesty? Are you there?"*

They broke apart quickly, and George cleared her throat. "I'm here, Roza. Are you all right?"

"No, I'm not all right. I was kept waiting till lunchtime to meet with this Lennox person and then she had the audacity to send me home."

George glanced at Bea. She knew Lennox King was a professional and her wife held her in high regard, so there must be a reason why she sent her home.

"Really? I was always led to believe Lennox was a very punctual and dedicated person. There must be a reason why you were kept waiting. Were you there on time?"

"Of course…I mean I might have been a little late."

"How late, Roza?" George asked her in a firm voice.

There was a long sigh and then Roza admitted, *"Maybe three hours, but I was out last night."*

Bea shook her head in disbelief, and George was more than a little embarrassed that her wife had gone to the trouble to set this up for Roza, and no doubt twist some arms to make it happen, and Roza was treating the job with disdain. Timmy's was everything to Bea, and George would not allow Roza to treat her position with disrespect.

"Yes, I and all of Europe knew you were out last night. Something I do not want to see repeated. The Queen Consort's reputation hinges on your behaviour at Timmy's, and I will not see that jeopardized."

"But George—"

"No buts. No more late nights, Roza. No more stories in the press. Turn up on time, and do as you are asked by Lennox King. Are we quite clear?"

There was silence on the other end of the line for a few seconds before a small voice answered, *"Yes."*

George felt sorry for her then and Bea mouthed to her, "Be nice."

"Roza, we love you and we want you here, but we each have a role we must play. You're representing our family when you are out at a nightclub or working at Timmy's. You are representing us, and you know how important that is."

"I know. It won't happen again, George."

Bea smiled and squeezed her hand.

"That's all I need to hear. Come to Windsor at the weekend—we'll go riding. On Sundays we have a big family meal just like the old days. Bea's parents join us and we have a great time."

"I'd like that."

George said her goodbyes and finished the call.

Bea said, "Sounds like Lex stamped her authority today. I knew she could hold her own."

"Hmm. I wish I could take Roza on some engagements with me. Try and teach her some responsibility, on the job as it were. Uncle Christian has left her to flounder under the microscope of the press without proper guidance on how to carry out her role. Unfortunately I don't think the PM would wear it."

Bea turned around to face George. "Then let me take her under my wing. You see things in a black-and-white kind of way, but I think we could connect. I'll ask her to girls' night."

George chuckled. Girls' night happened once a month, barring any official engagements, and Cammy and herself were banned from entering the palace cinema room where Bea and her friends watched films, drank wine, and ate snacks.

"I think she would love that."

Roza lay on her bed, her eyes sore from the tears that were now all cried out. After her phone call with George, she felt alone and guilty for disappointing someone she really looked up to. Maybe she was what her father, what everyone, said—selfish and a disappointment.

She clutched a small silver photo frame. In the frame was a moving picture of her mother, Queen Maria. A woman who had given her life, but who was a stranger to her.

As a child the silver frame had sat on her dressing table, and then at night she would take it to bed, hide it under her pillow, and imagine her mama coming into the nursery and reading a story before bed.

Roza imagined every moment of that scene. The story, her smile, her laugh, the smell of her perfume, and the song she would sing as Roza drifted off to sleep. Then as she got older she began to resent the woman she never knew, the perfect woman whom she looked so much like but could never hope to live up to.

Roza didn't look at the picture often these days, but she never travelled without it. She put the picture in her bedside drawer and lay on her side gazing at the news report playing on the TV.

It showed various pieces of footage of Thea as they reported the continuing search for her and the crime syndicate she was part of.

"Computer, pause video." The footage stopped on an image of Thea looking directly into the camera.

Rosa reached out to touch her face, but pulled back when her fingers went through the image. Fresh tears filled her eyes. When she looked at Thea, she felt a mixture of emotions. Hurt, anger, desperation, panic. Deep down she knew the relationship had been toxic for a long time, but she was trapped in a vicious cycle of emotional need for someone to love her and defiance towards her father. The more he disapproved, the more he pushed her into Thea's arms.

She held up her left hand and gazed at the ring on her finger. It weighed heavily on her, but there was a small part of her that didn't want to give up that one thing that represented a relationship of her own choosing and someone she had thought had cared for her.

"Computer, call Thea Brandt."

The computer responded and tried to connect to the number in her contact list. Roza knew calling was futile—Thea blocked her calls—but she just wanted to hear her voice. The voicemail recording played. *This is Thea Brandt. Please leave a message and I'll be delighted to get back to you.*

So polite. You'd never guess she was a criminal, but that's what Thea was—polite, charming, and terrifying, and Roza had seen all three.

She jumped when there was a knock at her bedroom door.

"May I come in, ma'am?" Perri called through the door.

Roza sat up quickly and wiped her fresh tears away. "Yes, come in."

Perri walked in and said nothing for a few seconds as she observed the evidence of Roza's puffy eyes and damp cheeks, but to her credit she said nothing. "I wondered, since you're back early for the day, if you would like to get out for a while."

"I wanted to go shopping, but Ravn insisted it wasn't possible with the paparazzi and everything."

Perri smiled warmly at her. "I wasn't thinking about shopping, and I've already cleared it with Major Ravn."

"If it gets me out of here, then I'm game." Roza got up and went to her wardrobe. "What should I wear?"

"Something comfortable."

❖

Roza followed Perri from a gravel car park up to a wrought-iron set of gates. Major Ravn and Johann were up ahead, already through the gates and checking what was beyond.

Whatever this place was, it was quiet on a weekday and she was sure there were no cameras waiting to take pictures of her. "Where are you taking me, Perri?"

Perri stopped at the gates and touched the bars as if remembering some nice memory. "This is a place where your mother used to come a few days a week, just to get away from it all. It's a secret garden attached to the large Edwardian house over there, but it's open to the public. Just wait till you see inside."

She opened the gate further and they went in. Roza couldn't see what was so special about it so far. There was a path, overgrown with weeds and wildflowers. Up ahead trees and plants followed the line of the path, and were so thick, she couldn't see what was ahead.

"Perri? Are you taking me to an overgrown jungle?" Roza moaned.

"Just around this bend in the path and you'll see this hidden gem."

Roza sighed. Perri had pulled her away from the comfort of her bedroom for this?

They rounded the corner and Roza gasped. "It's…it's…"

In front of them was an Edwardian sunken garden. Classical pillars with flowers and plants hung down and twisted around the stonework. The path they were on turned into a stone walkway that led along to a pergola at the other end.

"Beautiful, isn't it?" Perri said.

"Yes, it is. It's so quiet and tranquil."

"I know, you would never guess it was in the middle of London, would you? Let's walk along to the pergola."

They started to walk and Roza asked, "How did you know about this place?"

"Your mama used to come here all the time to sketch, when she wasn't at art college."

Roza looked around at her sharply. "My mama went to art college? I didn't know that. I mean, I knew she drew and painted—I've seen her pictures at the palace—but I didn't know she studied it."

"Oh yes." Perri stopped halfway along the walkway and leaned on the wall there to look down to the large pretty pond below. "She went to the London School of Art, just like your cousin Theo. Maria wanted to be an artist, before she met your father of course."

Roza joined Perri, leaning over the side. It really was so pretty here. A set of stairs led down to the pond where some ducks were swimming and playing, and one elderly lady was sitting on a park bench throwing bread to them. It was the only person she'd seen since they arrived. It was certainly a place to think and feel calm. All you could hear was the trickle of water and the birds in the trees.

Ravn and Johann stopped up ahead, and the others stayed further back behind them, securing the area.

"I never knew she was really serious about art," Roza said.

"She was very serious, and at that time she never thought she would have many royal responsibilities, so she could dedicate her life to art. She was only the oldest child of the King of Spain's second son, remember. Along with your Aunt Sofia, they didn't really expect to be in the royal limelight much. Then your mother met your father, and your aunt met your Uncle Edward."

No one had ever talked to her with so much freedom about her mother. Queen Maria was a touchy subject in the family, and she'd learned to stop asking questions after a while.

"Perri? What was Mama really like?"

Perri smiled but didn't look around. She kept looking down at the ducks frolicking in the pond.

"Maria was beautiful inside and out. Friendly, thoughtful, kind, and…serene. Yes, I would say serene, and that serenity touched all those who were close to her."

"I can't imagine it affecting Father. God knows what she saw in him," Roza said with anger in her voice.

Perri snapped her head around. "That's where you're wrong. Christian was a brash young man when Maria met him at a party. A brash and wild young man who went through ladies like they were going out of fashion. He was young, in the first year of university, and enjoyed every aspect of student life. He drank too much and partied too much, and his father, your grandfather, wasn't best pleased with him, I can tell you."

Roza couldn't believe this description of her father. The man she knew was cold, distant, a stickler for discipline and doing things in the correct manner. "What happened to him to make him so different?"

"Your mama. Let's walk along to the pergola."

At the end of the walkway they went into the classical stone pergola and sat on the stone benches there. Major Ravn and her team stood by the entrance.

The view was spectacular from here and Roza could quite imagine a young artist being inspired by the gardens. "So what happened?"

Perri chuckled. "Christian chased her relentlessly, but she was never going to be interested in someone who behaved like he did at the time. Don't get me wrong, she found him handsome and attractive, but she told me she was sure there was much more beneath the rebellious image he liked to show the world. So he told her he would prove to her he could be exactly what she needed, and he loved her, no matter how long it would take."

"I never even knew Father went to university," Roza said.

"He didn't, for long. Christian left in his first year and went back home to train at Denbourg's army officer training college. He was dedicated to his training, and it really made him a new man. A disciplined, helpful man who always thought of others before himself. He never forgot your mother and wrote her emails all through his training and first deployments. Maria said she gradually fell in love with him through his love letters, as they really were. He changed his life because of your mother, and won her love."

Roza stood and walked over to the side and tried to gulp back the confusing emotions she was feeling. She had always thought she resembled her mother and had none of her father in her, but going by this, she had more than a little of King Christian in her.

"I wish I had known that man. Not the man he is now."

"I know he has been hard to live with since Maria died. I think he felt she was the one who had made him a better person, and after she was gone, he shut away all his emotions."

Roza felt *her* emotions threatening to spill out. She took a deep breath and closed her eyes. How could someone so kind and gentle like Queen Maria love him?

They stayed quiet for about five minutes, taking the time to enjoy the secluded garden.

"Do you draw, Roza?"

"I used to. Not any more."

"You should try it again. Your mama found great peace here, and so could you."

"I'm not my mother, and I'm sick of people expecting me to be," Roza snapped.

Perri got up and walked over to Roza. "How do they?"

"Everyone. Father, Gussy, Aunt Sofia, you, the public. Everyone sees the royal rebel who is everything Queen Maria wasn't. I see the way they look at me."

"I think you're projecting your own fears on others."

She thought back to lunchtime when Lennox King walked into the office. She'd been so angry at being kept waiting, but even angrier when Lex dismissed her. "It is true. I've seen it all my life—I saw it this morning from this woman I'm meant to be working with. She looked at me like I was wasting her time, like I was a silly party girl."

Perri took out a handkerchief from her bag, and wiped away Roza's tears of frustration that had started to fall. "If you want to be treated differently, then don't give people the excuse to accept what is written about you in the media. I know there's more to you than those headlines, because any child of Maria will have such goodness and kindness inside them."

"I didn't give the best impression this morning."

"Then show this Lennox just how useful you can be. Show her the house of Ximeno-Bogdana-de Albert is not afraid of hard work."

"Maybe."

CHAPTER SIX

The next morning, Lex fought her way past the paparazzi in front of the Timmy's and finally got in the building. She immediately called security. "This is Lex. Get in touch with the police. We can't have our staff and clients having to go through that media scrum at the front door. We need barriers and proper police support. Thanks, and call me and let me know the outcome."

All this for a bloody princess who doesn't even want to be here.

When she arrived at her office floor, she was surprised to see Roza's security already in their positions. Conrad came rushing over to meet her.

"Lex, Princess Rozala arrived about ten minutes ago."

"Really?" The Queen must have backed her after all. Excellent. She approached the office door and nodded to Major Ravn. "Morning, Major, I've asked security to contact the police about the press outside. I'd appreciate your cooperation if they contact you."

"Of course. I'll speak to them. It would make sense to move the press pack across to the other side of the street, to leave access clear for those entering the building."

Ravn opened the door for her and she walked in to find Roza sitting at her new desk. As she did yesterday, she gave Roza a bow. "Good morning, Your Royal Highness."

"Good morning, Lennox. Is this early enough for you?" Roza asked sarcastically.

Lex just knew this woman was going to bring a whole heap of trouble to her life. "It's good enough, and it's Lex. Call me Lex."

Roza got up and strolled slowly over to Lex's desk and sat on the edge, her skirt riding up her thigh. She was wearing a more appropriate dress today, but it was still tight around her obvious curves and assets. Lex wanted to look, but knew that would be a mistake, so she never showed an ounce of interest. She sat back in her office chair and met Roza's eyes with indifference. Lex could see she was a temptress, but she was well practised in keeping control of her needs and wants.

"So what can I do for you first, Lex?" Roza's eyes dropped down to Lex's crotch and she licked her lips.

She was a beautiful girl but Lex knew when she was being played with, and she wouldn't allow it. Clearly, Roza was playing a game of control and Lex would not let her get the upper hand.

"Well, you're here to learn everything from the ground up, so how about Conrad teaches you how I like my coffee?" Lex laughed internally at the anger that instantaneously flared in Roza's eyes, before she took a moment and calmed down. Lex knew she had been a bit condescending, but she was simply showing Roza she could play just as well as her.

Roza stood and smoothed down her dress. "I am yours to command, *apparently*."

❖

Conrad and Roza were in the staff kitchen area. As ever, Ravn wasn't far away, and stood at the doorway of the kitchen. Conrad's hands were shaking as he made coffee for all three of them.

"Conrad?"

"Yes, Your Royal Highness?"

She touched his shoulder and he nearly jumped out of his skin. "Hey, relax. Listen, I'm not some stiff, scary royal. I'm just a normal woman—call me Roza."

Conrad looked nervously towards Ravn, who stood staring ahead. "Are you sure she'll let me?"

Roza turned to Ravn and said, "Ravn, stop looking so mean and moody. You're terrifying Conrad here. She's a pussycat really. How about we start again? I'm Roza—I like clubbing, dancing, and having fun."

Conrad finally cracked a smile and replied, "I'm Conrad, and I think your dress is just divine."

Roza burst out laughing. "See? We're going to get along famously.

So dish the dirt on Lex. If I'm going to be number one tea girl, then I need to know her likes and dislikes."

Conrad leaned back against the kitchen counter, visibly more relaxed. "That's the thing about Lex. She doesn't really have any dirt to dish."

Roza joined him leaning against the counter and sipped the coffee he'd made them. She couldn't believe someone as good-looking as Lex didn't have any dirt, and she had noticed Lex's good looks straight away. Even though she was annoying, infuriating, and disrespectful to her sometimes, she was an extremely good looking butch. "I don't believe that. Tell me."

"No, honestly. She lives a really clean life. Decaf coffee, fruit tea, protein shakes, and she gets lunch sent from a little local deli. Brown rice, chicken, veggies—super healthy."

Roza had noticed a fridge in the office filled with fresh fruit juices and bottles of protein shakes. *She has a great body—she must work out.* Roza was sure she could get her attention and tempt her.

"Okay, let's get this coffee back to her before she thinks I'm slacking."

Roza took in the coffee and placed it on Lex's desk. "Black coffee, decaf. I think I just about managed my first task."

"So it would seem, thank you. I've mailed you the link to the virtual mailroom. I want you to go through each item, and enter the details on a spreadsheet, and note which department they have to be referred on to. It's backed up from last week so there's a lot to do."

"Excuse me? You want me to go through mail? There's nothing better you can think for me to do than sort through mail?" Roza said angrily.

Lex didn't even look up from her own work and replied, "You're learning from the bottom up, remember? First coffee, then mail."

Roza didn't know what was more infuriating, being given such a menial task or the fact she didn't even look up at her. "You are the most disrespectful person I've ever met, you know that?"

"I'm not disrespectful. I'm just treating you as a normal employee, as I was requested to do. You can have more important work to do when you prove you can handle the basics. I won't put serious work in the hands of an amateur when it could affect this charity. Your first week is mail, and then we'll see how we go."

Roza clenched her fingers so tightly they went white, and her heart battered in her chest. She wanted to walk out, but if she did, Lex would have won. Roza remembered what Perri had said to her yesterday. *Then show this Lennox just how useful you can be. Show her the House of Ximeno-Bogdana-de Albert is not afraid of hard work.*

She gave Lex a hard stare. She would be the best PA Lex ever had, and she'd have Lex eating out of her hand.

A few days later Roza was starting to get into the swing of things, and actually enjoying her new nine-to-five timetable. Not going out every night till all hours was giving her energy she never knew she had. So much so that after a shower and change after work, Roza had Major Ravn take her to her mother's drawing spot in the Edwardian garden. Armed with some new pencils and a sketch pad, she was trying to recapture her love of art that she had lost many years ago.

The mid-March evening was bright and beautiful, and although a little chilly, she was quite comfortable drawing in the pergola of the garden, overlooking the pond and ducks.

As she drew, her thoughts turned to her day and the person who filled them, Lex.

Lex was fascinating to Roza. She was not only an exceptionally good-looking butch, but she was someone who embraced that part of herself wholeheartedly, much like Major Ravn, and could teach some of the men she had met about looking sharp and well turned out in their suits and ties.

Roza looked up from her sketch pad to Major Ravn, who was surveying the scene for potential threats as always.

"Ravn?"

"Yes, ma'am?"

"What do you think of Lennox King?"

Ravn took a few moments and said, "I think she is very easy to work with, straightforward, controlled, and a woman of her word, so far, to me."

Controlled, that was a perfect way to describe Lex. Her day and way of life seemed to be regimented. Decaf coffee and a protein shake in the morning, a fruit and vegetable smoothie at eleven, and then she disappeared from the office at lunchtime for an hour and a half every day, and returned to the healthiest lunch Roza had ever seen.

Conrad, with whom she had had an instant rapport, insisted Lex was everything she appeared. No dark secrets and no talk of any women in her life, which she found hard to understand.

Lex had a calm authority that was very sexy, but there must be a way to shake her and get under that controlled persona, and if there was, she was the girl to do it.

Roza looked down at her drawing of the pond and was pleased with what was developing. She was extremely rusty and it would take time to relearn some of the techniques she had learned in art class as a child, but the process was fun and brought calm to her day. It brought her comfort to know her mother had been in this exact spot doing the same as she was today.

She closed her eyes and listened to the birds chirping away and tried truly to connect with the spirit of this place and her mother, but every time she tried to clear her thoughts, Lennox King floated across her mind.

Roza had to admit, it was a change to meet someone who either didn't treat her with reverence or like a ticket to a glamorous night out, like some of her acquaintances. No, Lex didn't give her attention easily, but for some reason Roza wanted it so very much.

She packed up her things and said to Ravn, "I think that's enough for today. Time for dinner, I think."

I wonder what Lex is doing?

Since Roza had arrived at the beginning of the week, Lex had watched her work with quiet amusement. The look of determination on her face, and the intense fury that came over her when the computer did something she wasn't expecting or couldn't work out how to fix was sweet.

Sweet? Did I just describe her as sweet?

She was slowly learning that Roza's anger, though intense, would dissipate equally as quickly as it rose. Roza was certainly more complex than the short phrases the press used to describe her, like *party girl* and *royal rebel*.

They had managed to successfully get through a first week together. She was in no doubt Roza was simply determined to prove her wrong, that she could cope easily with the work given her, but as to whether Roza would lose interest over the next few weeks, who could say. The one thing Lex did know was she would deserve an honour from the Queen if she survived this.

Lex was just about to get her bag together for the gym when Roza came over to her desk with a satisfied smirk on her face.

"Finished," Roza announced.

"Finished? Finished what?" Lex thought maybe she was leaving or something like that.

Roza bent over the desk, giving Lex a free view of her cleavage. "Finished the work you gave me. All last week's mail logged and done, up to this morning. I emailed the spreadsheet back to you."

Lex had to admit she was surprised. The amount of tedious work she had been given should have kept her busy well into next week.

"That's quick. Are you sure you've done it correctly?"

"Positively. Check it yourself," Roza challenged.

While Lex called up the file, Roza came and sat on the desk, just by the side of the computer. She was so close, Lex could smell her perfume, and it smelled so good.

Lex checked down all the columns on the spreadsheet to make sure everything was right, and it looked perfect. "Did you send these on to the correct departments?"

"I did. You can check on that too," Roza said smugly.

"It's all right. I trust you. Well done then, Roza. I thought this would take you till next week, but I was wrong."

"So what's next?"

Lex got up and got a protein shake and water from the fridge. "Next is I'm going to the gym. Have an early lunch."

"You're very dedicated."

Lex put her things in her backpack and zipped it up. "Maybe, but I like to keep healthy."

"Which gym do you go to? Maybe I could use some exercise to wake me up at lunchtime," Roza hinted.

"No," Lex said flatly. "The gym is my private time."

"You're very rude, you know."

Lex swung the bag onto her shoulder. "Look, it's just my time to relax, okay? Away from here, away from everyone. Why don't you go out to one of the restaurants around here. You'd love them. Take Conrad—I bet he'd love to have lunch with you."

Lex observed a look of sadness and what she could only describe as loneliness.

"I can't just go out and have lunch. You've seen the press out there. I need to send out one of my security people for lunch, just like every day."

Lex found herself feeling sorry for Roza. She hadn't realized Roza stayed in the office every lunchtime while she was out. Lex tried to be upbeat. "You did an excellent job this morning. I'll get you some more work when I get back, and Monday you can do something a bit less tedious. We're never short of work to do at Timmy's."

Roza's cheeky smile was back. She got up and leaned over to whisper in Lex's ear, "I'm ready for whatever you want, Lex. In fact you'll have to keep up with me."

She pulled back, winked, and walked seductively out of the office. Roza's words and breath on her ear hit Lex hard. Her heart pounded, and her sex throbbed. No one had triggered that sort of reaction in a long, long time, and it frightened her. She grabbed her bag, and went out of the office quickly and without looking back.

Lex got through the rest of the day without either throttling or kissing Roza, although both had been viable options. She sent her home about four thirty and worked late, as usual. She went home to quickly change and headed back onto the late-night streets of London. Dressed casually in jeans, T-shirt, and jacket, she got lots of interested flirtatious looks as she walked down the street in a predominantly gay area of town. This part of London was filled with pubs, clubs, and restaurants, and happy well-adjusted people enjoying a spring evening together.

Lex would never describe herself as well adjusted, far from it—and that's why events today had disturbed her.

She stopped off by a corner café with tables and chairs outside and a darker more intimate seating arrangement inside. Lex walked through the door and heard her name being called.

"Lex, over here."

Lex smiled when she saw her friend, Vic. She made her way over to the table in the corner, and Vic stood and embraced her. "Thanks for coming, I appreciate it."

"You know I'm only a phone call away. I ordered you a decaf latte. I hope that's okay?"

Lex took a seat. "Perfect."

"So how's life, mate?" Vic asked.

Vic was always straight to the point, and that made her a perfect friend for her. Vic was a few years older than her, and the only person she could count as a friend, in her new life. The only one who could understand.

"Things have been good." Lex tapped her fingers on the wooden table nervously.

"But? I know something's wrong. I can tell when you're worried."

A waitress came and gave them their coffee, giving Lex more time. "Well, it's not really wrong. It's just…I had a reaction to something today that I haven't had for a long time, and it freaked me out."

Vic added lots of sugar to her coffee while Lex added nothing as usual.

"We have a new girl, a new *woman* working for us. I'm teaching her the business and—"

"Princess Rozala?" Vic asked.

Lex looked around them to see if anyone heard, but everyone was talking amongst themselves. "Not so loud. The press are camped outside the building, desperate for a story. I don't want my troubles to be splashed across the papers."

Vic laughed. "Princess Rozala is filling the papers every day. I've had a running commentary from June about her and her outfits."

Vic and her wife June were a devoted couple and an inspiration for Lex. "June can work with her then. The Queen Consort asked me to do her a favour and keep the princess busy while she's here."

"Is she a rebel as they say? I know there are a lot of people angry over this arms business, and her ex-girlfriend," Vic asked.

Lex immediately felt something new. She felt protective of Roza, and didn't want people to have a bad view of her. "She's obstinate and fiery, but hard-working, when she puts her mind to it." *And lonely*, she thought silently. "I think there's a lot more to her than what the media think."

Vic dipped one of the biscotti in her coffee. "If you think she has redeeming qualities, then she must not be that bad."

Lex stared into her coffee. "She's not, just misunderstood. Probably."

"So what's the problem? When you called, you said you needed to talk."

"I felt something today when I was talking to her, that I hadn't felt for a long time. Hunger."

"She's a beautiful girl. It's only natural to feel attracted to her," Vic said.

Lex shook her head vigorously. "No, you don't understand. Not attraction, I've felt that before. The intense hunger I used to feel before I..."

"Before you went on a binge?"

Lex nodded and touched the tattoo on her wrist. "It frightened me. That feeling when you have no control of yourself, or your wants and needs. I don't know why it's back after so long."

"If you want my opinion, you're conflating sexual attraction with the needs you had in the past, and how they made you feel."

"But sex was a big part of that. You know how I was." Images of Lex's past floated across her mind. She remembered one cocaine- and alcohol-fuelled party she'd attended at a famous actor's house. There were models, musicians, politicians, all enjoying his wild hospitality. It was one of the wildest parties she had attended, and she had been so drunk and high, she couldn't remember much, but she did remember being in one of the bedrooms with two women who were more than happy to accommodate any needs she had, given the money she had been throwing around, and then waking up in a police cell after the party was raided.

She would never forget the look on her dad's face when he came to pick her up from the police station, and she could still feel the shame and a sick sensation deep inside her gut. She had thought that was her rock bottom, but it took more than that feeling of shame to start her on the road to recovery.

"I know that, Lex, but one day you're going to have to separate a perfectly healthy need for sex from your destructive behaviours. You can't live the rest of your life running away from your natural needs. Today was probably just your body telling you to move on with your life. Find a nice girl to go out with, and enjoy it for what it is."

Vic was probably right in that her reaction was down to frustration. She would just have to work harder in the gym. "I can't take that chance. It's too dangerous a road for me to go down."

❖

Roza was bored. She stared at the computer screen looking at some websites while someone from her security unit got her lunch.

Now that she had gotten the work Lex gave her all up to date, there was nothing left to do. Maybe that was Gussy and George's plan—keep her bored, occupied, and out of trouble.

Her usual London trips consisted of shopping, lunching in the most fashionable restaurants, going to art gallery openings and book launches, and clubbing. She sat back in her chair and spun herself around. Did she want to do those things? Were they really so exciting? Not when she got home at the end of the day and found herself alone.

I want more. There must be more to life, more I can do.

The garden her mother visited popped into her mind. That would be a nice place to think, and she needed to think. She could feel she had reached a crossroads in her life, and finding the right path was vital.

There was a knock at the office door and Conrad popped his head around. "Ma'am, I have lunch for you. I was going for mine anyway and persuaded Major Scary to let me get yours."

Roza giggled. "Did Ravn hear you call her that?"

Conrad looked to his side where Ravn was obviously standing and guarding the door. "Uh…yeah. Can I come in before she kills me?"

Roza waved him in. "Quick, I'll save you."

Conrad hurried in with his bag of goodies and laid it on her desk.

"Oh, whatever you've got for me smells scrumptious." She looked up at Conrad who stood, looking a little awkward. "Sit down, will you? I'd love the company."

They settled at Roza's desk and started to eat.

"This is good."

"It's from a little Italian place around the corner. Not very healthy, but delicious." Conrad smiled.

"You're a man after my own heart, Conrad. I love everything that's unhealthy. Cheese, pasta, candy, and the one thing I couldn't live without—chocolate. Luckily, and infuriating for some of my friends, I don't seem to ever gain weight."

Conrad looked at her through narrowed eyes and said, "Bitch."

Roza burst out laughing. "Yes, I get that a lot, mainly when people think I can't hear them."

After talking for a while and enjoying their food, Conrad asked, "I hope you won't mind, and you can tell me to shut up if you want, but what's the Queen Consort like? Is she as sweet and adorable as she appears?"

"I don't mind, and yes she is everything she appears. Very kind, and extremely genuine," Roza said.

"That's nice to know. The Queen and the Consort are an adorable couple. It makes you hope for that sort of love in your own life, doesn't it?"

Roza felt a wave of sadness come over her. She put her fork down and dabbed her mouth with her napkin. After the hurt of her relationship with Thea, how would she ever find something like that?

"Yes it does."

Conrad must have immediately noticed the melancholy look on her face, and remembered Roza's love life was full of hurt at the moment, because he said, "I'm sorry, ma'am. I shouldn't have said that."

"That's okay. You probably know more about my sad love life than I do, since it's all over the press most days."

Rather than replying, Conrad smiled. "I forgot. I've got something else in my lunch bag that I got for us. It should cheer us up." He pulled out a box from a local bakery with two thick slices of chocolate cake.

"Oh God, yes," Roza said, "Can I marry you, Conrad?"

Conrad laughed and handed her a napkin and piece of cake. "Sorry, Princess Rozala. I'm looking for a handsome prince."

"Damn," Roza joked.

Just as they tucked into their cake, the office door opened and in walked Lex. "Afternoon, you two. Having fun?"

Roza looked up and felt a tingle of butterflies in her stomach that she hadn't felt in a long, long time. Lex looked different. She looked pumped, her cheeks glowed with health, and her eyes sparkled with energy.

Wow, Roza thought, but quickly tried to cover up her obvious lustful stare. "Quick, Conrad. The grumpy boss is back. Yes, we have had fun. We have enjoyed a delicious lunch full of unhealthy things, and now we're having chocolate cake." Roza held out a forkful and said in a low teasing voice, "Do you want some?"

She was sure she saw a flicker of something in Lex's face and a tightening of her jaw.

"No, thanks. I don't eat chocolate."

"You don't eat chocolate? How is that possible? It's my favourite thing in the world."

Lex smiled and sat down at her desk. "I'll need to remember that.

Conrad? Could you order me chicken, brown rice, broccoli, and kale please?"

Conrad got up immediately and started to clear the lunch things he had brought. "Straight away, Lex. Thanks for sharing lunch with me, Princess Rozala."

"No, thank you. Why don't we reconvene tomorrow at lunchtime and we can run down our grumpy boss?"

Conrad looked delighted. "You've got it. Thank you, ma'am."

She gazed at Lex and saw her smiling and shaking her head at Roza's joke. "You think we won't?"

"Oh, I'm sure you will," Lex said. "Now in true grumpy fashion, get back to work, Princess."

There was something about the way Lex called her *princess* that made her feel excited, and giggly like a schoolgirl. "Whatever you say, boss."

CHAPTER SEVEN

After three weeks together Lex was beginning to come to terms with having Roza in the office. In fact she was pleasant company for the normally solitary Lex. Although it was getting harder and harder not to fall under her spell, especially as Roza tried to flirt with her incessantly. Lex had no idea why—she didn't think herself anywhere near Roza's league.

In the beginning Lex thought it was just to prove the point that Roza could have her, but as she got to know her, she became doubtful. Underneath all the bravado, Lex suspected Roza was not what she portrayed.

Lex puzzled over this as she made her way back from the gym. She walked past the press pack who ignored her, thank God. It would have put an unbelievable strain on her if she had to put up with what Roza did.

She got in the lift, leaned back against the wall, and let out a sigh. *Roza.*

Roza was in her thoughts far too much these days. Sometimes Lex caught herself gazing at Roza while she thought she wasn't looking. In those moments she saw the beautiful, natural girl she was, but sometimes when Roza was in close proximity to her and she was flirting, it was torture not to give in to her body. Lex shook off the feeling and walked into her office after giving Ravn and Johann a nod.

Unusually she found Roza alone at her desk. "Hi, no Conrad this lunchtime?"

Roza gave her the sweetest smile and she felt her chest constrict.

"No, he had to go to the bank. He said to tell you he won't be long, and he ordered you lunch before he went."

"No problem. I had a few thoughts for the staff meeting tomorrow and some phone calls I need you to make. Can you come and take some notes?"

"Of course."

Lex sat down and was surprised when Roza came to sit on the edge of her desk, right beside her.

"I think you can hear me perfectly well on the other side of the desk, Roza," Lex said without looking at her.

Roza leaned forward into her personal space, and Lex had to stop herself from groaning at the smell of Roza's perfume.

"Why? Do I frighten you?" Roza whispered.

Yes. Lex could almost taste Roza's lips, and feel her nails tenderly scratching down her shoulders. She had to quickly regain control. "Don't be silly. This is just not the way to conduct office business."

Still Lex refused to look at her, but she soon felt Roza's lips brushing her ear.

"I think you *are*. I think you're frightened of letting go of some of that perfect control you keep on yourself twenty-four-seven."

All Lex could think about was kissing Roza until she begged Lex to touch her, and if she turned her head to look into her eyes, she was sure that's what would happen. *Stop, stop. Breathe.* "Get to the other side of the desk, and sit down, before I tell Ravn you're sexually harassing me."

Roza laughed and said, "Yes, boss."

Finally Roza sat down, but she crossed her legs seductively and gazed directly into Lex's eyes. "Okay, boss, what do you want me to do for you?"

Lex was so turned on she was getting angry. "Why do you do that?" she snapped. "Besides the fact I'm ten years too old for you, why do you flirt and try to get a reaction from me?"

Roza looked surprised at her anger, and snapped straight back, "I'm twenty-three—I don't think thirty-three is too old for me. My ex was twenty-seven years older than me."

Before Lex's mouth could engage with her brain she retorted, "Yes, and look how well that turned out."

As soon as she said it she regretted it. Roza's face crumpled and tears welled in her eyes. Roza stood and hurried to the office door.

Lex jumped up quickly. "Roza, wait, I'm sorry."

Just as Roza put her hand on the door handle she turned back. "I do it because I like you, and when you come back from the gym you have this glow, and your eyes sparkle with energy. I'm sorry you don't seem to like me. Maybe someone else will."

Roza left and slammed the door. Lex put her head in her hands. "Why did I say that? Why?" Roza was making it so hard to keep control. One minute she was this seductive woman wanting her attention, and the next she looked like a hurt little girl. She didn't know whether she was coming or going.

Roza came back about thirty minutes later and didn't talk to her for the rest of the day, and although the next few days were frosty they did start speaking again.

❖

While Roza waited on Conrad bringing lunch, she looked out the office windows and watched Lex cross the road and walk around the corner to the gym.

I wish I could see her there. Roza suspected it was the only place you could see under the strict control Lex kept on herself, if the sparkle she had when she returned was anything to go by. If she was an ordinary person, she could go over to the gym and ask to look around, but the ever-present press pack and Major Ravn and Co. would put a stop to that in three seconds.

But what if she wasn't Princess Rozala?

Conrad knocked and came straight in carrying lunch. "The cake shop had this amazing chocolate fudge cheesecake and I just couldn't choose—"

Roza wouldn't be distracted by chocolate cheesecake. All she could think about was the idea forming in her brain. "Conrad, I need to ask you a favour."

Conrad put the food down on her desk and said, "Of course. You know I'd do anything to help you."

"Well…" Roza sauntered over to him and sat on the desk. "I want to get out of here without being noticed, at lunchtime tomorrow."

"Okay, but how will you ever get by the press?" Conrad asked.

"A disguise. It'll be such great fun. Please, all I ever want is some time on my own. Will you help me?"

Conrad tapped his fingers on the desk. "Of course I'd want to help you, but Major Scary will notice."

"She won't, I have it all worked out in here." She pointed at her head. "Will you help me? Please?" Roza clasped her hands and begged.

Conrad sighed. "You better save me when Ravn tries to kill me." Roza laughed and gave him a big hug and kiss. "Thank you."

❖

The next day Conrad did as Roza had asked. As soon as Lex headed off to the gym, the plan went into action. Roza stood with Conrad outside the ladies' toilets. He handed her over a large rucksack. "Are you sure this is a good idea? Major Ravn will kill me."

"It'll be fine. It's my one chance to escape for a bit. Give me fifteen minutes, then distract Ravn and Johann, okay?"

Conrad sighed dramatically. "You be safe, okay?"

Roza kissed him on the cheek. "I promise."

She went into the private bathroom and locked the door. She was almost giddy with excitement as she pulled on the heavy men's clothes and made herself extra bulky.

Roza looked in the mirror and tied her hair up before putting on a nondescript woolly hat. Suddenly she started to get nervous. "Why am I doing this?" But she knew the answer right away. She wanted to see Lex in the only place she suspected her boss ever let her control waver and enjoyed the passion Roza knew she had underneath.

Roza carefully hid the bag out of view and peeked out of the toilet door. Conrad met her eyes and immediately started to talk in animated fashion to Ravn and Johann.

It's now or never.

She put her head down and made her way to the lifts quickly. Once she got into the lift alone and the doors shut, she let out a breath of relief. "Oh God. That was thrilling."

Roza made it down and out of the lift, but the big test would be if the press would recognize her in these layers of thick heavy clothes.

The doors opened automatically, and she held her breath, waiting for the blinding flashes that always came when she walked out, but there were none. The press continued talking to each other and looking utterly bored.

Yes! I did it.

Now she just had to keep her cool and make it to Lex's gym. She put her hands in her pockets, kept her head down, and hurried around the corner. It felt so exciting. She had no agents following her every move. This was so freeing.

Roza walked into the gym and up to the main desk. She tried to change her accent from the cut-glass English with a hint of a European twang she usually spoke with and hoped she could keep her cover.

"Can I help you?" the man at reception asked.

"Um…yes, I was thinking about joining and wondered if I could have a look around."

His eyes gleamed with the prospect of a new membership, and he was on his feet in a second. "Absolutely, I'll be happy to show you around."

Once he got someone to cover for him, he took her past the security gate and they walked upstairs to the gym. All the time he was giving her the full membership spiel about facilities, costs, and special offers, Roza was looking everywhere for Lex.

She was led through a set of doors that opened up into the gym proper. The space was impressive. One half was all cardio equipment, and the other was weight machines and free weights.

Roza still couldn't see Lex, but then she couldn't see the full weights section as it rounded a corner.

"Could we look at the weights section first?"

"Sure, we have every piece of equipment you could possibly want. In this section we have…"

She started to tune out again and then she saw Lex at last. She was up at the back of the room, walking towards the pull-up bar. Roza pulled her hat down to try and make sure she wasn't spotted by her.

Roza got as close as she could without getting spotted and continued to pretend she was listening to her guide.

She watched Lex pull up her body weight, and almost groaned out loud at the sight of pronounced muscles in her arms and shoulders with a light sheen of sweat coating them.

God, she's gorgeous. Roza could feel herself falling in lust on the spot. Her stomach clenched and a heavy beat started deep inside. She did groan out loud when Lex was at the end of her reps, and she pushed it one last time before letting go of the bars. Lex bent over trying to catch her breath. The look of the high undiluted pleasure on Lex's face was almost orgasmic.

The gym fell away and all she could see was Lex and all she could hear was her breath. Roza wondered if she looked like that when she made love.

I would love to make her feel that way.

Then, all of a sudden, Lex looked up, apparently aware she was being watched, and Roza ran, leaving her guide bemused as to what was going on. She ran out of the gym and around the corner, and then felt herself pulled into an alley.

She struggled, but the burly man pushed her up against the wall and pulled her hat off.

"Let go of me—"

He held his hand over her mouth, and it felt suffocating. "Calm down, Princess, or I'll hurt you."

She knew no one was coming to her rescue, as Ravn and her team thought she was still in the Timmy's building, so she let her body go limp.

"That's better. I've got a message from Thea."

Thea? She would send this guy to hurt me?

"Computer, play message," he said, and Thea's voice started to play from the phone on his wrist. *"Hello, my special girl. Do you miss me? I bet you do. Even after everything that's happened and how much you might hate me, I'll always be in your heart and in your head, won't I?"*

Roza felt tears come to her eyes. That was the fear she had. Thea was inside her, and she didn't know if she could ever move on, as the ring on her finger was testament to.

The message continued. *"I want you to get your father and his allies to call their dogs off me. I'm more powerful than you could ever imagine, and I will not allow my empire to fall. Remember what happened to your Cousin Theo? That will be nothing compared to what I am capable of. You know that's the truth, don't you?"*

Roza could only agree as she remembered all the times she'd felt frightened by Thea. She was capable of anything.

"Think about what I've said. Goodbye, my special girl."

The audio finished and Thea's man pushed his arm further into her throat. "You better listen to Thea, Princess Rozala, or you and your family will be very sorry."

In an instant he was pulled off her and punched to the ground. *Lex.* She had come out of the gym still dressed in shorts and T-shirt and was tackling Thea's man. Before Roza had a chance to think, Ravn and Johann rounded the corner, guns drawn and pointed at both Lex and her attacker.

"Stop and put your hands where I can see them. If you make a move, you will be shot without hesitation. Johann, cover the princess."

Lex lifted her hands in surrender and moved off the attacker underneath, and Ravn indicated to her with her gun to move to the side, and addressed the man holding up his hands as he remained face down.

"Move onto your knees and put your hands behind your head," Ravn ordered.

Roza gazed down at her saviour on the ground with new eyes, while Ravn and her security team patted down her attacker.

Lex had been so brave, and fearless. She could have just called the police, but no, *she* saved her. *She could have gotten killed, and it would have been my fault.* She closed her eyes and imagined Lex lying on the ground with a bullet wound, or it could have been Ravn, who had a wife and children waiting at home.

What had been an exciting adventure had turned into a nightmare and it could have been worse. This had to stop—she was selfish and unthinking.

Ravn had told Lex she could stand, and Roza threw herself into her arms, crying hard. "I'm sorry, Lex. This was all my fault. I'm sorry, I'm sorry."

Lex's arms engulfed her and held her tight. "Shh, shh...it's okay. Everything is fine." Lex pulled back and took her head in her hands. "Calm down. It's okay. I'm here."

She nodded and buried her face in Lex's neck. This was safe, *Lex* was safe, comforting, and she didn't want to let go.

The sounds of sirens arrived and Ravn left the attacker in her team's capable hands. Ravn knelt down beside her. "Are you injured, Your Royal Highness?"

"No, I'm okay, I'm okay."

Ravn held her hand out to Lex and they shook. "Thank you for taking care of Princess Rozala for us. That was dangerous, to tackle an armed man like that, but I'm forever in your debt."

"Thank you. I appreciate that," Lex said.

"I'll go and talk to the police and get the road blocked off before I get Princess Rozala back to St James's Palace. There could be others in the vicinity." Ravn left Lex and Roza alone together.

Lex must have become aware of how intimately she was holding Roza and gently eased her grip, allowing her to move if she wanted, but Roza didn't release her grip on Lex's neck. Lex continued holding her tightly.

As the man was dragged away to a waiting police car, he shouted, "Remember what she said, Princess. Don't be stupid."

"What happened?" Lex asked.

Roza struggled to talk through the tears that suddenly came without warning. "He pulled me into this alley to give me a warning from my ex."

"Your ex? The arms dealer set this up?"

Before they got a chance to talk any more, Ravn came back for Roza, and Lex finally released her. As Roza was escorted into a state car, she looked back at Lex, longing to still be in the comfort of her arms.

Roza got into the car and it pulled off, escorted by police sirens. Ravn was angry, she knew, despite the fact she was trying to hide it, and unlike in the past when she had slipped away from security, she felt terribly guilty.

She'd jeopardized lives all because she wanted to be nosy and see Lex in her private time.

"Ravn?" Roza said in a small voice.

Ravn glanced at her quickly and replied, "Yes?"

"I'm sorry for what I did today. I was childish, and innocent people could have gotten killed. It won't happen again."

Ravn looked surprised at her apology. "I can't protect you if I don't know where you are."

"I know, and you probably won't believe me straight away, but I promise it won't happen again," Roza said sincerely.

Ravn sighed and nodded her head. "I'll take your word on that, and I'll also give you a promise, Your Royal Highness. If you desperately want to go somewhere, talk to me about it, and I will do everything in my power to make it happen."

"I promise, I will."

They pulled into St James's Palace and found a worried looking Perri at the front entrance. When she got out, Perri pulled her into a hug. She was so not used to this kind of open affection, but no matter how annoyed she was to have a new lady-in-waiting thrust upon her, she enjoyed the offered comfort, and there was something soothing about being comforted by her mama's best friend. The one who knew her the best.

"Your Royal Highness, are you all right? Are you injured?" Perri asked.

"I'm unharmed."

Perri stared into her eyes and checked all over her body for injuries.

"Really, I'm okay."

Perri kissed her on the cheek and said, "I was so worried. Your brother is waiting by the phone to hear from you, and there are some people from MI5 waiting to speak to you in the drawing room."

Roza's heart sank. *I've caused so much trouble again.* How could she expect people to believe she was truly sorry about the arms scandal if she kept getting into trouble. She wanted to go and call her brother to explain, but she looked to Ravn for guidance.

"Go and speak to the prince, Your Royal Highness. MI5 will want to debrief me in any case."

Would Ravn as commanding officer take the blame for this? Another thing to feel guilty about.

George had been circulating around the room for an hour and desperately wanted to talk to her wife. They were on a three-day trip to Washington, DC, and were this afternoon hosting a reception at the British embassy.

Finally, after making small talk for too long, she spotted Bea was finally free. She walked over to her quickly before anyone else nabbed her, which was highly likely as anyone who met the Queen Consort seemed to instantly fall in love with her.

George walked up behind her and said, "You look beautiful, and all the men and some of the women are jealous I get you to myself later."

Bea turned, smiled seductively, and discreetly ran her fingers down the front of George's shirt, and gently pulled at her belt buckle. "There's no one else in this world I would want or would let touch me, so the duty falls to you, Your Majesty."

George leaned forward and whispered in her ear, "You are such a tease, but I'm willing to do my duty as always, Mrs. Buckingham."

Bea giggled and was about to say something else when Cammy came up to them, bowed, and cleared her throat.

"Excuse me, Your Majesties. The prime minister and Prince Augustus have both called to talk to you."

The flirtatious, happy atmosphere dropped away like a stone. "What's happened? Is it Roza?"

"I think you better talk to them yourself, ma'am."

George nodded and was about to tell Bea to wait here before Bea said, "Don't even think about leaving me behind. This is Roza we're talking about."

They both slipped away quietly to use the ambassador's office. Bastian and Lali were waiting for them.

George sat at the desk and Bea stood beside her, with a supportive hand on her shoulder. "Okay, tell me what's going on before I talk to the PM. I don't want to be taken by surprise."

Bastian stepped forward, and said to the computer, "Display Princess Rozala incident report." A series of images and video appeared from the CCTV cameras around the incident, and Bastian commentated.

"At twelve thirty today, Princess Rozala slipped away from her agents and made it to a gym around the corner from Timmy's. For reasons unknown as yet, she ran out of there and straight into the arms of one of Thea Brandt's thugs. He assaulted her and gave her a message from Ms. Brandt."

Bea gasped and clasped her hand to her mouth. "Oh God, poor Roza. Was she injured?"

"No, ma'am. I believe she just got a scare."

George watched as someone came running down the alley to engage with the attacker. "Who is that?"

"That is Lennox King. She pulled him from Roza and tackled him until the princess's agents arrived."

George looked up to her wife. "Lennox King from Timmy's?"

Bea nodded and George said, "Thank God she was there. This thug could have hurt her. Trouble just seems to follow that girl around."

Bastian interrupted, "I believe the PM wants to give you a full report."

"And no doubt to try and persuade me to send her away." George patted Bea's hand to ask her to step away from the screen.

"Don't send her away, Georgie. She's made great strides these last couple of weeks. She's turning up on time and actually working well, Lex tells me."

"I agree, it's good to give her days some discipline, but the PM will have some problems with that I assume."

"The prime minister is on hold, ma'am," Bastian said.

Everyone left the room, except for Bea who went to sit on the leather couch in the middle of the office.

Bo Dixon's image filled George's screen. "Prime Minister."

"Good evening, Your Majesty. I'm sorry to disturb your event."

"Not at all. My private secretary has shown me the special report you sent. Can you confirm Princess Rozala is safe and unharmed?"

"Yes, ma'am. She is just shaken by the whole incident. MI5 have spoken to her and her security chief at great length. The attack was meant to scare her father, brother, and government into scaling down the search for Thea Brandt and her associates."

George snorted. "King Christian and his prime minister will never allow themselves to be intimidated. I will assure them our security—"

"I'm sorry to interrupt, ma'am, but I think it would be wise for the princess to go home to Denbourg."

This was exactly what George was afraid of. If it had been three weeks ago, Roza would have jumped at the chance to go home, but now she was not so sure. Bea seemed to think she was enjoying the change of pace and feeling useful for once.

"You want me to send my cousin away?"

Bo appeared to be annoyed and frustrated speaking to someone she couldn't just give an order to—that was how things usually worked for her. That was the strange thing about the sovereign's relationship with her prime minister. Bo had authority over the government and ultimately the last word, but she wasn't able to simply order George outright.

"Yes, I think it's for the best, before Britain gets any more tainted by this arms scandal."

"Prime Minister, whether Ms. Brandt used Princess Rozala's name to attract contracts or not, the crime syndicate had many countries fooled. Let me speak to her and her security and we can talk again. I will not send away my family if they need me."

"Even if it damages your own country, ma'am? Your first loyalty is to Britain," Bo said.

George was furious at that last statement, but tried to keep her emotions under control. "I doubt there would be anyone who would doubt my loyalty to *my* country, Prime Minister."

Bo immediately tried to backtrack. "Oh, of course not, ma'am, and I would never try to suggest it. I will be back in touch with you when we have more information. Again, my apologies for the intrusion, and my best regards to the Queen Consort."

As soon as the call was ended, George exclaimed, "Bloody woman."

Bea was over to her in a second, and wrapped her arms around her and placed her chin on George's shoulder. "Ignore her, Georgie."

"She tried to question my loyalty to my country." George was so angry, but her fury started to dissipate with Bea's soft kisses to her cheek and jaw.

"Shh...don't let her get to you."

George let out a breath, as her anger started to calm. Bea always brought balance to her life. "Thank you, my darling. I don't know what I'd do without you by my side."

"It's where I was meant to be. Now call Cousin Augustus and then we can take it from there. I love you."

George lifted Bea's hand and kissed her knuckles. "I will. I love you."

❖

Roza sat on her bed with her head in her hands. *I can't believe I've caused this much trouble.* She had just come off the telephone with her brother, and George, after spending the afternoon being politely interrogated by MI5.

She was glad to give as much information as possible to try and protect her father and her brother, but it was draining, and now all she could think of was how safe and protected she felt in Lex's arms. That safety was one she hadn't felt before and she longed to experience it again, not that there was much hope of that. Lex never appeared interested when she tried to get her attention and flirt, except maybe last time when she was angry. Maybe she just wasn't Lex's type?

The thought made her even more depressed. Her phone beeped.

"Computer, play voice message."

"Hey, Roza, it's Cressie. I know you're having a hard time in London. How about I fly over for the weekend and we make some headlines together?"

The thought of making sensational headlines used to be fun— she'd thrived on it. It meant she got all the attention she wanted, although not always good. In the past month she had come to realize how her behaviour affected other people, especially today. Now, in this moment, she couldn't think of anything worse than having her life spread across the weekend news websites.

How she would face Lex on Monday, she didn't know. To explain why she followed her to the gym would be difficult and awkward to put into words.

Maybe she should have taken the opportunity to leave Timmy's when George had offered it. The truth was in the last three weeks she had come to enjoy going to Timmy's, working, laughing, and joking with Conrad, and spending time with Lex.

Roza threw herself back onto the bed and covered her face with her pillow. This weekend was going to be long and uneventful. George and Bea were overseas, and Theo had left this morning for a week-long visit to South Africa. Cousin Max was with his regiment and Vicki and Grace were busy with preparations for the Windsor Horse Show. Everyone was useful, but her.

Again she heard her phone beep. "Oh, Cressie, I don't want to go out, okay?"

She waited a few seconds and sighed. "Computer, play message."

"Roza, it's Lex. I know you probably have a lot going on, but if you could just take a few seconds to tell me you're okay, I'd appreciate it. Conrad is worried about you...well, me too."

Roza felt a rush of excitement flood her body, while the butterflies took flight yet again and flapped a million tiny wings in her stomach.

"Lex! Computer, play message again."

The computer did as instructed and Roza felt even more excitement. She jumped up off the bed and began to pace backwards and forwards. "I could call her, but then I'd have to explain this afternoon...and that's hard."

Argh! Should I call? Maybe...no, yes.

"Computer, call Lennox King."

As soon as she made the call, she realized Lex would see her with red puffy eyes, no make-up, and wearing her oversized woolly jumper. She quickly ran her hands through her long hair, but there was no point—she knew she looked a mess.

Roza was just about to cancel the call when she heard Lex's voice.

"Hello? Roza? Is that you?"

Uh-oh. She hadn't activated video call and the last thing she wanted was Lex to see her like this, but she wanted to see Lex's face more. And now, Lex's face was gazing back at her.

"Hi, I just called because of your text." Roza watched Lex look over every part of her face silently.

"Are you okay, Roza? You look—"

"A complete mess." Roza finished for her.

Lex shook her head. "No, that wasn't what I was going to say. You look hurt, and alone."

She was. Despite Perri being in the apartment, she felt so alone, but she just replied, "It's been a difficult day."

"Did that thug hurt you?" Roza could hear anger in Lex's voice.

Roza ran her hand through her hair. "Just a few bruises from being hit against the wall, but my doctor got rid of them."

"I'm glad to hear it. Conrad has been beside himself with worry." They shared a smile as Lex said that. It conveyed more than either of them wanted to admit or contemplate for the moment.

"Well you can tell Conrad the princess is fine, thanks to a valiant knight coming to her rescue."

"I wouldn't call myself valiant, but I wish I'd gotten there sooner. Why did that man want to harm you?" Lex said.

This was the hard part. The part where she had to explain why she was there in the first place, why she could have gotten herself and everyone injured or killed. Roza let her long hair drape over her face in a bid to hide her embarrassment and awkwardness.

"I need to explain about today, and…it's hard."

Out of the blue Lex asked, "Do you want to meet for coffee or something tomorrow? I know a nice little place. We could talk then."

The thought of spending time with Lex was both exciting and nerve-racking, but impossible. "I'd love to, Lex, but I really can't meet in a public place. Things were bad enough before with the press, but after today, impossible."

Lex's demeanour changed. She looked disappointed for a millisecond but put on her professional, impassive persona. "It doesn't matter—it was just an idea."

Now she really wanted to see Lex. Today in her arms, and now that split second of disappointment, showed her maybe Lex wasn't as cool towards her as she'd thought.

"But I'd really love to. You know you probably should see me, just to put Conrad's mind at rest."

Lex's smile was back. "You're probably right. What if you come to my house for lunch, something like that. Would that be secure enough? No one knows me."

"I'd love to come to your house," Roza said excitedly. "Can I talk to Ravn about it, and call you back? I promised her I'd be on my best behaviour from now on."

"Sure, no problem. Go find out and call me back."

CHAPTER EIGHT

Lex switched off the vacuum cleaner and looked around her medium-sized living room with a sense of satisfaction. "I think I might be finished…oh, bollocks!" She spotted dust and dirty marks on the large mirror above the fireplace.

She grabbed a duster from the back pocket of her jeans and some cleaning spray that was hanging from her side pocket like a gun in its holster, and set to work.

"Why am I even paying a cleaner every week, and why did I ask a bloody princess to lunch?"

Lex knew exactly why—the way Roza had looked at her in the gym, and the way she felt in her arms in that alleyway. When instinct had told her to look up in the gym, she couldn't remember a time she had met another woman's gaze and felt her blood run so hot. This was more than lust, it was need, just like she had explained to Vic. A need for something she was frightened would become addicting.

She stopped polishing the mirror and remembered holding Roza. She wasn't the rebellious princess then. She had clung to her like she needed someone, an anchor to cling to in the raging storm of her life. Lex had felt so desperate to protect her, but that job was not one she was qualified to apply for.

An incoming call from her mum interrupted her thoughts. "Computer, answer call." Her mother Faith's image popped up on the projected TV screen in the corner of the room.

"Hi, Mum."

"Morning, darling. Your father's here as well."

Lex's dad, Jason, came into the picture with his usual smiling, happy face. "There's my girl, are you all ready for the big visit?"

Lex sighed, put down her cleaning things, and walked over to the couch. "I think so. I mean, I've tidied, even though my cleaner was meant to have done it."

"Did you clean the bathroom?" Faith asked with a look of panic on her face.

"Of course I did, Mum."

Faith turned to look at her husband and said, "Maybe she should have gotten a new toilet seat, Jason. Do you think the princess would expect that?"

Lex groaned in frustration. "Mum, I'm not fitting a new toilet seat just because Roza is visiting."

"But she's a princess, Lex," Faith said.

She pinched the bridge of her nose and replied, "I'm painfully aware she is a princess, Mum. Last night her security people came by and swept the house with sniffer dogs, the lot. I don't know why I would have a bomb to kill her when I saved her the day before, but anyway I know how important she is."

"You saved her?" Faith asked.

Lex really didn't want to go into this. Fortunately the news media had only reported a passer-by had come to Princess Rozala's aid.

"Yes, but keep it to yourself. I don't want my name out in the public forum. It's bad enough as it is, trying to get into work past the cameras. I'd like to keep a low profile."

Faith and Jason grinned ear to ear. "We won't, darling, but we're so proud of you," Faith said.

But her dad added a word of caution. "Just be careful though, Lex. This Princess Rozala obviously has troubles at the moment. I don't want you to be hurt in the crossfire."

"I'll be fine, Dad."

"And the food? Is it all in hand?" Faith asked. "Maybe you should have gotten a caterer."

Lex smiled and shook her head. Her mum was doing more worrying than she was. "Yes, all prepared and ready to go in the oven. No problems. Trust me, I won't dishonour the King family name or anything."

"She has it all under control, honey bunny," Jason said before kissing his wife on the lips.

"Do you two have to be so sickly sweet all the time?" Lex said.

A third head popped up behind her mother and father. "You don't have to live with them."

Lex smiled at her sixteen-year-old sister. "Hey, baby sister, keeping out of trouble?" Lex asked.

"Barely. I can't believe you've got Princess Rozala coming to lunch. She is *gorgeous*! Like a fashion icon of our time. Try not to poison her, okay? I've tasted your food, and I don't want to have to visit you in prison."

"Very funny."

Jason looked at her seriously. "I've read in the media the kind of lifestyle Princess Rozala leads, and I just want you to be careful. Okay?"

Lex gulped hard and rubbed her thumb over the tattoo on her wrist. "I will, Dad. Don't worry. It's just one lunch—I doubt I'll see her socially again."

She checked the time. "Listen, I better run if I'm going to be ready on time."

They said their goodbyes and Lex ran upstairs to get changed.

She was just spraying on some aftershave when she heard a car. Lex looked out of her bedroom window to find Major Ravn opening the car door for Roza.

Roza glanced up to the window and gave her a sweet smile and a wave, and her heart started to thud with excitement. *No, no. No way am I feeling this.*

She closed her eyes, started to breathe deeply and to take a moment to calm herself, before running downstairs.

Lex opened the door to find herself looking at Major Ravn and not Roza. "Good afternoon, Ms. King. I would like to have a look around the house while Princess Roza gets settled."

"Of course. Feel free."

She stood back and Ravn entered while talking to her team through a concealed device. "I've gained entry. Johann, take the back door, and the rest of you patrol the street as discussed."

As Ravn started to look around, Roza walked up the front steps looking so different from how she usually did at the office. She was dressed casually in a pair of tight blue jeans, flat pumps, and a pretty little figure-hugging jumper. She was beautiful in such a simple way. This was the girl she'd seen in the alley—this was the real Roza, she was sure.

"You look lovely."

Roza reached out as if she was going to touch Lex's arm, but pulled back quickly. "Thanks. You look different out of a suit. I didn't think you did casual clothes," Roza joked.

Lex crossed her arms feeling a bit bashful. "I'm quite different at the weekend. Please, come in."

"Sorry about all this fuss," Roza said pointing to Ravn as she disappeared up the stairs. "I promised I'd be on my best behaviour after yesterday."

As Roza stepped in, Lex awkwardly reached out for a handshake, but Roza took her hand and leaned in to kiss her cheek, which stunned Lex for a few seconds.

"Come through to the living room." Lex opened the door and Roza walked into the room, decked out in warm colours and real wood floors and furniture.

"This is a sweet room," Roza said.

Lex ran her hand over the short hairs at the nape of her neck bashfully. "Thanks. Please sit down."

Ravn came in to inform them she would be guarding the door while she visited.

"Thank you," Roza said. "I'll call when I'm ready to go." Ravn bowed and left.

Lex ushered her towards the couch and Roza indicated a group of photo frames set in pride of place on a side cabinet.

"Is this your family, Lex?" Roza picked up a frame with a beautiful older couple in it.

"Yep, that's my mum, Faith, and my dad, Jason."

Roza was mesmerized by the moving image which captured the couple holding each other, laughing together and kissing. "They look so happy."

Lex crossed her arms and laughed. "Yes, they are. Too happy, my sister and I think."

"You have a sister? I would have loved a sister. Is this her?" Roza picked up another frame.

"That's my baby sister, Poppy."

Roza could see Lex was proud of her sister, and her family. This was a different side to Lex, one that was not on show at the office.

"Poppy is beautiful. Will you tell me about them?"

"If you like. We can talk while I serve lunch." Lex directed her through to the kitchen and told her to sit at the kitchen table.

Everything was set beautifully—tablecloth, napkins in silver ring holders, and a thin vase of flowers in the middle of the table.

"This is perfect. Flowers too?" Roza asked.

Lex took out the salmon fillets she had cooked from the oven. "Yes, I picked them from the garden."

Roza felt the butterflies that seemingly appeared every time she was in Lex's company these days. "That's sweet," Roza said.

"To be honest, I wasn't sure they weren't weeds, but I took a chance."

Roza giggled. Lex was really making an effort, and to be honest Roza didn't feel she deserved it. "Something smells good."

Lex brought over the plates and laid one in front of her. "Thanks. I hope you'll like it."

"You're going to feed me something really healthy, aren't you?"

Lex nodded. "Yep, I'm going to show you healthy can taste good. We're having salmon with chilli and ginger, steamed green beans, and potatoes."

"Beautiful," Roza said. "I have to say I'm surprised. I never thought someone like you could cook."

"Too butch?" Lex took her seat and poured some sparkling water in both their glasses.

Roza chuckled. "Maybe."

"Well don't get too excited. I learned to make five or six dishes well, and apart from that I'm lost. When I started being healthy, I had to learn. Before that I lived on takeaways," Lex said.

Roza took her first bite and hummed in pleasure. "This is delicious."

"Thanks," Lex said. "I hope you don't mind the sparkling water. I don't drink."

"Of course not. I don't like to drink at lunchtime, despite my reputation. Can I ask you something I've been wondering?"

"Of course."

"Why all the health food, protein drinks, decaf coffee? You're very dedicated."

Roza noticed Lex shift in her seat a little uncomfortably and reach for her glass of water quickly.

"I came to a kind of crossroads in my life. I was out of balance, and I needed to find out how to right it again."

"Hence the organic superfoods." Roza smiled.

Lex took a bite of her food and nodded. "I don't let any poisons in my body any more."

Poisons? That was a strange way to describe it, but she sensed it was a somewhat sensitive subject so she moved on. "So, tell me about your family."

As soon as she mentioned Lex's family, a broad smile erupted on her face. "Well, they live in a little village in Buckinghamshire. It's rolling hills as far as the eye can see, farms, and not much else."

Roza was surprised. She expected Lex to be from a metropolitan background. She couldn't quite picture her fitting in with the country set. "I wasn't expecting that. You don't seem the country type."

Lex sat back in her chair and sipped her water. "I always wanted to live in London from when I was a teenager, and I would say I never appreciated the virtues of country living until I spent time living the excess of London life. Now I live for the holidays when I can go home."

Roza leaned her chin on her palm. There were certainly hidden depths to Lennox King and she wanted to know more. "Tell me about your parents and your sister."

"There's not a lot to tell really. We're a pretty average bunch, not as exciting as your family, I'm sure."

Roza rolled her eyes. "You'd be surprised. So, tell, tell."

"My dad was a surgeon at the local hospital, but he's retired now. My mum ran her own catering company, which she sold when dad retired so they could spend time with each other. They are...a very close couple. Sickeningly sweet, Poppy thinks. I did too, but now I'm older I appreciate how rare that kind of relationship is."

"Aw, that's sweet. Imagine being so much in love you want to spend more time with each other. Most couples can't stand each other after being together that long. What about Poppy?"

"Poppy is wonderful, intelligent, and funny. She's sixteen going on thirty, she thinks, and the best baby sister anyone could have, and I'm under orders not to do anything to upset or annoy you because she thinks you're"—Lex put on a high-pitched, girly voice—"super cool and totally gorgeous. I think that means she likes you."

Roza laughed and said shyly, "I have at least one fan."

Lex reached out and covered her hand, and Roza felt the warmth spread up her arm. "More than one."

It looked as if Lex regretted the action because she pulled her hand back quickly, and said, "Eat up and we can have dessert in the living room, and talk some more."

❖

Roza put her empty dessert bowl on the coffee table. "That was delicious."

Lex had kindly bought chocolate cheesecake and ice cream, despite the fact she didn't eat that sort of thing. Roza enjoyed every mouthful with exaggerated pleasure, trying to tease Lex, but she just laughed. Something had changed between them. The teasing and gentle flirting was jovial, natural, and sweet. It was no longer a game to make Lex lose control.

There was a lull in the conversation and Roza knew it was time to explain herself, but she felt really nervous. "I have to tell you about yesterday."

"You don't need to say anything."

"No, I do. I want you to understand." Roza pulled her legs onto the couch, crossed them, and allowed her hair to fall like a curtain around her face. "I was being childish, just because you said it was your private time. I suppose it was intrusive, but after a rocky start, we were getting on much better, and I wanted to know you better. You are so serious and restrained all the time and I thought I would see more of who you are while you were doing something you loved. Then I thought it would be a bit of fun, to show I could escape, and get past the photographers."

"I don't know how you did that," Lex said. "But when I looked up I knew it was you."

"How did you know I was even there, and how could you tell it was me?"

Lex was silent for the longest time, as if she was choosing her words carefully.

"I don't know, something just told me I had to look up at that moment, and then—your eyes."

Roza hadn't realized they had gradually gotten closer to each other. She gazed at Lex's powerful arm resting on the back of the couch, inches from her hair, and ached for her caress. "I didn't think you'd noticed me."

"Surely everyone notices you."

"The princess yes, not Roza."

"You think I know the difference?" Lex asked.

"Now, I know you do." Roza felt Lex's longed for fingertips stroke her hair. She turned slightly and saw Lex's tattoo on her wrist, up close. The tattoo that Lex touched like a talisman, that seemed to give her strength. What did it mean?

She saw a look of panic in Lex's eyes when she realized what she was doing. Lex jumped up quickly, and said, "I'll get us some coffee. How do you take it?"

"A mocha, with an extra shot and a dash of hazelnut and chocolate shavings," Roza joked.

"I'll bring coffee and milk." Lex winked at her.

She returned with a tray of tea, coffee, and biscuits and said, "I thought the major and your team would like something too."

She's adorable and she doesn't even know it. "That's kind. I'm sure they'll appreciate it, thanks."

When Lex returned, the intensity of the moment appeared to have dissipated, which was probably best.

"So, this man who tried to hurt you. Am I allowed to ask about who he was, or will Major Ravn kill me for asking?"

"No, I can tell you," Roza said. "I'd like to tell you, but it's difficult to know where to start."

Lex poured her coffee and handed it to her. Lex was astonished at how different Roza had looked since she had been here. The woman with attitude and a chip on her shoulder and the seductress were nowhere to be seen, and had left a young woman who surprisingly gave the impression of being very innocent.

"Just tell me whatever you feel comfortable with."

Roza twisted the ring on her finger. "I know you've read about my ex-girlfriend."

"Yes, I'm sorry about what I said when we argued." Now that Lex knew Roza better, she could quite understand how someone older and ruthless like Thea Brandt could have taken Roza in.

"That's okay. Well, she sent him."

Lex could feel the same anger that had hit her in the alleyway when she saw that thug with his hands on Roza. "She sent him to hurt you? Why?"

Roza shrugged. "She's on the run, feeling the pressure of the joint UN forces looking for her. You have to believe me, Lex. I would never have been with her if I had known what she was doing. She was up to some shady dealings, and she always had money to burn, but she would never talk about her business."

"Of course I believe you. Not that my opinion matters."

"It matters to me," Roza said firmly.

Lex didn't quite know how to respond to that, so she said, "You looked terrified when I found you. Was it being in contact with her again? Did that frighten you?" When Roza looked down and didn't respond right away, Lex said, "I'm sorry. That's a personal question."

"No, I don't mind. You're right. The attacker didn't frighten me as much—it was her. She has this hold over me…inside…and I can't shake free. I haven't told anyone this or been able to explain. You know the way someone can frighten you or make you walk on eggshells around them with just a look, and not lay a hand on you?"

Lex nodded. "I've never felt that but I understand what you mean, and I know what it is to be afraid."

Roza tilted her head and gazed at her questioningly. "What could possibly make a big, strong person like you afraid?"

Lex gulped hard and rubbed her thumb over the tattoo on her wrist. "That's a story for another day. I better clean these things up."

"Let me help you." Roza helped her clear the dishes and take them through to the kitchen.

As they packed them in the dishwasher, Roza said, "You said you were quite different at weekends. Since you're like a monk Monday to Friday, what do you do for fun?"

"I go rock climbing and go to a kickboxing club—that's where the gym comes in. I need to constantly work on my upper body strength at the gym for both."

Roza gazed longingly at Lex's shoulder and biceps muscles proudly displayed in the tight designer T-shirt that clung to them. "I can see that." She so wanted to lean forward and kiss Lex then. Normally she wasn't shy about using her body and assets in order to get what she wanted, but this was different. Lex was different. She appeared to be immune to her charms and that saddened her. "I've never done anything like that. At school I always managed to have a stomach ache whenever we had to do those sorts of things. Where do you do your climbing?"

"When I'm in London, I go to this fantastic climbing centre, but when I'm visiting my parents, I can do real climbing, or go hiking and camping."

Roza rolled her eyes. "Oh, you'd get on so well with Her Majesty. George adores hiking, sailing, all that tough stuff."

Lex quirked an eyebrow. "I take it you're not as keen on the outdoors then, Your Royal Highness?"

"You're right. I prefer to hike around designer clothes shops."

"My sister tells me you are a style icon," Lex said.

"Oh, I don't know about that. I enjoy beautiful clothes, and I try to wear all the up-and-coming designers in Denbourg. I learned early on if

I wear something, the fashion writers cover it and the public buy from them." Lex just smiled at her and she realized that might have sounded bad. "I'm not trying to be big-headed or anything. If I'm going to be splashed all over the world's press, I might as well publicize young designers in the industry."

"No, you're right. It's not just charities that need promotion nationally and internationally. I think that's a good way to use the publicity you get."

Roza thought this was the perfect opportunity to bring up an idea that had been bouncing around her head. "Can I ask you something, Lex—about work, I mean?"

Lex leaned against the kitchen worktop and crossed her arms. "Absolutely. Ask away."

Roza couldn't stop herself drinking in Lex's solid, confident form. The way her jeans hung around her hips made her weak at the knees. *Come on. Get it together.*

She closed her eyes for a few seconds to try and centre herself. "I wanted to get your permission to work on a little project I've been thinking about, to help the charity. I'll still be your personal tea girl and do all the other tasks you want me to learn."

"Tea girl?" Lex raised an eyebrow.

"You know what I mean. So can I work on my secret project?"

"Why do you need my permission?"

Roza felt like playing Lex and took a step towards her. "Because you're in charge."

Lex took a step forward to match hers so they were now close. Roza saw something in Lex's eyes then, the hint of interest she had crudely tried to elicit in their first few weeks together.

"Oh? I'm in charge? Who are you and what have you done with Princess Rozala?"

"This is the real Princess Rozala."

Lex leaned forward and Roza licked her lips as she inched towards her. Roza's heart thudded and the butterflies in her stomach flapped their wings excitedly.

She's going to kiss...

They jumped apart quickly when Major Ravn knocked at the kitchen door. "The car is ready when you are, Your Royal Highness. You wanted to be back at St James's Palace by five."

Roza felt her cheeks grow warm and Lex turned away quickly. "I'm coming, Ravn. Just give me five minutes."

When they were alone again, Roza turned to Lex. "I'm sorry, I have to go. Perri is taking me out to the theatre tonight, but I've had a wonderful afternoon."

"You are very welcome, Your Royal Highness."

She had the feeling Lex was using her title to put some distance between them. Time to leave.

CHAPTER NINE

Since the day they'd nearly kissed at Lex's house, Roza had noticed that as much as they were becoming friends, Lex always kept a distance between them. Whenever Roza would try to get closer, or touch Lex innocently, she pulled away and found an excuse to put distance between them.

Roza was quite certain they were attracted to each other, but why Lex didn't want to show it, she had no idea. Whether Roza was ready to move on was another matter. The strange thing was, many weeks into her job at Timmy's, Roza still didn't know anything about Lex's love life, but Lex and the rest of news-reading world knew all about hers.

Lex had given her the task of monitoring the charity's social media, and she was working on her super-secret project. She had used all of her contacts with the rich and famous to raise some much needed money, plus she had organized a party at a top London club where there would be a dinner and charity auction for all her VIP friends. She nearly had everything she needed to present Lex with a portfolio of donors, donations, and party details.

She was just waiting on one more donor getting back in touch, a big media mogul, to complete her plan. Roza rechecked her figures on the computer screen, and rubbed her hands together with excitement. "I can't wait to see Lex's face. She's going to be so happy with me."

The satisfaction of doing good for others was exhilarating, and something she wanted to continue on with. *Maybe I can get involved with some Denbourg charities when I get home. Gussy would like that.*

Roza looked at the time: three thirty. Lex had been out at a meeting for the afternoon and the time seemed to drag without her there. She was just about to go and seek out Conrad's company when Lex came in the door.

Her heart soared and she rose to her feet to go and meet Lex as she struggled with a tray of hot drinks, her briefcase, and some packages.

"I thought I'd bring in coffee," Lex said, handing the tray of drinks to Roza while putting her packages and case on the desk. "Yours is on the left."

"Great, I could do with a pick-me-up." Roza looked at the takeaway cup and it was marked as a mocha, extra shot, with a dash of hazelnut and chocolate shavings. "You remembered."

Lex's smile gave Roza the urge to kiss her and run her hands through Lex's short hair.

"Of course I remembered, Princess. I listen to everything you say."

Roza gulped hard and tried to think of something to say that didn't involve *kiss me* or *touch me*, but she was at a loss. No one had ever listened to her like Lex did. She was usually someone to be placated, or kept happy, or out of trouble, but never listened to.

"Did you have a fun meeting?" Roza managed to say.

"Planning and building meetings are never fun. How about you?"

"It's been fun doing the social media output, and I was working on my super-secret project."

"Great, I can't wait to hear all about it. Oh…" Lex picked up one of the bags she had brought and handed it to her. "I was looking for a taxi and I walked past this little exclusive-looking chocolatiers. So I went in and got you something."

Roza put down her coffee and gingerly took the iconic gold and black bag from a famous London haute chocolatier. She couldn't quite believe Lex had done something so sweet. "You bought them for me?"

Lex hung her suit jacket over her chair and came to lean on the front of her desk. "Of course, you love chocolate. Open them then."

Roza slid out a silver box tied with a ribbon. The chocolates were packaged in the shape of a jewellery box and she knew from personal experience that inside were four sliding drawers filled with delicious and very expensive chocolates. These were not the kind of thing you'd normally bring back with coffee to go.

"You shouldn't have bought me these," Roza said.

"Why? Does Major Ravn not allow you to accept gifts of sweets and chocolates? Do you need your royal taste tester to try them first?" Lex joked.

"Very funny. I think after the alley incident, Ravn considers you part of the keep-Roza-out-of-trouble team. No, I know how expensive these are. You didn't have to do that for me."

"I know I didn't, but I did, so eat and enjoy them."

Roza clasped the box to her chest and said, "Only if you share one with me."

"I don't eat sugar, you know that. I can't remember the last time I ate any sweets or a chocolate bar."

Roza had an intense craving to play with Lex. She sauntered over and placed the chocolates on her desk. "Oh come on, Ms. King. You can't be so puritanical all the time." She ran a fingernail slowly along Lex's tie. "Sometimes you've got to give in to pleasure."

Lex immediately stiffened, and her jaw visibly tightened. "What do you want from me, Princess?"

Kiss me and make love to me on your desk, she thought, but said, "Taste the chocolate with me. Come on, break one little rule. For me?"

"I might as well. I break all sorts of rules when it comes to you." Lex sighed.

Roza felt like she had won some sort of victory. She quickly opened the first drawer in the box and took out two squares of tasting chocolate wrapped in foil.

"Now to appreciate the fabulousness of chocolate, you have to taste it like a fine wine, slowly and with consideration."

"I don't like slowly," Lex said with a low tone that surprised and excited Roza.

She had a sudden flash in her mind of Lex lifting her onto the desk and pushing past her underwear and inside her fast and without preamble.

"You can't take something special like this fast. Watch me."

Lex shifted her position on the desk and loosened her tie as Roza's teasing began to make heat spread throughout her body. What she had thought would be a simple little gift had only served to amplify the attraction between them. She watched Roza slowly open the foil to reveal a dark chocolate.

"You have to use all your senses to achieve the most pleasure. First, you smell." Roza brought the chocolate to her nose, closed her eyes, and inhaled. "Each chocolate has a different aroma, fruity, spicy, hmm…this one is deep and spicy."

Lex's breathing rate increased and she couldn't take her eyes from Roza as she experienced what was clearly unadulterated pleasure.

Roza opened her eyes to meet Lex's and said, "The next sense is sound." Roza broke the chocolate square in half. "A good quality chocolate will have a good snap. Did you hear it?"

Lex nodded, unable to speak and caught in Roza's haze of seduction.

"Then there's touch. Rub the chocolate between your thumb and forefinger and it should start to melt slowly."

Roza took Lex's hand and placed her fingers on top of hers so she could feel Roza's fingers rubbing the chocolate, but it wasn't chocolate Lex was imagining rubbing.

Lex had not experienced such an erotic scene in her life. She wanted Roza and wanted her now.

"Eat it," Lex blurted out. She couldn't wait for the payoff of watching Roza enjoy the chocolate. The anticipation was killing her. She was so aroused that she felt the hunger tingle in her stomach, a feeling she hadn't had to control in a very long time.

"Patience. You can't just eat it. It needs to be savoured," Roza replied.

Lex pulled her hand back and gripped the edge of the desk in desperation, in an effort to stop herself from grasping Roza and kissing her.

Roza held her gaze, drawing out the moment as long as possible, before saying, "Now the best bit."

Lex didn't breathe, she couldn't breathe. The anticipation was killing her, and all to watch Roza eat one piece of chocolate. It would have sounded ridiculous to her under any other circumstances, but in this sensual, passion-filled fog that hung between them, that piece of chocolate going between Roza's lips was her sole focus.

"You place a square under your tongue, and let it melt…slowly." Roza took a square and popped it under her tongue. Lex groaned in frustration and, finally losing control, grasped Roza's hips and turned her against the desk.

Roza's eyes went wide with surprise and Lex took the second square from her hand and popped it in her own mouth, and started to chew immediately.

She couldn't stop herself from wanting to taste what Roza did straight away.

Roza hummed in pleasure.

Oh God, thought Lex. She hadn't wanted someone so much in a long, long time. The hungry feeling was low in her stomach and growing stronger with each passing second.

"It tastes good, doesn't it?" Roza asked in a breathy voice.

"Yes." Lex was in a kind of turmoil. She felt out of control. Her needs were taking control and she couldn't afford to let that happen. *Get out. Take a breath.* "I need to take a few minutes. Enjoy your chocolate."

She turned and walked out of the office, never looking back. As she passed her PA, she said, "I'll be upstairs, Conrad. I won't be long."

❖

Bea walked into George's dressing room just as Cammy was helping George on with her suit jacket. Bea never lost the excitement she felt every time she looked at her partner. She was gorgeous, and had a special something that made Bea weak at the knees.

"Your Majesty." Cammy stopped what she was doing and bowed.

Cammy was not in her uniform this evening, as she and George were attending a European football final at Wembley Stadium in London, although she was still dressed very smartly in a three-piece suit with her concealed weapon under her jacket.

"Looking smart, Captain. Lali is in the drawing room if you want to see her before you go."

Cammy grinned from ear to ear. She asked George, "Is there anything else you need, ma'am, before we go?"

George picked up her aftershave from the dressing table and splashed it on. "No. We've got bags of time. Go and talk to Lali."

Cammy bowed to them both and left.

Bea walked into George's arms, slipping her hands underneath her jacket. "Mmm, I love the way you smell," Bea said.

George kissed her head and let out a breath. "I've missed you this afternoon. Where was your appointment?"

Bea tensed up. "Oh, it was a nutrition specialist Lali has been seeing. I thought I could speak to her about what I should be eating and drinking to keep my energy up. You know?"

George looked into her eyes seriously. "Are you feeling tired? You've taken on a lot recently."

She had to get George to stop worrying about something that wasn't there. "No, I just thought it never hurts to look at your diet and nutrition. Anyway, I missed you so much too, but I *won't* miss being with you tonight watching football. Besides it's girls' night."

George chuckled. "I know. Luckily Cammy and I can always find something to occupy ourselves with on girls' night."

"So what film are you watching tonight?" George asked.

"The new one with Story St. John. It's not out for another month, so we get first look."

Being Queen and Queen Consort had its perks. The film distributors always made new films available to them when requested.

George narrowed her eyes and gave her a look of mock annoyance. "Uh-huh. Story St. John? What a happy coincidence. She has a film coming out just in time for girls' night."

"She plays a hunky soldier in it, I'm told," Bea said with a smirk.

"I'm sure. What kind of name is *Story* anyway?"

Bea giggled and smoothed her hands across George's chest. "Don't be jealous. You are my hunky soldier and sailor, Bully."

Story St. John, one of Hollywood's top action heroes who was also a lesbian, had danced with Bea at a big Hollywood bash on their American trip. The lusted-after star had tried to gently push the boundaries of propriety and flirt with Bea, to George's annoyance. Since then Bea had softly teased George about her.

George surprised her by taking off her jacket and draping it over the chair, and advanced on her with a dangerous smile and a look of want in her eyes. Bea's heart started to beat fast as she walked backwards and came to a stop against the wall, just inches away from one of the large forward facing windows of Buckingham Palace.

"What are you up to, Bully? You've got an engagement, and I've got guests arriving."

George boxed her in against the wall, and whispered in her ear, "I think you need to remember who makes you moan, who makes you groan, and who makes you come, while you watch your movie."

"What if someone comes in?" Bea said.

George popped the button on Bea's jeans. "They'll knock first."

Bea looked to the side and they were inches from the window that faced out onto the Royal Mall, which was always busy with tourists. "What if someone sees us? The tourists or—oh God."

George didn't hesitate to slide her fingers into Bea's sex. "Mrs. Buckingham, you're awfully wet for someone who thinks this is a bad idea."

"I'm always wet for you, Bully." She pulled George into a kiss and groaned into her mouth as George's fingers skilfully rubbed her clit. Bea jumped in fright when she heard footsteps coming towards the door that connected to the hall. The fear of being caught was frightening but thrilling. "Go inside, please."

George smiled slyly and whispered in her ear, "What if someone catches us. Catches their Queen Consort being fucked up against the wall?"

Bea immediately groaned. "Yes, yes."

George pressed two fingers deep inside her. Bea's hips started to buck and she tried to push George's hand deeper.

"Oh, you'd like that," George continued to whisper, and Bea's breathing got faster. "You'd love one of our footmen to walk in and see what a bad girl you are."

Bea's orgasm wasn't far away when the footsteps returned outside the hall doorway, and there was a knock at the door.

Bea tried to stop, but George kept going. "Someone is going to see how bad you are."

Again there was a knock at the door, and Bea's hips began to take on a life of their own. All she could think about was being caught with George inside her.

She grasped onto George's neck and cried, "I'm going to come, I'm going to come."

George bit and kissed Bea's ear, before whispering, "The door handle's moving, they're coming in."

That was all she needed. Bea's orgasm exploded in her sex and waved down her legs. If she hadn't had George holding her, she would have fallen to the ground.

"Oh God. I can't breathe," Bea said hoarsely.

George chuckled and eased her fingers from Bea's depths.

"That was a new one—" Bea was transfixed by watching George suck clean the fingers that had just been inside her.

George pulled them out of her mouth with a pop and said, "Remember that when you're watching Story St. John on the big screen."

Bea laughed and said, "I love you, Bully."

❖

Bea met Roza and walked her to the palace cinema. When they walked through the door, Lali, Holly, and Greta were lined up and all gave her and Roza an exaggerated curtsy.

"Very funny, girls." Bea turned to Roza. "They do this because they know how much I hate it. Girls, meet Princess Roza. Roza this is Holly and Greta and you know Lali."

"Hi, nice to meet you all."

They all gave Roza another curtsy and Holly said, "Come in, come and get a drink. We've got the new Story St. John film."

Greta butted in, "Who Holly has a girl crush on even though she's straight."

Lali and Greta laughed as Holly gave them an indignant look. "I do not."

Roza had never had girlfriends like this before, who laughed and teased but really cared for one another. She had thought Cressida, her now former lady-in-waiting, was her friend, but really she was a friend for hire. Cressie was happy if she was riding the coat-tails, sharing in her VIP treatment, but not this, sitting together in a relaxed setting sharing popcorn and drinks.

Bea took Roza's hand and guided her over to the leather cinema seats. "Sit down and tell me how you're getting on at Timmy's, while they fight it out."

Roza immediately thought of Lex and the simple kindness she had shown her today by bringing her chocolates. "I like it a lot. I love working with Lex, although sometimes she can be a bit too serious."

Bea laughed. "She is a serious person. Very conscientious, and determined to make Timmy's the best it can be, but she's also very caring."

Roza looked down at her hands in her lap and said out of the blue, "She bought me chocolates today."

"She did?" Bea said with surprise.

"Yes, and I never thought she even noticed me," Roza said sadly.

Bea was silent for a moment as the other women took their seats, waiting for the film to start. "Do you want her to notice you?"

Roza nodded. "She's got this icy, stoic façade and keeps all her emotions and reactions under wraps, but sometimes I can see more in her eyes."

The girls erupted into applause when two footmen came in with cocktails, juice, and bags of popcorn.

"Mojito, Your Majesty, Your Royal Highness?" Sam offered from the drinks tray to Bea and Roza.

"Eh, no. Just orange juice for me. Thank you, Sam. Roza?"

Roza gladly took one of the delicious looking cocktails. Lali looked back from her seat in the row in front and said, "Are you ready, Bea?"

Greta piped in, "Yeah, Holls is getting desperate for some Story St. John."

"Yeah, go ahead." The lights went down and the titles started to roll.

"You have wonderful friends, Bea," Roza whispered.

Bea took a sip of her drink and put it back in the cup holder. "They are the best friends I could hope to have. We all met at university, and have been inseparable since. I'm lucky Lali and Holly agreed to work with me. It keeps me sane having them around in this goldfish bowl."

"That is lucky. I've never had friends like that."

Bea lifted up two bags of popcorn and offered one to Roza. "Chocolate covered popcorn?"

"Oh God, yes. Chocolate popcorn and Story St. John? Perfect. Thanks for inviting me, Bea."

Bea patted her hand. "You know, you're always welcome with us, Roza. I want you to know you're not only family, you're a friend, and welcome to my group of friends."

Roza felt a bit emotional at Bea's words. The Buckingham side of her family were so kind, so loving, and so very different to how she had been brought up. "Thank you. I really appreciate it, and thank you for giving me the chance to work at Timmy's. I'm having a great time."

The film started with an action shot of Story St. John running through a jungle in army fatigues with a rifle strapped to her back.

Greta, Holly, and Lali all wolf whistled at the screen.

"You would think they'd never seen a good-looking woman in their life," Bea joked.

Without thinking, Roza said, "I've met Story a few times, and she is good looking, but she's not as hot as Lex." *Oh God! Why did I say that?*

Bea turned around to face her with a smile on her face. "You like Lex?"

Should she try and cover up her attraction or just come clean? She popped a piece of popcorn into her mouth and nodded. "Yes, I do. I like her a lot."

"What about Lex? How does she feel?"

"I think she likes me, but I get the impression she's scared, not of me, but of being attracted. If you know what I mean."

"I do. Lex is a deep, complex person. Give her time and I'm sure she'll warm up."

Something in what Bea had said nagged at Roza. "Do you know something, Bea? Something about her life?"

Bea turned her attention back to the screen. "No, I don't think so." Then she clammed up.

Bea knew something, Roza was sure of it.

CHAPTER TEN

R oza finally got her reply from the media mogul and was ready to show Lex her super-secret project. She got into work nice and early and excitedly waited for Lex to be done with her staff meeting before getting her on her own. Roza emailed her the project folder and walked over to her desk.

"Lex? I sent you the project I've been working on. Could you take a look at it?"

Lex gave her a big smile. "Of course I will. Sit down."

Roza took a seat at her desk and eagerly awaited while Lex scanned her work. Her silence and faltering smile started to worry Roza. "Is everything okay? I've worked my way through all my contacts, and as you can see they all have really large numbers next to them. I've used my status for good and made a lot of money. The charity auction I've made plans for will be packed with rich people who'll pay a fortune to have dinner with a royal."

Lex's continued silence worried her. She so wanted Lex's approval, in fact she craved it. After all her excitement, she was now starting to worry. Surely she couldn't have her numbers wrong?

Finally Lex glanced up from the report with a look of annoyance. "Is this really what you think charity is? Persuading other rich and influential people to part with money they probably wouldn't even miss?"

Roza struggled to find her words and she stumbled. "Well, charity is about making money for others, so we can make their lives better. Isn't it?"

Lex sighed, walked away from her desk, and gazed out the window. "I haven't told you this before, but I was a stockbroker in the city and dealt with billions of pounds every day. I used to think money was what was important in life. Money was the endgame—but not any more."

Roza was surprised. Lex didn't seem the cutthroat money-making type. She was extremely businesslike and professional, but she couldn't imagine her caring about making money for money's sake. She was too caring for that.

"I could make a call right now and get donations of a million pounds or more. That is not the point. Charity is about more than that, and if you think the world's problems can be helped with charity champagne receptions and celebrity auctions, then I obviously haven't been teaching you correctly. Give me a minute."

Lex walked out of the office and left Roza confused, angry, and unappreciated. She thought she had done something to be proud of at last, and yet someone still found fault.

Eventually Lex came back in and said, "Grab your coat. We're going out. I've cleared it with Major Ravn."

❖

Lex and Roza sat in the back of the Denbourg state car, and were driving in a convoy to the address she had given to Major Ravn. Roza sat at the very far end of the seat, clearly wanting to put a distance between them. Roza never said a word to her and continually stared out the window.

She felt bad about hurting Roza's feelings, but she had to if she was serious about learning the business and what it took to run a charity. Lex had to teach her it wasn't as simple as picking up a phone and getting money from your rich friends.

Ten minutes into their journey, Roza finally asked sharply, "Where are we going?"

"We're going to one of our newly completed Timmy's play centres. I try to come once or twice a week."

They pulled into a car park and stopped in front of the entrance. Lex got out, and Ravn opened the door for Roza.

"I called ahead to let them know we were coming." Lex walked through the front door of the centre, and was met by a nervous-looking manager and play supervisor. Lex noticed that as soon as Roza saw them, she immediately dispensed with her moody look and smiled brightly, and it warmed Lex's heart.

"Princess Rozala? May I introduce the play centre manager, Kristen Davis, and play supervisor, Donna Gordon."

Roza shook hands with the two surprised women and said, "Thank you for allowing me to visit. I'm working with Ms. King at the moment"—Roza gave her a pointed look—"and she thought it would be beneficial for me to see how everything works here."

Roza never failed to both surprise and impress Lex. Despite her protestations to the contrary, Roza handled royal life with great ease, and made those that met her feel comfortable and relaxed. If you had to define being royal as a job, Roza was an expert at it, although she so often tried to hide it.

Both staff members curtsied, and Kristen said, "We're so happy to meet you, Your Royal Highness."

"Carry on as normal—we'll show ourselves around," Lex told them.

Lex led them off down a corridor, with only Ravn following them. The rest of the agents were placed around the perimeter of the building.

As they walked Lex said, "Thank you for being so nice to them. I know you were annoyed with me."

Roza shook her head. "Again you think the worst of me. Just because I'm annoyed with you doesn't mean I would take it out on the people I meet."

"I suppose that's fair, but I'm not trying to upset you—I'm trying to teach you and show you a different perspective."

Roza stopped and looked back to Ravn, who had stopped and looked away discreetly, placed her hand on Lex's chest, and moved inches from her lips to whisper, "Teach me everything you know then, Lex. I am your willing pupil." Roza gave her a cheeky smile and started to walk off as Lex tried to control the bolt of lust that hit her low and hard.

Lex took a couple of breaths and tried to calm her body and regain her ever important control. Every instinct was telling her to take Roza in her arms and kiss her until she begged for more. That was what the old Lex would do, but the new Lex used everything in her power not to give in to that. Apart from her own problems, she knew Roza deserved so much more than a quick encounter, but it was becoming harder and harder not to touch her. She wanted Roza so much, she could almost taste her.

She hurried to catch up with her and Roza asked, "So what is this place? It's not like the other hospice centres."

"No, they are a relatively new addition. With the Queen's and then the Queen Consort's patronage, we got a huge injection of cash—"

"So money *is* important?" Roza said.

"Of course it's important, but there are some things worth more than money and that's what I'm here to show you. Anyway the Queen Consort wanted the charity to diversify into new areas, not only hospices, but facilities for children with special needs, as well as children coping with illness."

"That was a good idea." As they passed some more nervous members of staff, Roza smiled sweetly at them, which was good as the staff looked terrified of Ravn, who walked behind them.

"They have various areas to help children of different ages. A mini movie theatre for the older kids, a games room for all the latest video games, rooms full of state-of-the-art play and sensory equipment."

They approached a pair of double doors, and Lex whispered as they walked into a large open room. "There is a theatre group in this morning, so we need to be quiet."

A group of actors dressed in brightly coloured clothing were dancing and singing for a group of children who were laughing and shouting along with the show. The lights in the hall were down low, so only a few of the play workers noticed their arrival, but the children remained oblivious as they stood by the back wall.

Roza watched the little show intently, and started to laugh along with the children. "This is a great idea."

"It's important to get the kids laughing," Lex whispered. "They have such a hard time during treatment, and other difficulties they have to endure, but laughing for an hour or so can really make their lives so much brighter."

"I can imagine that."

Roza asked all about the centres—how many were there, and were they going to build more? The whole program was inspiring to hear about and she was moved to watch the little kids so happy.

When the show wound up, one of the girls in the audience, dressed in a pink tutu and fairy wings, noticed Lex and came hurrying over. "Lexie! Lexie!"

Lex immediately dropped down to her knees and opened her arms to scoop up the little girl. "There's my Princess Summer."

Roza was awed as she saw an entirely different side of Lennox King. She noticed the discreet medical paraphernalia attached to the girl, and her heart ached for her.

Lex said to the girl, "I brought a special friend to meet you today, Princess."

Summer smiled at Roza. "This lady, Lexie?"

"Yep, this lady is a real princess, Summer, and she's from a country called Denbourg, where her daddy is the King."

When Roza saw the awe and nervousness come over the child, she knelt down beside her and held out her hand. "Hi, Summer. My name is Roza."

"Wow! You're a real princess?"

"I am. You look like a beautiful princess too. I love your fairy wings."

"Lexie brought them for us," Summer said happily.

Roza turned her gaze to a bashful looking Lex, and her heart gave a great big thud, like it was hit with a sledgehammer. If she hadn't been on her knees she was sure she would have swooned.

I might be falling for you. The thought came straight from her heart and shocked her with its intensity. She knew she cared for Lex, and was so attracted to her, but this was the first time she thought she might be falling into something deeper.

Lex must've noticed something because she put her hand on the small of her back. "Are you okay?"

She nodded quickly and wasn't given any time to dwell on her feelings as Summer asked, "How did you learn to be a princess?"

Roza straightened the little girl's toy tiara. "I've not been the best princess to be honest, but…" She looked at Lex and said sincerely, "I'm trying to be better."

The smile Lex gave her made those infuriating butterflies flap a million tiny wings in her stomach. She wanted to kiss Lex so badly. This feeling was so, so different from what she'd felt for Thea. It didn't feel wrong or rebellious, or give her the constant sense of anxiety she felt with Thea. This was right and good.

Summer's mother joined them, as well as some of the other children.

Roza talked to Summer's mother about her condition and the problems it imposed on all their lives. It opened up her eyes and she thought she understood why Lex brought her here.

As they were leaving, Summer asked, "Will you come back with Lexie and teach us princess stuff?"

"I'd love to."

❖

On the journey back to the office, Roza was quiet. Lex hoped their visit had made her think.

Once they walked into Lex's office, Roza said, "I think I know what you meant earlier."

Lex sat at her desk and leaned back in her seat. "Oh? What was that?"

"You can't simply throw money at charity. You have to actually take part. Give your time, your dedication, your service to others."

Lex smiled. "You've got it in one, Princess."

Roza's cheeks went bright pink, and she lowered her eyes demurely.

God, you're beautiful.

"I was thinking," Roza said. "Could I go back and spend time with Summer and her friends, maybe give them princess lessons?"

She could clearly see the excitement Roza had at the idea. But what would happen when she lost interest, or left as she would inevitably have to? "I don't know if that's a good idea. If you start something like that, you can't just not turn up because you have a cocktail party, or a book launch to attend. Summer isn't a pet."

"You don't know me, Lex." Roza's fury surged. "I might have had a very active social life, but I'm not a bad person. If I make a commitment to spend some time with a sick little girl, I'm not going to let her down. I'm not the shallow socialite you think I am." Tears tumbled uncontrollably from her eyes. She grabbed her handbag and stormed out of the office.

Lex held her head in her hands. "Fuck! What did I say that for?"

Conrad popped his head around the door and asked, "Is everything all right, Lex? What happened to Princess Roza? She's left with her security agents."

She was doing so well. *They* were doing so well, and she'd hurt her. "I didn't believe in her, just like everyone else in her life."

❖

The next morning couldn't come quickly enough for Lex. She had tried to call Roza a few times last night to apologize, but got no answer.

She got into work early and waited and waited, hoping Roza would come in today, and to her relief she did.

Roza walked in and without looking at her sat at her desk.

Lex immediately went to her. "Roza, I'm really sorry about what I said yesterday. I was thoughtless and unkind. I tried to call you a few times last night but I couldn't get through."

"I wasn't out drinking at a club or champagne party, if that's what you think. My phone number is changed regularly for security," Roza snapped.

Lex knelt down by Roza's chair. "I didn't think that. Listen, I'm sorry, can we start again? I was wrong to say that to you. The more I've gotten to know you, the more I know what a kind, caring girl you are. I was just trying, in my unthinking way, to make sure you understood what committing your time, not just money, to a little girl like Summer and to the play centre meant. I didn't know when I started, and I'm not a princess—although I'd make a pretty good one, I think you'll agree?"

Roza chuckled and her eyes twinkled, making Lex's heart happy. "No, you are a King, never a princess."

"I suppose you're right," Lex said with a smile, and without thinking she held Roza's hand gently. "What I'm trying to say is, I worked in the City, and money and making it were everything to me. Then I had to…*reassess* my life due to certain circumstances and I had to get a new career. I thought, hey, I'm good at making money, I can do that for good now. Then I came face-to-face with what that money does. Summer, the kids, and the staff it makes possible, and the people it helps. When I first saw a group of kids, a group of kids who were ill, some who had no hope of recovery, laughing and singing because of one of the entertainers and the play workers we provided, the scales dropped from my eyes. This was what I was meant to do with my life."

Roza looked into her eyes with what she could only describe as passion. "That was beautiful."

Lex felt herself respond to her. There was nothing she could do but inch closer and closer to Roza. She wanted her so badly in this moment. Then she thought about who Roza really was, a princess of Denbourg, and how she couldn't allow herself to give in to the craving she had for her.

"Yeah…well, enough deep and meaningful conversation, we have work to do. I just wanted you to know why I took you there yesterday and why you need to be really committed to someone in that kind of vulnerable situation."

"I understand, Lex. I want to help you and do something meaningful for once. Will you let me?"

Lex stoop up and thought for a second. "How about you rethink your secret project, after knowing what you've learned yesterday. I'll give you a budget, and I want you to come up with a fully costed plan. If it's suitable for Timmy's, I'll give you the money to go and do it."

Roza jumped up and threw her arms around Lex. "Thank you. That's a great idea. I'm going to knock your socks off with my plan."

"I don't doubt it." Lex eased herself from Roza's arms and went back to the relative safety of her desk.

After a few minutes, Roza asked, "Lex? Why did you leave your job in the city?"

"That is a story for another day. Are we all good now, Princess? No bad feelings?"

"None. Let's get to work, King Lex."

❖

Roza worked tirelessly on her project while spending time at the play centre a few days a week. The group of children who came to play with her grew larger, and as it did she sourced toy dress-up kits for the kids. Princesses, knights, toy swords and helmets, tiaras, and of course the essential fairy wings.

Roza knelt on the floor and gathered the children around her in a circle. She had a dress-up box next to her and had a storybook in her hand. The little excited faces gazed up at her and tugged her heartstrings. She was so glad Lex had brought her here.

"Okay, princesses and valiant knights. Today we're going to do something a bit different with our lessons. Princesses and knights don't just have to look the part, they must always go on great quests and serve their people."

She held up her book. "This book is called *The Dragon of Crystal Mountain*, and we are going to vanquish it."

The children cheered and edged ever closer to the dress-up box. "Before you choose your parts, remember not all princesses need to be rescued. Some are warriors with swords, and some knights like fairy wings. Choose the costume you feel suits who you are."

They didn't need a second invitation, and after ten minutes they were ready to play. Roza took Summer's hand—the little girl was now dressed in fairy wings and a sword—and led the children over to the play castle in the corner. There she had hobby horse toys waiting for them.

"Everyone get your horse and saddle up. We are going on a quest to find the dragon of crystal mountain!"

All the children shouted and squealed with excitement. Roza opened her book and started to read, "Once upon a time, in a faraway land, the kingdom of Agrar was plagued by a dragon who lived in crystal mountain. The good and brave of that kingdom gathered together to go on a quest to crystal mountain…"

❖

Lex had a meeting with the centre manager while Roza was hosting her princess lessons in the large playroom. After she was finished she made her way along to see her. Major Ravn and Johann stood guard outside the door.

"Major. Everything all right?" Lex asked.

Ravn smiled, something she didn't often do. "Everything is good. Take a look."

Lex gazed through the windows in the doors and watched Roza, who was dressed in jeans and a casual top today, on a hobby horse, riding around the room.

"She's changed so much," Ravn said, "thanks to your influence."

The children cheered and laughed at something Roza said, and she was engulfed by hugs.

"No, she had it all inside her. She just needed someone to listen and pay attention to what she said." *And I'm frightened I'm falling for her.*

When Roza spotted her watching she came to the door. "Come on, you, we need another valiant knight, and you fit the bill, Lex. Oh, and you too, Ravn. We need a dragon."

A bemused Major Ravn was dragged into the playroom.

❖

When they got back to the office, Lex headed up to the roof garden. She needed some space, and time alone to process what her heart was feeling. She walked up to the edge of the roof, leaned on the barrier, and took some deep cleansing breaths. *This is so hard.* Lex already knew she was beginning to have more than feelings of lust for

Roza. She knew she cared about her deeply, but when she saw Roza down on her knees playing with the kids, kids who might not see their next Christmas, and showing them so much care, she realized she was starting to fall for her.

Being around Roza each day was getting to be so hard, and the hunger she was feeling terrified her. She heard the fire door open and just knew who it would be.

"Lex?"

Roza's very voice made her shiver. "I'm here."

She appeared at her side and leaned on the barrier beside her. "Why did you disappear?"

Because I wanted to set you on my lap and kiss you for the rest of the day. "I just needed a breath of air," Lex said.

"Oh, okay." It sounded like Roza didn't quite believe her.

Roza's hand slid along the railing until it covered her own. She knew if she snatched it away, Roza would be hurt, so she just gave in to the feeling of her touch.

"Playing with the kids was so much fun today, wasn't it?" Roza asked.

Lex nodded. "The kids love you, and they love meeting a real princess."

"I've never really been around kids much, but I enjoyed it enormously. I think Major Ravn enjoyed playing the dragon," Roza joked.

Lex couldn't help but laugh, remembering the stoic agent stomping around after the kids. "Yeah, I would never have thought Ravn would be the playing type."

"She's devoted to her wife and children, so I think she's used to it. You were the perfect valiant knight yet again." Roza inched closer.

"I had fun too." Lex was eager to get the conversation onto boring work. They both obviously had feelings and Roza seemed eager to act on them. "You're doing good work. I'm proud of you. How is your project coming on?"

"Good, I should be able to show it to you soon. Lex? Would you look at me? I can feel you trying to pull away from me every time I get closer to you."

Lex sighed and turned to face her. "Roza, I'm a lot older than you, and you've just come out of a relationship."

Roza looked down at her hand and pulled off the ring Thea gave her. "I think it's time to move on with my life."

She dropped the ring over the side of the building and it was gone. Lex didn't know what to say. This was so hard.

Roza caressed Lex's cheek and said, "There's so much I want to tell you."

Lex couldn't stop her arms circling Roza's waist. No matter how bad an idea this was, or how hurt they both could get, she couldn't stop the desperate pull towards Roza's lips.

"Lex, please?" Roza pleaded breathily.

They were about to kiss and there was nothing Lex could do to stop it. Her body demanded it. Their lips came together softly, and Roza moaned. As Lex gave in to the kiss, all her practised restraint was gone. The hunger that had been smouldering inside her was set on fire. She felt desperate, needy and Roza was the only one who could assuage her.

Roza moaned deeply, slid her fingers through Lex's short hair, and grasped at it desperately.

Lex pulled back to breathe and was about to kiss Roza again when the fire exit door opened and they jumped apart. Lex quickly tried to calm herself from the passion-filled fog in her head.

Mel from PR stared at them with a smirk on her face. "Oh, excuse me. I'll come back later."

She never comes up here. The enormity of Lex's fear was back. If anyone found out about them, it could cause them both so much trouble. Lex felt like she was shaking apart inside. One touch of Roza's lips and she wanted more, and her body demanded it right now. *I'm losing control.*

"I think we'd better go back to work."

She took a step away and Roza grabbed her arm to stop her. "Don't run, Lex."

Lex looked down at the ground and tried to get ahold of herself. "Roza, I don't know if that's a good idea."

"No, it is. Give us a chance. Will you have dinner with me tonight? We could talk."

She couldn't tonight, and she knew it would hurt Roza. "I can't. I have a prior engagement."

Roza let go of her. The sadness was evident in her watery eyes. "What engagement?"

"It's personal."

Roza said nothing but walked away without looking back.

Why do I always hurt people?

Chapter Eleven

The community centre hall was busy tonight with many old and a few new faces. Lex sat down in the circle of chairs and the meeting began. After the new members were welcomed, the floor was open. Lex didn't always speak, but tonight she felt she needed to so she stood and said, "My name is Lennox King and I am an addict."

She got the affirmation of a round of applause from her fellow group participants.

"I've been clean from drugs and alcohol for six years, and I'm so very thankful for every day of those six years."

Lex looked across to where her friend Vic was sitting and smiled. Vic had been with her every step of this journey from the first time she'd stepped into this Narcotics Anonymous meeting, after leaving residential rehab, and she couldn't have met a better friend, or sponsor.

Like her, Vic had been a successful businesswoman, owning and managing a series of pubs and clubs. Now she dedicated her life to her family, and her four whole food supermarkets in the London area.

Lex launched into her story, drawing strength from what she had overcome and where she was today, but she couldn't get away from the guilt she felt at turning Roza down.

After the meeting broke up, Lex stayed to talk with Vic.

"You looked worried when you spoke tonight," Vic said.

Lex leaned forward and stared down at the hard floor of the community centre. "I think I'm falling for Princess Rozala."

"What? You were just attracted to her when we talked last and—"

Lex looked up at her and admitted, "It's always been more than attraction. It's been different since I first met her. She got under my skin and now she's into my heart."

Vic shook her head in disbelief. "You sure know how to pick 'em.

After all these years of no one in your life, you pick a princess of one of the most influential European countries on the world stage."

Lex couldn't help but smile sadly. "I know, it's crazy. We kissed today, and I nearly couldn't stop."

"Jesus. What does she feel?"

"I think she feels the same or at least thinks she does. She asked me to dinner tonight and I had to say no of course. She was hurt, and that tears me apart. People have let her down before and all she wants is someone to love her."

Vic sighed. "Julie told me about Princess Rozala's ex, the arms dealer."

Lex nodded. "We've both got a lot of baggage, and besides the fact her family would never accept an ex cocaine addict to be the partner of the second in line to the throne, I'm terrified of how she makes me feel and how I'll feel when she leaves—and she *will* leave me sometime. I crave her. She's all I can think about."

"Why do you think you feel that desperate craving for her?" Vic asked.

"I really don't know, Vic. I don't know what to say." There were no answers she could find, or maybe wanted to find.

"Okay then, why did you take drugs?"

That was the question she had worked around her head every day since her first day in rehab, and there were many different levels to it. "I was desperate for the next high, the next hit of warmth, of acceptance. I wanted love and was frightened I would never find what my parents have."

Vic smiled, as if she was pleased Lex had worked it out for herself. "You want love and you're falling for Princess Rozala, partly because she is aching for the same kind of love."

Lex felt a heavy load slide off her shoulders at admitting that, and recognizing why it scared her so much. "What should I do? It can never work out long term. I would be an embarrassment to her."

"I know that's not true. If you explore your feelings, you may get hurt, but if you don't, you will definitely get hurt. You need to tell her who you are, and what you've been through."

"That is the terrifying part."

Vic chuckled softly. "I know. When I met Julie, I put it off and put it off, and when I did talk about it, I got more love than I could have ever imagined. I didn't believe I was worthy of love, but with each passing day, I started to believe."

Lex stood and gave Vic a hug. "Thank you. You're the best friend I could have, you know that?"

"Oh, don't get all lovey-dovey and emotional on me. I'm too butch for you—go and show it to your princess."

Lex laughed out loud. "Yeah, you are. I'll call you."

She was suddenly full of energy, and anxious to talk to Roza. Maybe she could face these feelings and see where they went, even if it wasn't forever. Roza needed love and Lex wanted to give her it.

Roza was huddled up on the couch in her St James's Palace apartment. The TV played in the background, and she cuddled her wool blanket as she watched absently. She had cried herself out earlier, and as much as Perri tried to get her to talk, she just couldn't explain the hurt she had felt this afternoon.

She was sure Lex was going to admit what was between them, and there was nothing she wanted more, but as soon as they were disturbed, Lex shut off to her, and ran. It hurt when she'd turned down her offer of dinner. Maybe she read it wrong—maybe Lex just didn't want her.

Perri came into the living room and leaned against the door. "Are you sure you're okay, Roza?"

"I'm fine. Just a little tired." Roza gave her a small smile.

"I've hung up your clothes for tomorrow, so I'll go back to my apartment and read for a while. If you need me, don't hesitate, okay?"

As she had gotten to know Perri, she'd come to understand why her mother loved her so much. She was caring, kind, and gentle. Gussy had been right, as much as she'd protested at the time. Having someone around her who knew her mother so well was nice.

She got up and walked over to Perri, and surprised her by giving her a hug. "Thank you for looking after me. I should have said that before. I've been a spoiled brat, and I'm sorry."

Perri hugged her back tightly and said in an emotional voice, "You're a good girl, Roza. You've been working hard and your mama would be proud of you."

They heard a knock at the door, and Perri went to see who it was. Roza was delighted when Theo came in carrying two large pizza boxes and ice cream.

"A little birdie told me you didn't eat supper. I hope you're hungry," Theo said.

Perri must have called him. She couldn't help but smile and feel uplifted by her exuberant cousin. "I could eat a horse."

After stuffing themselves with pizza, they both sat with their feet up on the coffee table and ate their ice cream out of the tub. They were watching a historical TV show about knights on white chargers, and armies fighting to the death for the throne of their kingdom.

Theo pointed his spoon at the TV. "You know what I don't understand? Why they fight so hard to steal each other's throne. I couldn't think of anything worse than being King."

"Or Queen," Roza added before eating another spoonful of her favourite raspberry ripple ice cream.

"Exactly. Imagine waking up every day knowing there's a diary filled with events for you to do, from now until the day you bloody die. You can't do what you want, or go where you want, and everyone deferring to you all the time." Theo shivered.

"It's bad enough being spare to the heir. Being both so close to the throne, and yet so far away," Roza said, "without being locked in that gilded cage for the rest of your life."

Theo laughed. "Yes, it's not very flattering being a spare anything, far less being the spare heir. I've told George often enough, if anything happens to her, I'll kill her."

Roza put her ice cream tub on the table as she laughed at Theo. "You're too funny. It's strange, isn't it?"

"What's strange?"

She took a sip of her drink and sat back on the couch. "It's strange how things turn out. Both George and Gussy are really similar. They're serious, responsible, hardworking, and they were born as the heir to the throne. How lucky is that? Can you imagine the chaos if we had been born first?"

"I think Bea and her republicans would have had a case for abolishing the monarchy in that case. God! The thought is terrifying. I keep telling George to hurry up and make some babies. I want to be kicked down the line of succession as quickly as possible."

"Me too," Roza agreed. Once Gussy was married, she didn't think it would be long before he and his fiancée had children. They were a very loving couple, and she envied them that. "Do you think George and Bea will have children soon?"

Theo chuckled. "I think George would have wanted to get Bea in the family way on their wedding night if she could have. She loves children and has always just wanted a family of her own. Bea on the other hand wants time to settle into her role first, and I don't blame her. She has got one hell of a job to learn everything from scratch, and she's doing fantastically."

Roza had to agree wholeheartedly. Bea was doing an astonishingly good job, having not been brought up in royal life. "I can imagine them with lots of kids in tow, just like Gussy. Then we won't be the centre of attention any more," Roza said with a smile. "No more spare to the heir."

Theo lifted his glass. "Let's drink to that. No more spare to the heir, as soon as possible please."

They clinked their glasses together and drank a toast. "So," Theo said, "tell me about Lennox King, and why has she got you so upset tonight?"

Roza knew he would ask sometime, but could she tell him the truth? She was desperate to tell someone, so she just came out with it. "I'm falling for her and she doesn't want me." Roza surprised herself at her frankness.

"Bloody hell. I never saw that coming. What about Thea? Do you still..." He looked down at her ring finger, and said, "Ah, you got over her then."

She pulled her blanket up to her chin, feeling cold and shivery from the ice cream. "I wouldn't have, if it hadn't been for Lex. She gave me the strength to let go of the part of her that was inside me."

"Then that's good. I can't imagine Lex wouldn't return your feelings, Roza. You're gorgeous."

"Thank you, but looks aren't everything. There's a part of her she's keeping secret from me, and I don't think she wants to talk about it."

"I know what a big deal it was for Bea to walk into this royal life. It's a huge ask, but this Lennox is an idiot if she doesn't want you."

Roza's phone rang on the arm of the couch. "Yes, Johann?"

"Sorry to disturb you, Your Royal Highness, we have Lennox King downstairs. She would like to see you."

Roza jumped to her feet and Theo mouthed, "Who is it?"

"Um...okay. Send her up." Roza dropped the phone on the couch and began to frantically run her fingers through her hair. "It's Lex. She's on her way up."

"That's good, isn't it? If you have feelings for her, then you should talk," Theo said.

Roza sat down with a thud and rested her head in her hands. "I'm a mess. My hair looks like it's been dragged through a hedge backwards, I've no make-up on, and I've got big puffy eyes from crying earlier."

"Oh, shut up." Theo moved along the couch to Roza and gave her a hug. "You look beautiful. I'll go and let her in on my way out, and I want you to text or call later with a full report."

Roza gripped Theo's hand tightly and kissed him on the cheek. "Thank you, big cousin. You really cheered me up."

"Good, I'm always here for you. I'll go and let Lennox in."

Lex was led through the grand entrance to St James's Palace by Johann. The grand staircase, paintings, and rich furnishing that she saw as she walked in served to remind her how different they were. How could an ex-addict be accepted into this world? But she needed to show Roza the real her, and let her know her feelings, no matter the price.

They came to a halt outside an apartment, and Johann knocked on the door. To Lex's great surprise, Prince Theo answered. She bowed her head immediately.

"Princess Roza is waiting for you in the living room."

"Thank you, Your Royal Highness."

Theo gave her a hard stare for a few moments and said, "The Queen and I love Princess Roza very much, so be careful with her and her feelings, okay?"

That was a warning if ever Lex heard one. "I understand you very clearly, sir. I will try my very best not to do anything that would cause her pain."

Theo stood back to let her in, and then went to his own apartment. Johann pointed her in the direction of the drawing room.

The door was open but she knocked on the door frame before entering. Roza met her eyes and all the reasons why this was a bad idea drifted away. *She is beautiful.* "Hi, can I come in?"

"Sure, sit down."

Lex could tell Roza had been crying and it made her feel even guiltier. She set the wine she'd brought down on the coffee table, then handed Roza flowers. "These are for you."

"Thank you. They're beautiful."

What to say now? This was going to be the hard part. "I called Lali Ramesh to get permission to visit you. I don't have your new number."

"I'll give it to you before you go."

There was a long silence before Lex took a breath and began. "I wanted to explain why I couldn't spend time with you tonight."

"You don't need to justify yourself to me. You're free to do what you want or go out with anyone you want."

Lex could hear the hurt in her voice, and the guilt slithered around in her stomach. "I know I don't have to, but I want to. I want you to know everything about me."

She picked up the wine and handed it to Roza. "I thought this might help."

Roza looked at her quizzically and then read the label. "Non-alcoholic wine? What—?"

"I couldn't be with you tonight because this is my NA meeting night. Narcotics Anonymous. I'm a recovering drug and alcohol addict."

Roza's eyes went wide for a second and then to Lex's relief she took her hand. "But you're so healthy, with—"

"With what I put into my body. Yes, that's why. I vowed I'd never abuse my body the way I did when I took drugs and drank."

Roza put the bottle back down and asked, "Can you tell me about it?"

"I will. It's important I tell you, but no one at work knows about this, except for the Queen Consort."

"I promise I will never tell anyone, Lex."

Lex smiled, then gripped her hand and squeezed it. "I know. It's just hard to talk about. I feel so guilty about that time in my life. When I graduated from university, I joined a prestigious trading company. I seemed to have a talent for figures and making money, and made a lot of money. I loved the high of trading, it made me feel invincible, and I loved the lavish London life that went with it. Champagne, parties, and women were simply a perk of that lifestyle, but—"

She faltered, but Roza moved closer to her, and held her hand tighter. "But? You can tell me. I'm listening."

Lex took a deep breath and prayed Roza wouldn't hate her after she told her this. "Soon I was hungering for that high of making money all the time and fell into the worst excesses of London life. I snorted cocaine, drank to excess, and used sex to try and maintain that high all the time. Soon the cocaine wasn't having the same effect on me.

I couldn't get that same high, so I started mixing it with alcohol and drinking it. It gives you a bigger high but it's one of the worst things you can do to your body. My work life was becoming affected and I was getting deeper and deeper in debt."

Lex stared at the floor as she told her story, unable to meet Roza's eyes. "My family tried to help, but nothing could stop me. I was so ashamed at bringing this to their door. The stress of the situation, my job, and the effect of the cocaine finally came to a head when I collapsed at work and was taken to hospital. The cocaine abuse was giving me heart problems and I came very close to dying, but I didn't, and my dad got me on a residential drug and alcohol rehab course."

If Lex was expecting shock or condemnation she couldn't have been more wrong. Roza lifted her hand and took off her watch, to reveal her tattoo. She traced her fingertip across the Roman numerals there and said, "This is the date of your sobriety, isn't it?"

Lex nodded. "Yes, six years now I've been clean."

Then Roza placed a soft kiss on her wrist and said, "I'm so proud of you, Lex."

Roza gave her a soft smoky look that started the heavy beat of want inside her, but she was terrified of going where her body wanted her to. The last time she gave in to her body's needs, she'd brought so much pain to so many people.

Roza continued to caress her hand, letting their fingers intertwine, and then moved so close their foreheads were touching, lips inches from each other.

"What are you doing?" Lex asked.

"Caring about you. Is that okay?"

Lex must have shown her terror because Roza whispered, "Why do I frighten you so much? You always try and pull away, or run away, every time we get close."

Roza parted and licked her lips, making Lex feel like she was being drawn to her like a siren. "My body craves you the way I craved when I was an addict. I could become addicted to you."

Roza took Lex's hand and placed it on her heart. "This. What we are starting to feel between us? It isn't bad. It could never be bad. You don't have to be afraid of it, of wanting me, Lex."

She leaned forward and started to place delicate kisses on Lex's face, and in between kisses whispered, "Not all addictions are bad. They're only bad if they bring you pain. If you allow yourself to feel what's in your heart, you would only feel happiness." Roza moved her lips to Lex's ear and whispered seductively, "Happiness and pleasure. Kiss me, please?"

There was a desperate need in Roza's voice that she just couldn't fight any longer. Lex softly pressed her lips against hers and simply melted into her. Lex heard her moan when she slipped her tongue in to taste her mouth, and Roza climbed onto her lap. Lex grasped a handful of her pert round buttocks and felt Roza's hips start to rock into her groin.

This was too soon, so she reluctantly pulled her lips away from her. "Princess, we need to stop."

Roza looked worried and unsure of herself. "Why? Don't you want me? What did I do wrong?"

Lex cupped her cheek and tried to comfort her. "Hey, hey, you did nothing wrong. Of course I want you, but you deserve more than a quick fumble on a couch. You deserve so much more."

She saw tears well up in Roza's eyes. "No one's ever said that to me before. Everyone always wants something from me."

Lex took Roza's hand and kissed her palm gently. "Then no one's ever treated you the right way before. You are a special, wonderful girl, and despite the fact you are a princess already, you deserve to be treated like one."

Roza looked emotional and stayed quiet for a few seconds, then slid back into her seat. Lex lifted her arm and she gratefully snuggled into her chest. "My cousins are playing in a charity polo match on Saturday. Would you come with me?"

Lex should have said no, but with the raw emotions they had just shared, and with the nervous shyness Roza had just shown her, she didn't have the heart to let her down. Roza was right. Her addiction for her didn't need to be bad, but Lex wasn't naive. Roza's family would never accept her, so in the end her addiction would break her heart, but at least Lex could make Roza happy for now.

"I'd love to."

CHAPTER TWELVE

L ex pulled through the large iron gates at St James's Palace and
saw Major Ravn waiting for her at the front entrance. What a
strange way to start what would really be her first date with Roza.
Even stranger—when she left the house this morning, she was sure
she was being watched. She didn't know how or why, because no one
knew anything about Roza and her, but she had the impression that the
blacked-out van she had spotted across the road had something to do
with it.

Major Ravn opened the door and said, "Good morning, Ms. King.
We need to scan you and the car before Princess Rozala goes with you.
I hope you don't mind?"

Lex got out and left the car open for Ravn. "Of course, Major.
Anything that keeps Princess Roza safe. And call me Lex."

"Thank you." She signalled over to her second in command.
"Johann, sweep the car for me."

Johann sprang into action and Ravn took Lex over to the side, and
started to use a small handheld scanner all over her body.

"If you would prefer to drive us in your state car, I don't mind."

"It's okay," Ravn replied. "I want the princess to have as normal
a day as she can, but there will be some security measures that I'd
ask you to cooperate with. A large number of the British royal family
will be at the charity polo day, as well as Princess Rozala, so security
is tight. Especially after Thea Brandt's threat to the Denbourg royal
house."

"Whatever I can do to help or make things easier, please tell me."

Major Ravn finished her scan. "You're all clear." She took out an
air syringe and held it for Lex's inspection. "This will place a barcode

under your skin, allowing you to move freely around the royal box and other park areas. It will disintegrate harmlessly by this evening. Do you consent to using it?"

Lex took off her suit jacket, and rolled up her shirt sleeve. "Yes, whatever you need. Is there anything else I need to be aware of?"

Ravn administered the painless injection, and checked to see if she could read it. "My team will have cars in front and behind you. If anything untoward happens, follow the car in front and it will lead you to safety. As I said, security will be tight at the polo match. There will be undercover Denbourg security and MI6 agents patrolling the grounds. This is a joint operation, so just be aware if the princess is threatened in any way, there will always be someone nearby to protect her. So please allow them to take you to safety."

"I will. Thank you."

Major Ravn looked her dead straight in the eye, and said, "One more thing, Lex. Treat her well. I'm under direct orders from her brother, Prince Augustus, to stand in his stead, and protect her from anything like what Thea Brandt did to her, and I will do that as if she was my own little sister. She's a lot more vulnerable than people think."

When someone like Major Ravn gave a thinly veiled warning like that, only a fool would fail to heed it. Lex was well built and extremely confident about protecting herself, but the Major was in another league.

"Message received, Major. You'll have no worries for me."

Ravn nodded just as Johann came over with a concerned look on his face. "Major? We found a tracker on Ms. King's car."

"What?" Lex said.

To her relief, Ravn was not looking at her in an accusatory way. She simply asked, "Have you noticed anything unusual yesterday or today?"

"Yes, this morning I couldn't shake the feeling I was being watched, and there was an unusual looking blacked-out van sitting across from my house, but no one knows who I am. The press don't know who Princess Roza is working with inside Timmy's."

"Someone obviously knows something now. Johann, make sure the car is clean and we'll carry on as normal. Just be extra vigilant. I'll get Princess Rozala and Lady Linton so we can leave."

❖

Roza looked over at Lex nervously gripping the steering wheel of the car. They were slowly approaching the entrance to the polo grounds, and security was moving the VIPs through as quickly as possible. She had been quiet ever since they'd set off, and Roza had begun to wonder if Lex regretted coming here with her. The security and craziness of royal life were likely to put anyone off.

"Lex? Is everything okay?"

"Hmm? What?"

Lex hadn't even heard her. Maybe she had read too much into last night.

"You're quiet, and seem really nervous. If you didn't want to come today, you should have just told me."

"Of course I wanted to come. It's not that." Lex nervously drummed her steering wheel. "It's…well this isn't my first time at one of these charity polo events."

"No?" Lex was full of surprises.

"Yes, my bank hosted a VIP tent at two of the big dates on the polo calendar. This was one of them. I was never near the royal tent of course, but the one my bank organized was flowing with champagne, money, and, for a few of us, cocaine. It makes me nervous coming back here."

Roza put a hand on Lex's thigh and grasped it gently. "I wish you would have told me. I'd never want you to come somewhere that makes you feel uncomfortable."

Lex grasped her hand and squeezed. "No, it's fine. I don't want you to think I don't want to be here with you. I do. But it still gives me a sense of fear, facing my past. There were so many people like me there then. Alcoholics, drug addicts, sex addicts, or all three."

She understood Lex's fear. She had been around those types of people ever since she was old enough to drink and party. Rich people who had money and no responsibilities. The excess of that life could eat you up.

"Listen to me, all you have to be nervous about is meeting my family. The royal tent is what I described to my brother as domestic, from Dowager Queen Adrianna and my aunt, Queen Sofia, down to all the children of the family, plus dogs running and barking all over the place. It might give you a headache, and there will be champagne, but nothing is done to excess there. If anyone gets out of hand, Queen Adrianna gives you a swift smack in the behind with her walking stick."

Lex laughed. "Thank you, Princess. You've made me feel so much better."

"While we're waiting, could I tell you about the project I've been working on?" Roza asked.

"Your super-secret project?" Lex said in a stage whisper.

She play-hit Lex in the arm. "Hey, be serious, or I'll tell Ravn on you."

Lex chuckled. "Okay, okay. Go ahead."

"I was thinking about Summer and what was important in her little life. To her being a fairy-tale princess is a dream that she loves to play out, whereas other children might want to play at being the warrior king, a footballer, a movie star, things like that. You know?"

"Uh-huh, go on."

Roza turned around in her seat, and became animated. "Well why don't we give them their dreams? Someone like Summer could have a day of being a princess at Windsor Castle, little James, her friend who talks nonstop about football, we can get him involved in playing with his favourite team in a friendly match, things like that. I've made the phone calls, I've costed the days, the food, the drink, everything. What do you think?"

Lex's impassive look soon changed to a broad smile. "Well done, you've really listened to what I've tried to teach you. It's a wonderful idea."

"So is it something we can make happen?" Roza asked.

"If I check out the financials on your report and they all work out like you say, you can have the budget and set this up as a part of Timmy's charity, and you can be its patron."

Roza was so happy she squealed and just about threw herself onto Lex's lap. "Thank you, Lex. It's going to be so much fun. Something that's my own, something I can be proud of." Roza placed kisses all over her face, just as the line of cars started to move.

"Hey, you're going to shock the security guards."

Roza sat back in her own seat, and giggled. "I don't care. I'm happy."

Lex took her hand and said seriously, "You've done well, Princess. I'm proud of you, and your family will be proud of you."

"That would make a first," Roza joked.

"Well they're going to know all about it. First thing Monday, we'll make plans for a launch for…What do you want to call this programme?"

Roza had come up with this name almost as soon as the idea. "The Dreams and Wishes Foundation. What do you think?"

"It's perfect."

❖

Bea felt a wave of dizziness and clutched the chair beside her. The royal tent was hot and stuffy inside, and she hadn't been feeling her best today.

"Are you all right, sweetheart?" Sarah, her mother, was sitting beside her and clearly noticed her swoon.

"I'm fine, Mum. Just a little bit out of sorts. I think I need to cool down."

Sarah took her hand, and looked concerned. "You're working so hard, Bea. You need to slow down a bit."

"I've got to, Mum. It's my job. I'll go and get a drink and ask them to turn down the temperature."

She walked to the back of the tent where staff manned the food and drinks tables. A young footman bowed and asked, "What can I get you, Your Majesty?"

"Could I get a glass of iced water, please, Sam?"

"Of course, ma'am."

While Bea waited, she gazed around the massive tent which was much more of a grand enclosure. This was a big family affair. Everyone was either a relative or friend and the atmosphere was relaxed. Royal nephews, nieces, and grandchildren ran around playing. Lali, Greta, Riley, and Holly had joined them for the day.

The dogs yapped and ran around playing, all except Shadow, Baxter, and Rex, who were standing by her dad, Reg, who was a bit of a Pied Piper when it came to dogs. Reg was chatting with George's uncle, the Duke of Bransford. They had struck up a friendship soon after they had met. Uncle Bran was an enthusiastic horticulturalist and farmer, and Reg had visited his estate many times to help him with planning improvements. Now that Reg was retired, it was wonderful for Bea to see him keep an interest in his first love.

"Here's your drink, ma'am."

"Sam, could you get them to make the temperature cooler?" Bea asked.

"Right away, ma'am."

She took a drink, and the cool liquid instantly made her feel less wobbly on her feet, but she still felt queasy. *Maybe I need to eat.*

Thoughts of her own ailments fell away as George strode confidently into the tent. She had been taking some of the children to see the horses. She had one of Viscount Anglesey's little girls up on her shoulders, and Greta and Riley's little boy, Charlie, by the hand.

Since her cousin Julian's betrayal, George had made a concerted effort to heal the family and bring his wife and children back into the fold, and separate them from their father's dishonour, while he spent his days in a secure facility.

Luckily, unlike their father, they loved their cousin George, as did Greta's children. It meant so much to Bea that the whole royal family were bringing her friends and family close. She watched George lift little Elizabeth from her shoulders and give her a kiss before the girl ran off with Charlie.

Bea felt like she would melt on the spot. George looked both so attractive and adorable at the same time. Something about her polo team uniform of white jeans and thick brown belt, brown leather riding boots, and the Windsor team jersey emphasized her tall, powerful form. But that powerful form was softened by the gentle way she interacting with the children.

God, I want to have your children. She looked down and realized she had been rubbing her stomach as she thought that.

"It can't be. It's too soon," she muttered to herself. Bea shook her thought away and watched George stop to say a word to Cammy, who was standing with Lali. Then George stopped for a word with Bea's mum, but something Sarah said made George frown. She immediately set off toward Bea at a fast pace.

George took Bea into her arms. "Are you okay? Your mother said you were dizzy."

Bea laid her head on George's chest, allowing her to hug her. "I'm fine."

George sighed. Bea had been working so hard lately, and she never complained but George had seen the tiredness in her eyes. Her wife had always had an uncompromising work ethic, but since becoming Consort, she had worked relentlessly.

It would have been hard enough to get used to the pace of royal engagements, but Bea had taken on the patronage of an enormous number of new charities. Deep down George believed that Bea felt a slight sense of guilt about the great privilege she now enjoyed. She needed a rest, and fortunately they would be going to Balmoral for their holidays in a month's time, and she would make sure Bea rested and was well taken care of.

George tightened her hold on Bea and kissed her sweet-smelling hair. "You said you were fine this morning when you felt sick."

"It's just too hot in here, and I probably need to eat. Sam is going to make sure the climate control is made cooler."

"But—"

Bea pushed away slightly and gave her the mischievous, sexy look that made her skin hot. "Do you know how delicious you look in this uniform?"

"You're just trying to change the subject...oh God." She groaned as her wife's hand slid under her polo shirt and her nails scratched across her stomach, and the fire was lit inside her. "God, don't do that, when I can't do anything about it," George said.

Bea chuckled and whispered, "I want you in this uniform. I want to go down on my knees, open up your belt, and—"

"Oh no, no, no. I'm not listening. No more, or I'm going to explode." George could see the entire scene play out in her head and she simply couldn't let Bea finish that thought.

"Okay. I'll stop, as long as you promise to wear this for me tonight," Bea said, looking far too pleased with herself.

"Anything you want, my darling. I am yours to do with as you please, Your Majesty." George took her wife's glass of ice water from the table and took a large gulp. "You're right, it is too hot in here."

Bea looked over her shoulder and smiled. "Oh, look, Roza's arrived. Remember, don't be all intimidating to Lex. Be good."

George watched Bea walk off with a gentle sway to her hips, which mesmerized her. *She winds me up so tightly and expects me to be good?*

❖

Lex felt the collar of her shirt grow ever tighter as the cool gaze of Queen Georgina fell on her. Roza was currently receiving a hug of welcome from the Queen Consort, while she stood awkwardly behind.

She could feel many pairs of eyes on her as she waited. Perri was sitting beside the elder ladies of the Buckingham family, and she was sure she was the topic of conversation as Perri gazed over at her.

Everyone here was very protective of Roza, and that was a good thing, but nerve-racking if you were the one walking into the lion's den.

Bea greeted Lex like an old friend and introduced her to George, who gave her an overly firm handshake.

"Pleased to meet you, Your Majesty," Lex said.

"Likewise, Lex. I understand from my wife that you and Roza are doing great things at Timmy's."

"I'm only doing my job, ma'am, but Roza is doing wonderful things. She's keen to learn and has come up with her own charity programme."

"We make a good team," Roza added.

Lex saw the Queen's gaze fall on their clasped hands. It would have been obvious to anyone there was more than just friendship going on.

George was just about to say something more when Theo popped his head into the tent and shouted, "George, we're up."

"Coming," George replied to him, then looked Lex in the eye. "I'll find some time to talk to you later, I hope."

"I'm at your service, ma'am," Lex replied.

George shook her hand again and pulled her in close. "Be very careful with my cousin, Lex. I am extremely protective of her."

"Of course, ma'am," Lex said.

George kissed her wife goodbye and left the tent, and Lex let out a breath.

Bea giggled and joked, "Don't worry, Lex, I won't let her chop off your head."

Great. She could imagine how much more protective they'd be if they knew about her past. She wondered if Bea had already told the Queen.

❖

George and Theo cantered around the playing field, while Lex, Roza, the Consort, and her friends sat on lounge chairs at the side, enjoying a picnic.

Lex topped up Roza's fizzy apple juice from the bottle in the picnic basket and said, "Are you sure you don't want champagne, Princess? I don't mind if you drink around me. I'm okay with it."

Roza leaned over and kissed her cheek. "No, I don't want to bring those things around you, and I don't need them when I'm with you."

Lex's heart gave a happy sigh. Roza was everything she'd ever dreamed about. "Okay. Whatever you want."

All the friends started to cheer when George passed the ball to a teammate who then went on to score a goal.

"Oh God," Holly said to her friends. "If only I had known how gorgeous these polo players were, I'd have come a lot sooner. Who was that Adonis who scored? Number four? He fills out his uniform so well."

"Holls, you find so many nice men and never give them a second date. You're breaking hearts all over London," Bea joked.

Holly pointed at herself and feigned innocence. "No way. I'm just choosy. I want to find my perfect Mr. Right."

Bea rolled her eyes. "Of course you are. Cammy, do we know who number four is?"

Cammy had the biggest smile on her face. "I do indeed. That is Captain Quincy. *She* served with Her Majesty and me in the Royal Navy."

Everyone burst out laughing and Holly looked perplexed.

"Maybe that's where you've gone wrong—maybe you need to look for Ms. Right," Bea joked.

Holly stuck her tongue out and said, "Very funny."

Lex felt Roza shiver. "Are you cold?"

"It's a bit chilly, but I don't want to miss George and Theo," Roza said.

Lex got up and brushed her suit down from the blades of grass on it. "I'll go and get your shrug from the car. I'll just be five minutes."

As Lex walked out of the Royal Enclosure area, she heard someone shout her name. She turned around and her heart sank. Lula Ambrose. Someone from her days as an addict, who had worked as a PA at her investment bank,

"Lex! It's you." By the level of her voice, the sway of her walk, and the drink in her hand, she clearly hadn't given up any of the addictions they had shared.

Lex looked around nervously as everyone around them stared. "Lula, how are you?"

When Lula got close she threw her arms around Lex, spilling the champagne down Lex's jacket.

"Shit, be careful, Lula."

"Is that all you have to say to me? I haven't seen you in so long, Lex. Remember how much fun we used to have?"

Everyone was really looking at them now. All she needed was for Roza to see Lula hanging all over her. "What are you doing all the way over here? The bank's VIP tent is on the other side."

Lula pointed to her nose and sniffed. "I had to meet someone to make a little purchase, you know what I mean?"

Lex knew exactly what she meant. They had done cocaine together here, often enough. Now she cursed her luck that she would meet Lula of all people here.

"I'm lost now, Lex. I can't find my way back."

Lex weighed up her options. She didn't want anyone who could report back to Roza to see her like this, so she took Lula by the hand and set off to take her back herself.

"Where are we going, Lex?"

"I'm taking you back." Lex led her through the lines of horseboxes to the other side of the grounds.

Lula went from giggling to whining the whole way. At one point she stopped dead. "Lex, let's have some fun like we used to."

The memories of doing drugs and having sex in a semipublic place flooded back to her. The memory was horrible, and yet in her weakest moments she still craved that darkness.

Lex's moment of hesitation allowed Lula to push her up against one of the trailers, and she kissed her.

Lex pushed her off, but that just made Lula more determined. She looped her arms around her neck. "Come on, Lex. You know you want it." Lula pulled out a bag of white powder and waved it in front of her. "Let's have some fun."

"I don't do drugs any more, Lula. I've been clean for six years."

Lula just laughed at her and said, "You know that'll never last. I've tried too, but you and I are the same. We always want that instant thrill."

Lex felt paralysed with fear. Fear that she wasn't strong enough, not good enough. When she thought back to everyone in the royal tent looking at her questioningly, inside her demons were telling her she'd never be good enough, she would never be good enough for Roza.

Lula pressed the bag against her lips. "You can almost taste it, can't you? Almost feel the rush? Nothing feels better."

Lex groaned and she closed her eyes. She could feel it, taste it. Nothing felt better…Then she saw Roza in her mind saying, *I'm so proud of you.*

She remembered the feel of her lips as she kissed her, and found her control. She grabbed Lula, turned her back against the trailer. "No, I don't want this. I'm clean and that's the way I'm going to stay. I know something that feels better, and she's waiting for me back over there."

When she turned to point back over to the playing field she saw Roza standing at the end of the line of horseboxes, looking shocked, and with tears rolling down her cheeks. She looked back at the way she was standing with Lula pushed up against the trailer, and her stomach sank.

I've fucked up everything.

She let go of Lula and started towards Roza, but Roza turned on her heel and ran off.

"Roza! I didn't…" She let the sentence die on her lips. What was the point? She was never going to be more than a drug addict.

CHAPTER THIRTEEN

Lex chased after her, but all hope deserted her when she saw Ravn escorting a distraught looking Roza into the state car. Once she was in safely, Ravn stared back at Lex with a look of disgust and disappointment.

Once they left, Lex wandered slowly back to her car, craving everything that was toxic to her. Her mind kept saying, *One drink won't hurt, just one.*

Lex got into the driver's seat and held her head in her hands. This was why she told Vic she shouldn't fall in love, or become involved with anyone. She was always one stressful situation away from a drink or a hit.

My past is always going to hurt me.

For the first time since rehab, she felt like crying. She thought working hard and giving her service to others would be enough to give her life meaning, but it wasn't enough any more. Now she had tasted what love might feel like, had tasted Roza, and she knew she would have that craving for the rest of her life.

She sat back in the seat and noticed Roza's shrug in the passenger seat. She lifted it and put it to her face and inhaled Roza. She looked at herself in the driver's mirror, and said, "I can't live without putting this right." Even if their relationship was impossible, she couldn't go on with her life knowing that Roza thought the worst of her.

Lex drove over to St James's Palace but wasn't even allowed past the front gate, orders from Major Ravn.

She left a message that the agent on the gate said he would pass on, but who knew if he would, so when she got home she sent another message on her phone, and just prayed Roza would read it.

❖

Roza felt dazed, confused, and so terribly hurt, but she did know she had to find out the truth for herself. When she had seen the woman kiss Lex it felt like the bottom fell out of her world. She could never have pictured Lex doing that to her while she was on a date with her. Thea, yes, but not Lex.

Roza knew she had to talk to Lex face-to-face, especially after she got her message. Ravn drove her across London to Lex's house, and when they stopped, Ravn said, "Are you sure about this? She's upset you enough already."

"Yes, I'm sure. I need to talk to her. Would you have believed Lex would go off with another woman while she was with me?"

Ravn was silent for a few seconds and said finally, "No. I wouldn't have thought she would, but just make sure you are not being duped."

Roza leaned over and kissed a surprised Ravn on the cheek. "Thanks for looking out for me."

"I'm here in your brother's stead, so I'll always take care of you."

Roza smiled and got out of the car. She looked up at Lex's living room window and saw her looking back at her.

Please, Lex, please have an explanation. I think I might love you.

Lex let her in and they went into the living room. "Thank you for coming. Can I get you tea, coffee, I think I might have juice—"

Roza sat on the couch. "Just tell me the truth, Lex. I don't care about anything else. Do you know how much it hurt to find you in another woman's arms? I brought you to meet my family. I thought I meant something to you."

Lex dropped to one knee in front of her. "You did, you do. What you think you saw wasn't what it looked like."

"That's the usual excuse, but it certainly looked like she was kissing you, and you pushed her up against the trailer. Do you know how many times I found Thea in that position? But she just laughed at me, and I ran after her like a puppy. I'm not going to put up with that any more."

"Roza, I swear to you, I did not kiss her. She was someone I knew from my days as an addict. She spotted me when I was on my way to the car."

"So how did she get you behind a horsebox with her tongue in your mouth?"

"She didn't," Lex said with frustration. Lex got up and started to pace. "She was drunk, drugged up, and acting stupidly. I wanted to help her back to her VIP tent and leave her there but she launched herself at me. She kissed me and I tried to push her away but—"

"A big strong person like you couldn't push off a little woman like her?"

Lex got up quickly and turned her back on Roza. "I was fighting my cravings, okay?" Lex nearly shouted. "She had a bag of cocaine and was trying to talk me into hitting it with her."

Roza was shocked. "But you're clean now."

Lex turned around and said quietly, "I still crave, I'll never stop craving, especially when I'm stressed."

Roza stood and approached Lex. "Why were you stressed?"

"I was meeting your family, who just happen to be the British royal family, who also just happen to be particularly protective of you because of how your ex treated you."

Roza reached out to touch Lex's cheek. "I know they are a bit protective but they were still nice to you, weren't they?"

"Of course they were. It's me." Lex beat her chest with her fist. "My demons inside tell me I'm not good enough, that I'll never be accepted. When I take drugs, it dulls those demons for a while." Lex cupped Roza's face with her hands, and hoped the absolute truth would get through to her. "I was so close to giving in and I thought of you. I thought about you saying you were proud of me and how good it felt to kiss you. Believe me, I did nothing wrong."

Roza closed in on her lips, and whispered, "All I've ever wanted is for you to look at me the way you looked at her."

"I was looking at her like I wanted to get away," Lex said desperately.

Roza wiped away her tears furiously. "I want you to look at me like I look at you."

Lex replied, "You think I don't? I want to kiss you every time I look at you. You're the most infuriating woman I've ever met, and sometimes I just want to shut you up with a kiss, but you're a princess and so far out of my league."

Roza grasped her shirt and said, "I believe you about what happened. Make love to me?"

"No." Lex shook her head. "Not like this, you're upset."

"Why do you have to be so noble all the time?" Roza snapped.

Lex took her hand and kissed it softly, even though all her body wanted to do was touch her. "Because no one has ever treated you the way you deserve. You don't have to give up your body to me just to receive love and affection."

Roza slipped her hands around Lex's neck and scratched her fingernails down the nape to her collar, triggering a heat that waved all over her body. "Kiss me. I want you, Lex."

Lex was using every last ounce of her restraint. She wanted Roza so badly, but she didn't want to take from her the way everyone else had done. She wrapped her arms around Roza and whispered into her ear, "I don't want to be like everyone else has been in your life."

Roza pushed back from her in frustration. Tears ran down her cheeks, sadness and longing evident in her eyes. "If you don't want to be like everyone else has been in my life, then give me love. That's all I've ever wanted."

The heartfelt plea reached somewhere inside Lex, deep in her soul, and she could not refuse it. No matter what the future held, she was certain her purpose was to show Roza love as long as they were in each other's lives.

She cupped Roza's cheek and wiped away her tears with her thumb. "Go and tell Ravn you're staying."

❖

When she came back, Roza stood by the living room door, suddenly feeling nervous. This was what she wanted, but what she had asked of Lex was not something Thea had ever given her, and that was something she craved but was scared of at the same time.

Lex sat on the couch and beckoned her over. She held her hand out to Roza. "Come here."

Roza held her position, scared to take this final step. What if she shared this with Lex and she was rejected by someone else in her life?

Lex seemed to read her apprehension. "You don't have to worry about anything, Princess. Sit down, we can talk for a while." She pulled her down to sit beside her. "I don't want anything from you, only what you want to share with me," Lex said.

"Lex, I want to tell you something."

Lex sat back and opened her arms. Roza rested her head in the crook of her neck. "What do you want to tell me?"

How could she explain? Why was it so hard to admit all the

worries and pain she had kept locked up inside for so long. "It's hard to explain."

Lex smiled and stroked her hair. "I'm here to listen if you want to talk."

Roza closed her eyes and just spoke from her heart. "Everyone always thinks I'm promiscuous—well, experienced at least. I went to parties, drank a lot of champagne, and people started to make assumptions, especially in the press. It suited me to have that reputation because I knew it would horrify Father."

"And you were always wanting his attention, even if it was negative?" Lex said.

Lex always seemed to understand even before she explained. Roza nodded. "Yes, I suppose. People that were interested in me were always disappointed when I left them at the end of an evening. They wanted the badge of honour of sleeping with a princess, and when they didn't get one, they often made up a story to sell to the press. In reality I only ever shared myself with Thea."

"Because you loved her?"

In Lex's arms she felt so safe. Safe enough that she could unburden what she had kept locked up tight. "I thought I loved her. Really I think I was emotionally dependent on her. Unlike the others I met, she knew I was not this tough party girl. She realized early on I was quite innocent in the ways of love and sex, and she played me."

Tears started to fall from her eyes as she explained what she had kept locked up inside.

"The first time was okay but she became selfish, and said I was boring, that I was a pillow princess, and put me down all the time. She blamed me for her straying with other women."

Lex tenderly stroked away her tears. "She was just trying to control you emotionally, Princess. She used you and used your position, and I hope you know I would never do that."

Roza nodded. "I know you wouldn't. Do you think I'm boring?"

"You are the most beautiful woman I've ever met, and you're in my head constantly. You make me crave you, Roza. I've never craved anyone in my life before. When I look at you, all I want to do is touch you, and make you come hard and fast because I can't wait to take it slow. Does that sound like you're boring?"

Roza clambered up onto her lap, and clasped her hands to Lex's cheeks. "I want you so much, Lex. I think I'm starting to fall—"

Lex silenced her by kissing her hard on the lips, and Roza met her passion with equal fervour and started to grasp at Lex's shirt, trying desperately to pull off her tie and undo her buttons.

Lex pulled back and struggled to pull off Roza's T-shirt, then discarded it. Roza quickly unclipped her bra and allowed her soft, full breasts to tumble free.

Roza watched Lex still and gaze longingly at her breasts, and reach out to cup them with her hands.

"Oh, Jesus," Lex said.

Roza placed her hands on top of Lex's and encouraged her to squeeze whilst her hips started to move in instinct, longing for her touch.

Lex closed her eyes and leaned her head back as if she was savouring touching her. When she opened them again, there was a desperate hunger in Lex's eyes that made her heart beat faster and ache inside.

"Do you know how much I've wanted to touch you ever since I met you?"

Roza shook her head. "I didn't think my flirting affected you."

"Affected me?" Lex brushed her thumbs over Roza's nipples whilst never taking her eyes off her. "You didn't flirt, you teased me relentlessly. When you teased me with the chocolate, I wanted to make you come there and then."

"Oh God." Roza was so turned on she started to touch her own body, and popped the button on her jeans.

Lex caught her hand and stopped her from going any further. "You teased me so much, and I need you so much that I can't wait any longer. I need to make you come and come on you."

Roza attacked her mouth with kisses, then pulled Lex's hand to the fly of her jeans. She felt hot, throbbing, and so yearned for Lex's touch.

Lex sat forward and, to Roza's surprise, lowered her to the rug on the floor, and immediately started to unbutton Roza's jeans.

"Oh, and there's nothing wrong with being a pillow princess." Lex smiled. Lex sucked her nipple into her hot mouth and gently bit down with her teeth, causing Roza to shout out. Lex swirled her wet tongue around Roza's painfully erect nipple, making her arch her back and moan. "I'm very much a top, and I would think it my great honour to have you as my pillow princess."

Roza giggled. "You couldn't be anything else but a butch top,

Lennox King." She was so turned on and desperate for Lex's touch that Roza grasped her own breast and squeezed.

Lex kissed and licked her way up her chest to her neck and softly bit her chin. "I want to make you come, Princess."

Roza gasped in surprise when Lex pushed past her underwear and straight into the warmth of her sex.

"Yes, baby," Roza moaned, and helped shrug off her jeans before setting to work on Lex's button and fly.

Lex split her fingers and rubbed the outside of Roza's clit, making her hips buck. "You're so wet, Princess."

All Roza could think about was Lex's fingers inside her. "Take your trousers off and come with me, Lex."

Lex kicked off her own trousers and slipped two fingers deeply inside Roza. She gasped out loud and Lex stilled allowing her to get used to the feel. When she felt Roza's hips start to move, she straddled her thigh and started to pump her fingers and her own hips.

The feeling was incredible. Nothing she could have imagined would have compared to the feel of Roza and the sounds she was making.

Roza grasped her short hair and pulled her down and into a kiss. Lex swirled her tongue around Roza's mouth as her own orgasm built up fast.

Lex groaned when Roza reached down and held the hand that was fucking her. That was such a turn on for Lex. "You like that?" Lex gasped.

Roza nodded and responded by arching her back and raising her thigh so Lex got a harder contact. "I love it. I want to come with your fingers inside me. I'm going to come soon, Lex."

Lex hastened her thrusts, and although she felt like she could come at any moment, she slowed her hips on Roza's thigh because she wanted to see her as orgasm flushed all over her body.

Roza's breaths shortened to gasps and Lex could feel her walls start to grasp her fingers as Roza's orgasm started to pulse.

"Oh God, harder, please…"

"That's it. Let go." Lex made sure to take in everything as Roza's orgasm surged over her. When Roza's nails pressed into her shoulders and she yelled out in passion, Lex couldn't help but restart her thrusts on Roza's thigh.

It didn't take long for her orgasm to hit as she was wound up so tight. Lex gasped and then let out a long, deep groan. Her orgasm was so intense it was almost painful, but as her body gave out, Roza's loving arms wrapped around her, and hugged her tightly.

"It's okay, I feel it too," Roza whispered.

Lex was shaking. It had been so long since she felt something like this, but she had never in fact experienced something so intense. She felt destroyed—her heart and soul had been conquered by this woman, and it was truly frightening. How was she ever to recover when she left her?

Roza kissed her and stroked her cheek. "I think I'm falling in love with you, Lex."

Lex leaned up and, still breathing hard, looked into Roza's beautiful eyes. "You are everything to me, Princess." Lex felt if she didn't say she was falling in love too, then somehow their parting, when it inevitably came, wouldn't be quite so heartbreaking. But even as she thought it, she knew it wasn't true.

Roza chuckled. "You couldn't even wait till you got me to the bedroom?"

"I don't do delayed gratification. It's one of my weaknesses."

Roza caressed her face tenderly. "We'll have to work on that then."

❖

The next morning Roza opened Lex's large fridge and stared at its contents. The fridge was a testament to Lex's controlled and ordered life, but one thing Roza had learned from last night was that Lex couldn't control her passionate self. Once Roza had broken through that stoic shell Lex kept around herself, and teased out the wild, hungry part, there was no stopping her. Lex was right. She couldn't do delayed gratification, and that seemed to be a fundamental part of her psyche.

Roza suspected that was why she had to keep such control over her daily life, because if she didn't her addictions might return.

Lex was not only a passionate, fevered lover, she was also unselfish to the point that Roza had to beg for mercy and sleep. The warmth from her memories spread throughout her body, and those parts of her that were sensitive this morning ached again.

She took out a bottle of ice-cold water and took a big gulp to cool down.

As she looked through the healthy vegetables and salads, desperately trying to find something remotely unhealthy for breakfast, she thought back to what Lex had said about teasing her with the chocolate she bought her, and it gave her an idea of how to maybe show Lex waiting could be good too.

Chocolate, she thought. What she wouldn't give for some pain au chocolat and a mocha, but sadly all Lex stocked were food bags of what looked like prepared meals, bottles of water and other health drinks, and drawers full of fruits and vegetables.

"God, does she have anything remotely tasty?"

"It depends what your definition of tasty is."

Roza jumped out of her skin. She turned around and found Lex standing in her boxers and a T-shirt, arms crossed.

Roza grasped her chest in fright. "You nearly gave me a heart attack."

Lex stalked towards her, pushed the fridge door shut, and boxed her against it. "Do you know how sexy you look in one of my shirts?"

Roza pressed her lips against Lex's and whispered, "How sexy?"

"So sexy that I'm willing to go and hunt and gather you breakfast and a large mocha from the coffee shop on the corner, since my spinach and kale smoothie won't interest you."

Roza giggled. "I must be very sexy then."

Lex kissed her softly and tenderly, before saying, "Thank you for believing me last night."

"I had to. I care about you too much not to." Roza wanted to say *love*, but she'd noticed the sentiment wasn't returned last night, and she didn't want to ruin the morning-after together by putting Lex on the spot. She felt deeply inside that Lex was falling in love with her, but she sensed she was scared of getting hurt. Roza determined she was going to show Lex that they could be together and her family just would not have a say.

"I care about you too." Lex punctuated her declaration with a kiss on her nose. "Shall I go and hunt and gather then?"

"Yes, please. If you could spear some pain au chocolat, I would be eternally grateful."

Lex bowed and said, "Your wish is my command, Your Royal Highness. I think my spear will be accurate enough."

"Oh, really?" Roza grabbed the hem of her boxers and pulled her towards her. "Good with it, are you?"

Roza felt alive with Lex. Everything about her excited and lightened her heart. She was surprised when Lex lifted her and turned to set her on the table. "That's for you to find out."

Roza slipped her hands down the back of Lex's boxers, grasped her muscled backside, and pulled her to her sex.

Lex had that fiery passion in her eyes again, and she leaned in to push Roza down on her table. When Lex's lips came to hers, Roza whispered, "Pain au chocolat."

Lex's head fell onto her chest and she started to laugh. "Oh, Princess, you are such a tease."

"But you love it. Now go—hunt, gather, and all that tough stuff."

Lex let out a breath. "Pain au chocolat. On its way. Are Ravn and the team still outside?"

Roza nodded. "Ravn and some of the team went home last night and left Johann and the rest. They were relieved at six this morning."

"Okay, I'll bring enough for everyone. I'll just take a shower."

"Can I come?" Roza asked with a smile.

Lex shook her head. "No way. You'll drive me insane, get me worked up, and then ask for breakfast. I'll go myself, Princess."

CHAPTER FOURTEEN

The day of the Dreams and Wishes press launch arrived, and Roza was nervous. She stood in the shower and let the hot water hit her face as she tried to wash away the knot of worry inside her, but it didn't work.

She switched off the water and stepped out to dry herself with her big fluffy towel. Roza wrapped the towel around her hair and caught herself in the steamed-up mirror. "Who am I trying to kid. I shouldn't be doing this."

Roza had a lot of experience courting the press cameras, trying to evade them, and leaking them stories to infuriate her father, but she'd never held a press conference to announce something good, something really important. The thought of answering questions about something that she had personally worked on was scary.

Lex will be there.

Roza let out a breath and wrapped another towel around her body. She walked out into her adjoining bedroom, where Perri was hanging up her outfit for the day.

"What do you think, Roza? The blue or the cream outfit?" Perri asked.

Roza's eyes were immediately drawn to the blue designer jeans, cashmere blue and white nautical style sweater, and navy blazer.

"The blue. It's perfect for an outdoors play day."

Perri smiled brightly. "That was my first choice too. We're getting to think alike."

Roza laughed. "More like I'm growing up, and dressing more appropriately."

Perri walked over and grasped her by the shoulders. "I'm so proud of you, Roza. You've done so well since coming to Britain, and your mama would be proud, especially at what you're doing today. Children's charities were always her favourite."

"I just hope I don't make a fool of myself."

"Of course you won't." Perri led her by the hand over to her dressing table to sit, and began to brush her wet hair. "You will be wonderful. You've worked hard on this idea."

Roza looked at her in the mirror. "I'm scared."

"Why are you scared?"

Roza tried to find the words to explain her fears. She let out a long breath. "I'm afraid no one will take me seriously. I'm afraid I'll freeze and not know what to say, that I won't be able to give my speech."

Perri kept on brushing her hair, despite the fact that all the tugs were gone. Roza found it soothing, and she wondered if her mother would have done this sort of thing for her.

"You won't. I have every faith in you, and Lex has faith in you— that's why she's given you this project. Don't think about the media's expectation of you. Be your own person and start forging a new path. The press will just have to follow you, and your new path."

Roza reached to her shoulder and took Perri's hand. "Thank you. I'm so thankful I have you in my corner."

Perri gave her a kiss on the head. "I always will be."

"Can I ask you something?" Roza asked.

"Of course."

"What was Mama like as a mother, to Gussy, I mean. Was she a hands-on mother or did she leave it to nanny?"

"Hands-on?" Perri laughed. "She never had Gussy out of her arms, if she wasn't on official royal duties. Your mama was determined from the start, despite the old-fashioned Denbourg courtiers, to be as normal a mother as possible. She took Prince Augustus everywhere she could, the park, animal farms, fairgrounds, and unless they were out of the country, she and your father put him to bed each night. The King read him a story and your mother sang a lullaby."

As Roza listened to a description of Gussy's childhood that was so different to her own, tears started to fall from her eyes.

Perri hugged her from behind. "I didn't mean to upset you, my little Roza."

Roza wiped away her tears. "It's okay. I like hearing about Mama, and what Father was like. I'm just sad I couldn't have known that kind of family life. When I was a little girl I thought my nanny was my mother for a time, then when I was able to understand a bit better I felt sad, and I'm ashamed to say angry, that she'd left me with Father. He never held me, never played with me. I always thought that I was to blame for her death."

"Oh, Roza, I'm sorry. I should have come back to the Denbourg court and helped your father bring you up. His heart was broken and I felt that I was a reminder of what he had lost."

"Just like me," Roza said sadly.

"Don't think about that. Think about how proud you're going to make your mama today."

Roza smiled and nodded. Maybe she could make the family she'd always wanted with Lex. If Lex would just talk about it, and not pull away.

The grounds at Windsor were a hive of activity already when Princess Rozala arrived. There were tents for food, face painters, candyfloss, popcorn, and every kind of fun snack you could think of. There were fairground rides, a mini-castle playground, and a pirate ship for the children, who were all dressed up as their dream characters.

"I feel sick, Lex."

Lex took her hands and said, "You have nothing to be worried about. You're going to make a short speech, then play with the children. That's easy. You've seen the kids out there? They are having a blast, and it's all thanks to your hard work. If you get nervous or tongue-tied, just imagine you're reading the speech to me as we did at the office."

"I'll try my best," Roza said.

"That's my princess. You are going to smash it." Lex pulled her into a hug and kissed her brow. "Let's go."

They walked out of the tent and immediately the flashes of the media cameras dazzled her eyes. As they had arranged, Summer was waiting outside for Roza. She took her hand, and Summer gave her the brightest smile.

"You look pretty, Ms. Princess."

Summer always made her smile, no matter how she was feeling. "Thank you, Princess Summer. Let's go and see your friends."

Lex had dropped back behind her security and all Roza could think of was that Lex should be by her side.

The children and the play workers sat cross-legged on a platform area that had been built for Roza to give her speech. Behind the children the press and photographers sat waiting on their story. They had already been warned by Timmy's PR executive not to ask any questions about the arms scandal or the growing speculation over Roza's mystery lover, but whether they would stick to that was another matter.

The play workers and children began to clap as she approached the podium. Her prepared speech waited for her. She gripped the side of the podium hard, and read the first few lines of the speech in her head.

You can do this.

When she looked up into the glare of the press lights, she couldn't see the children any more. She saw her father the King, looking at her with disappointment in his eyes. Her mouth immediately dried and her throat started to close.

The flashes of the cameras seemed to become blinding, as panic gripped her. The King was impatient and looked at his watch. *"Get on with it, Rozala. I knew you'd never be able to do this one simple thing."*

In desperation she turned to her right and saw Lex calmly smile back at her. She closed her eyes for a second, and tried to imagine speaking to Lex. When she turned back to the audience, her father was gone and a smiling Lex was there in his stead.

Roza's body started to calm, and she began the speech.

"Queen Maria, my mother, once said that the care of our children reflected our hopes for the future of our world. Those words have always echoed in my heart, and I felt it my duty to carry on her wishes and try in one small way to show my hope for the world. During my time working at Timmy's, I have come to see what a difficult time a child's illness is for all the family. But the things that can bring relief are play, imagination, and laughter. The Dreams and Wishes Foundation will be a charity dedicated to providing the means for giving every child their own dream and wish. That could be becoming a princess like my friend Summer there"—Roza pointed down to the little girl who was now sitting with her mother, and there were collective *aww*s from the assembled crowd—"or an astronaut experience for the day..."

The rest of the speech went perfectly and Roza took the first few questions from the press equally as perfectly, knowing she had Lex's support right behind her. Lex along with Perri and her developing relationship with Ravn made her feel more secure than she ever had.

"Princess Rozala, could you tell me if you have the support of the Queen and her Consort for this venture?"

Roza smiled. "Of course. The Queen graciously allowed us to use the grounds of Windsor to launch this new arm of Timmy's, who as you know are vigorously supported by Her Majesty, the Queen Consort."

Smashed it, she thought, just as Lex had said.

A well-known reporter from one of the more tabloid-style websites stuck his hand up and she had no choice but to accept.

"Yes?"

"There are reports that the royal rebel has a new lover in her life, can you comment on that?"

Roza heart started to beat hard. She'd known this would happen. Someone was bound to ask an awkward question, but using all the grace she could muster she smiled politely and said, "We're here to talk about the children."

She pointed to another more reputable journalist, but the previous questioner shouted in a loud voice, "One can only hope this new lover doesn't have the arms to send good British and Denbourg troops home in body bags."

Roza's stomach fell and she started to shake, but in a second Lex was by her side and took control of the press conference. "We will now move to the play tent where the princess will host a tea party for the children."

Roza couldn't move but she felt Lex's gentle touch guide her away from the podium. She wasn't aware of much, but as they walked into the play tent that had been set up for the tea party, she heard Lex say to Ravn, "Major, could you get our PR to give us ten minutes before they lead the children in."

They entered the tent and after a brief word the caterers left them alone in the vast space. Lex wrapped her arms around her and tried to calm her tears. "Shh…it's okay. I'm here now."

"No matter what I do, no matter how I try and change, I'll always be the royal rebel, won't I?"

"Hey, that was only one gutter tabloid reporter. You did fantastically well. I was so proud of you."

"You were?"

Lex took a handkerchief from her top pocket and handed it to her. "Of course. Dry your eyes now."

Roza dabbed her eyes carefully, so as not to smudge her make-up. "I wish I'd never met Thea. It hurts me to think of our people being injured because of her weapons."

"She would still be hurting people with her weapons whether you'd known her or not, so don't even think you are to blame. Concentrate on the good things you've done today. I was so proud of you out there."

Roza pressed her palms against Lex's chest. "Really? You were?"

Lex cupped her face and gave her the sweetest of kisses on the lips. "Of course I was. You looked beautiful, and you spoke confidently and warmly."

"I froze up at the beginning. I kept seeing my father watching me, but it was the thought that you were there that gave me strength."

Roza wanted to tell Lex how she felt, but maybe this wasn't the best of moments. "Lex, would you come with me tonight to the palace banquet?"

Lex sighed. "We've already been over this, Roza. If I go as your guest, it will be all over the media. They already know you're seeing someone over here."

"I don't care if they know."

"You should. Your family will not be happy when they see my history. It's only going to cause us both pain."

"My family doesn't have a say in my choice of partner."

"You're being naive." Lex walked a few paces over to the refreshment table and took a sip from one of the bottles of water.

"Lex, I'll be the only one not in a couple. I'll be on my own at one of the most controversial receptions the UK has ever had, with a roomful of homophobes from Vospya."

Lex stood with her hands in her pockets and sighed. "The reception is tonight, all the seats will be taken."

Roza hurried over to Lex and grasped her hand. "If I can get you a seat, will you come with me? Please? For me?"

"Oh, all right. If you can get a seat, which you won't. It's too late."

Roza giggled. "Thank you. We better let the children in for their tea party. Go and tell them." *I'm going to make this happen.*

Bea was in her office at Buckingham Palace, dealing with her correspondence. As ever Rex lay by her feet, sleeping and guarding her. She had no engagements today, because of the state visit. When she and George had gone to greet the president and his entourage at the airport and escort them back to the palace, it had been the hardest thing she had ever had to do. Normally a visiting head of state was led back to the palace by royal carriage and a parade of mounted horse guards and military dignitaries, but with President Loka and the demonstrations and protests over his visit, it was thought best to bring them quietly by state armoured car.

Every smile and piece of small talk took a great toll on Bea. She was only too glad to leave George to have a private audience with him while she made sure all the preparations were done correctly.

Lali handed her a letter on her computer pad and said, "This is the last thing that needs your signature, ma'am."

"Thanks. Is the banquet room ready to view?" Bea asked.

"Yes, whenever you're ready."

Bea sat back and stretched out her arms. "What a day."

"How was the wonderful President Loka?" Lali asked.

"Oh God. So infuriating. I let George do the talking, and I could barely get a word from his wife. Probably ground down by a lifetime with him."

"No doubt. How was he with both of you? I mean, he must despise everything about you both."

"He was cordial but looked at me with disgust. I don't think he dared do that to George." Bea got up and smoothed down her dress, and Rex bounced to his paws. "Believe me, tonight is going to be hard. I don't know how on earth the prime minister thinks this is a good idea."

"You know Bo Dixon, Bea. She uses whatever means to get what she wants, and she wants President Loka's trade agreement. It's all about money at the end of the day."

"You're right. I think Bo would sell her soul to the devil for more power and influence."

"I think she might already have done that," Lali joked.

Bea chuckled and Lali quickly called down to inform the master of the household, Sir Hugh Blair, they were on their way.

"Come on, Rexie, we're going downstairs."

They left Bea's offices and started to walk down the grand corridors of Buckingham Palace.

Bea rubbed her stomach, and Lali must have noticed because she said, "Are you all right? Feeling sick again?"

"No, it's settled a bit. I'm just nervous. This is the first banquet I've organized myself and my first walk-through without the Queen Mother. If I get anything wrong—"

"You won't get anything wrong. You're a professional."

Bea took Lali's hand and said, "Just don't let snooty Sir Hugh talk me into anything."

As they laughed, Lali's phone buzzed. "Lali Ramesh. Yes? I'll ask Her Majesty, please hold."

"It's Roza," Lali said. "She's popped in on her way from her press event at Windsor. She wondered if she could have a quick word."

"Of course. Get her to meet us at the stairs. We can talk and walk."

CHAPTER FIFTEEN

Roza waited nervously at the top of the grand Buckingham Palace staircase. What if Bea wouldn't let her bring Lex? Maybe George would disapprove. All these thoughts ran in a constant cycle around her head.

She spotted Bea walking down the corridor, with her faithful dog Rex beside her, and she felt better when Bea waved to her with a big smile. Roza loved the Queen Consort—she was so welcoming and easy going, so unlike the people that normally populated royal life.

When she reached Bea, Roza curtsied. "Thank you for seeing me at short notice, Your Majesty."

"Don't be silly. You can pop in anytime." Bea hugged her and gave her a kiss on each cheek.

That was yet another thing that was different about George and Bea, Roza mused. They were happy to see family whenever they asked, as long as they had no previous appointments. At home she even had to make an appointment to see her father.

"Let's talk while we walk. We're on our way to check the banquet preparations in the ballroom," Bea said.

Roza fell into step beside Bea, with Rex leading the way and Lali following behind.

"How was the foundation launch?" Bea asked.

"It went really well, apart from a couple of awkward questions from one reporter." Roza sighed.

"There's always one, I've found. You've done well, Roza. The Queen and I are so proud of you."

Roza had to gulp down the emotion she felt welling up in her. This was the first time in her life people were actually praising her. Perri, Lex, George, and Bea. Her brother loved her unreservedly and had always been on her side, but he was usually trying to get her out of whatever scrapes she had gotten into, not praising her.

"That means a lot. Thanks, Bea, but I could never have gotten this off the ground without Lex. She's been so strong for me, giving me confidence and helping me in any way possible."

Bea slowed and stopped as they got near the ballroom. Bea had seen the adoration Roza had for Lex at the polo, but she had also seen wariness in Lex's eyes, as if there was part of her she was holding back. "How are things going with Lex?"

"We are very close, but she won't give a name to what we are together. She thinks my family won't accept her past, and I'll leave."

Bea remembered that fear that George would leave her eventually. "I can understand that fear, Roza. I felt I would lose George, that a more suitable woman would be found, but George made me believe. You have to do the same. Why don't you take control and tell your brother about Lex, gauge his reaction?"

"Yes, I think I will. Would you mind telling George how serious this is?" Roza asked.

"If that's what you want."

"It is," Roza said. "I want to show Lex that we can be together, and that brings me to the favour I need to ask you. Would it be possible to bring Lex with me tonight, as my date? I know it's short notice but…"

"It's all right by me. Lali? Could we fit her in?" Bea looked to her friend who was checking through her computer pad.

"There were a few cancellations. It's just a matter of rejigging the seating plan, and Sir Hugh may be a bit testy about that."

Bea rolled her eyes. "Don't worry. I can persuade him." Bea looped her arm through Roza's and said, "Come help me look over the ballroom."

Two footmen bowed and opened the large ballroom doors. The first glimpse was spectacular. The light from the large chandeliers made the gold plates and glasses sparkle with radiance.

There was a collective gasp from the three women, and Bea said, "It's beautiful."

They walked in and all the staff bowed or curtsied to Bea and Roza. There was Air Marshal Sir Hugh Blair, Master of the Household, Simpson the senior page, and the royal florists.

"This looks wonderful. Well done, everyone."

Sir Hugh inclined his head in a bow. "Thank you, Your Majesty."

"I wanted to show Princess Rozala how wonderful everything looked."

Bea saw Roza barely restrain a chuckle, knowing the bombshell she was about to drop, messing up the entire table plan.

"It's spectacular, Sir Hugh," Roza said animatedly.

"You're too kind, Your Royal Highness." Then turning to Bea he said, "May I talk you through the seating arrangements first, ma'am?"

Bea walked to her and George's seats at the head of the table and gripped a chair. "Before we do that, Sir Hugh, I have a tiny little adjustment in the seating plan."

Sir Hugh and Simpson looked at each other nervously. Bea knew it had taken days of planning to get this table looking as incredible as it did. The lighting, the groaning dishes of fruit, the sparkling gold cutlery and plates, and now she was about to shake it all up.

"Princess Rozala would like to bring a guest, and Lali tells me there have been cancellations in the days running up to the dinner, so can you add one more place?"

Sir Hugh and Simpson gulped hard, and were just about to protest when Bea said, "Princess Rozala thought it would be impossible at this late hour, but I said no, our Master of the Household and senior page are the best in the business, consummate professionals who'll have no trouble fitting your guest in."

Bea gave him her biggest smile, and watched the panic in his eyes as he knew she had boxed him into a corner.

He put on his best fake smile and said, "Of course, ma'am. No trouble at all."

Yes! I'm good. Bea turned to give Lali and Roza a sly wink when a wave of dizziness turned her world upside down, her knees turned to jelly, and the last thing she heard were voices shouting, "Your Majesty!" Then her world went black.

George ran down the corridors of Buckingham Palace, closely followed by Cammy, hurrying towards her private rooms. She had been talking with the Yeoman of the Cellars about the drinks for tonight's banquet, when Cammy came to tell her Bea had taken ill.

As soon as she heard, she ran. Nothing else mattered but getting to her wife.

Footmen and women looked startled and bowed quickly as she tore down the hall to her rooms.

"George, calm down, man," Cammy shouted from behind, but nothing could calm her until she had Bea safe in her arms.

She burst into their drawing room to find Bea sitting on the couch, with Dr. Chris Brown, the Head of the Medical Household and Physician to the Queen, checking her vitals, and Lali standing behind her.

"Bea? What happened?" George rushed to her side and knelt in front of her.

"I'm fine, Georgie. No need to panic. I just had a little dizzy spell."

George cupped her cheek with her hand. "Fainting is not nothing. Cammy said you collapsed in the banqueting hall. Dr. Brown? What is the Queen Consort's condition?"

Dr. Brown looked too conflicted and struggled with her words. "Her Majesty is settled and is in good health."

"Well? Why did she faint?" George saw the doctor and Lali look nervously at their shoes. "There's something I'm not being told, and I want to know what it is, now."

Bea said to Dr. Brown and Lali, "Could I have a minute alone with the Queen?"

"Of course, ma'am," Dr. Brown said, and Lali led her out.

When they were alone, George kissed Bea's palm and said, "Tell me what's wrong. You're scaring me, Bea."

Bea smiled at her and stroked her hair tenderly. "There's nothing to be scared about, I don't think anyway. It was meant to be a surprise. I wanted this to be special, magical, but I didn't expect to keel over and feel sick as much as I have."

George felt all the blood drain from her head to her toes, and her mouth dry up. Somewhere inside she knew what this meant, but her brain was too full of cotton wool to process it.

"You have been feeling sick a lot," George said in a monotone.

Bea sighed. "I didn't know for certain until this week and I was going to tell you at Windsor, at the weekend, in our family home."

George's heart was beating out of her chest. "Our family home?"

Bea laughed gently. "Kiss me, Bully?"

She was confused but leaned forward to kiss her wife on the lips. Just before their lips met Bea whispered, "I'm pregnant."

She heard the words but somehow they didn't make sense. "You're...you're pregnant?"

Bea grasped George's hair and nodded her head. Her partner wasn't slow by any means but Bea suspected that George had wanted this for so long, that she couldn't quite comprehend it was real.

"I know what you've wanted for us, and I know that I was a bit reluctant so early in our life together, but I listened to what you said about making a family from our love and I was certain I wanted it too."

"You're having a baby?" George said with a squeak.

Bea nodded. "I'm having your baby. I hope you don't mind that I went to the clinic myself, but I wanted to give you a surprise—"

Bea was engulfed in a hug. "Oh my God, you're having our baby. I love you, I love you."

George kissed her deep and hard, then pulled back with tears in her eyes. "Thank you, my darling. You've made me the happiest woman in the world."

Bea joined her partner in shedding tears. The moment was overwhelmingly emotional. To share such joy with George—in this moment she wondered why on earth she had waited so long to share children with her.

She took George's hand and placed it on her stomach. "I can't wait to share this experience with you, and watch you holding our baby."

"I promise you both that I will always take care of you."

"Kiss me," Bea said.

❖

Bo studied the file on her computer silently, while her private secretary, Felix, waited on her response.

"I was contacted by the royal correspondent at the *Daily Speaker*," Felix said. "They had a tip-off from someone inside Timmy's that Princess Rozala and the director, Lennox King, are having an affair. Due to the rumour that Number Ten isn't in favour of having the princess in the country, they wanted a nonattributable quote on this new development."

"What does intelligence say about Brandt's current activities?" Bo said.

"We don't have a location, but the internet chatter is that her group are slowly building their caches of weapons. As soon as targets are found, they will be taken out."

"You know as well as I do how embarrassing this could be for us. The Queen insisted Princess Rozala's presence was a family matter, and refused to think about the damage to Britain's reputation. All we need is for a terrorist action to be linked to the deaths of any UN military personnel and we are up to our necks in the shit."

"You're not wrong, Bo," Felix said.

Bo sighed with frustration. "Roza is getting too much good publicity with all this charity work. The more popular she is, the less pressure I can bring to bear on the Queen about getting rid of her. There is going to be a shitstorm when Thea Brandt is caught, and the princess is going to be the first port of call for the world's media. I don't want Denbourg sharing this scandal with us. This is their problem. I want that spoiled brat out of *my* country."

Bo sat back in her chair and crossed her legs nonchalantly. "Wouldn't it be unfortunate for this file on Lennox King to fall into the hands of an irresponsible journalist?"

"Or several irresponsible journalists?" Felix said, feigning innocence.

"Quite." Bo smirked.

"If you'll excuse me, Prime Minister, I have some work to do."

George sat in a comfortable armchair enjoying a predinner drink and a quick look through the evening news, while Holly put the finishing touches to Bea's make-up. As usual on a formal occasion, the dogs were banished so as to not leave their marks on the Queen's and Queen Consort's fine clothes.

"I think that's everything, apart from your jewellery. Do you want me to…?"

"It's okay, Holls. I'll be fine from here," Bea said.

Holly smiled and gave her shoulders a squeeze. "Good luck, Your Majesty."

George stood as Holly curtsied to her on the way by. "Congratulations again, Your Majesty."

"Thank you, Holly."

Bea walked to her full-length dressing mirror and placed her jewellery case on a side table.

George couldn't get over to her quickly enough. Bea looked absolutely beautiful. She was wearing a cream-coloured evening gown, with her hair swept up, allowing a tantalizing glimpse of Bea's neck and shoulders. The feminine look was in contrast to George's white tie and tails, but they both wore the blue sash and diamond badges of royal authority.

After all the many lonely nights in the past and getting ready for these sorts of events alone, George adored these times, and now that Bea was pregnant, it was even more special. She slipped her hands around Bea's waist and rested her hands on her abdomen. "You look radiant, Mrs. Buckingham."

"And you look handsome, Georgie."

George sighed with utter contentment. "You've made me so happy, you know that?"

Bea turned her head so she could look at George. "You're not upset I went to the clinic without you?"

George held open the velvet box and let Bea put on the diamond and sapphire earrings that matched the necklace beside it. The set had been given to Bea by the Dowager Queen and remodelled in a more modern setting.

"Not at all. It made finding out all the more special. That's why I gave my stem cell donation as soon as we were married, so that no matter what we could have a child."

Once the earrings were on, George took out the necklace and stood behind her to fasten it. George secured the necklace and placed delicate kisses along her shoulders and neck, inhaling her gorgeous perfume as she went. "You smell wonderful."

Bea sighed in pleasure. "So? Would you like a little prince or princess?"

"I don't care. As long as it and Mama are healthy and happy."

Bea turned into George's arms. "Oh, I feel our first baby disagreement looming."

George looked puzzled. "Why?"

"I've made lots of compromises in becoming your wife, entering the royal family, and leaving my republican roots behind me—I think you'll agree."

George nodded. "I know. You made a monumental decision to enter this gilded cage with me."

"But after all that, if you think I'm going to let our little child call me"—Bea put on her poshest accent and said each syllable slowly—"*Mama* like a posh kid, you've got another thing coming. I'll be Mummy. You can be Mama."

George laughed. "We won't argue over that. You can be called whatever you wish, my darling, but I must also say I am not a mama either. It doesn't fit who I am inside. I'm more of a papa but people won't see me as a papa. It's hard to explain."

"I understand, sweetheart. Don't worry, we'll work it out."

George kissed Bea on the forehead so as not to smudge her wife's lipstick. "You always understand."

"And I always will. This baby is going to have some crazy life." Bea sighed and smoothed her hands over George's lapels.

"I know the world will go loopy when we announce this, and the baby will be followed by cameras every day of its life just like I was, but I promise I will do everything in my power to control the media storm."

Bea nodded. She knew that was true. George always fought to keep their lives as private as possible. "When should we tell Theo and the family? I hope you don't mind Lali and Holly knowing. It was hard to keep it from them."

"Of course not. Why don't we tell them after our first scan, just to make sure everything is okay first? It's only a few weeks."

"Sounds perfect. Speaking of family, Roza popped in today," Bea said, "out of the blue."

"Oh? How was she?"

"Great, her charity event at Windsor went without a hitch, but she had a few awkward questions about a mystery suitor the press think she has."

"I take it you mean Lennox King. I thought they were just casually dating."

Bea turned around and took her hands. "Come and sit with me."

George was led over to the couch and they both sat. "What's wrong?"

"They have become lovers, and Roza cares for her very much," Bea told her.

George rolled her eyes. This was the last thing Roza needed, more romantic problems. "And what does Lennox say about it? Are her intentions to have a relationship?"

"I don't know what her long-term intentions might be, or if they would ever get the chance. Lex has some past issues that she believes would hamper Roza if the press found out about her."

Now George was worried. "What past issues?"

Bea took her hand and said, "Now don't get worked up and worried."

"Tell me," George said flatly.

Bea gave her a potted history of Lex's past and tried to reassure her that her addiction issues were all behind her.

"Cocaine and alcohol? You knew and you didn't tell me?" George couldn't hide the fact that she was angry.

"I was told in confidence about it—besides it didn't affect her work."

"I should have known." George got up and started to pace. "If the press get ahold of this, it could cause yet more embarrassment for King Christian, not to mention the kind of influence Lex could have on her if she goes back to her addiction."

"Don't be such a hypocrite, George," Bea said angrily. "How many drug and alcohol charities are you patron of?"

George was taken aback by Bea's anger. "Many, I—"

Bea got up and faced her. "Exactly, and you have given countless speeches about giving people second chances, and third and fourth chances if need be, but if it touches your family it's different?"

She couldn't answer against that. "You're right. I'm sorry, I'm simply worried because Roza has just come out of a dreadful relationship, and she is extremely vulnerable."

"I know that, but Lex has been clean for six years and is utterly devoted to her health and well-being. Besides, her strength is exactly what Roza needs."

"Of course you're right. So what does Lex say on the matter?"

"She believes King Christian and Prince Augustus will not allow a former drug addict in the family."

"She may be right. Uncle Christian is very old-fashioned."

Bea placed soft kisses on George's face. "Well maybe you could speak to him and vouch for Lex."

George looked sceptical. "Hmm…perhaps."

Bea heard police sirens and shouts from outside. She walked over to the window. The protestors had been at the gates of the palace all day, but now the police and security officers were trying to get the VIP cars through the gates of Buckingham Palace without getting eggs thrown or generally harassed.

She hugged herself and sighed. "I can't believe we have to roll out the red carpet for this horrible man. I would have been out there protesting if I hadn't met you."

George came up behind her and wrapped her arms around her.

"We are the servants of the government and the people, Bea. We talked about this. As monarchs we don't get a choice who we entertain, or meet—it's your democratically elected prime minister who wants him here."

"I know. It's just hard."

"I would suggest we can make a statement to him by the way we receive him with dignity, and show him the values of the United Kingdom, and what could be better than two gay women doing that, eh?"

"I suppose you're right. I'm going to be extra gay for him," Bea joked.

"That's my girl."

Chapter Sixteen

L ex paced around her hotel room. Major Ravn had suggested she get ready and be collected from a discreet Mayfair hotel, to make security easier. And Ravn had been right. Over the course of the day, the press had started to gather outside Lex's home. They clearly knew she was the mystery suitor but thankfully they didn't know about her past—yet.

She walked over to the large hotel room windows and stared out over the London skyline. *What am I doing here?* No matter how much she felt for Roza, she knew it was going to end badly, and that was frightening.

God, I could do with a drink... The thought came from nowhere and it was terrifying. That was the first time in years she had thought about drinking. Lex rubbed her face vigorously and said to herself, "Get ahold of yourself."

She touched the tattoo on her wrist and started her deep breathing exercise.

Her feelings were bringing her demons from their slumber and she would need to work doubly hard to keep them in check.

There was a knock at the door. "Ms. King? Are you ready?"

Was she ready? As soon as she walked out that door, the press would have every rumour confirmed.

When she lifted her hands to quickly check her hair, she noticed she was shaking ever so slightly. On instinct her eyes went to the brandy, whisky, and vodka decanters, sitting on a silver tray at the side of the room.

"Ms. King? Are you there?"

In that split second, she could almost feel the burn of the whisky as it would go down her throat.

Again there was a knock at the door.

"I'll be right with you."

Lex took a long breath and let it out, before heading for the door.

❖

When Lex saw Roza in the car, all of her immediate fears went away. She was elegantly beautiful in a long green evening dress, her hair held up by a diamond tiara.

She took Roza's hand and kissed her palm. "You look beautiful, regal, and elegant and you take my breath away."

Roza giggled shyly and then leaned in to straighten her white bow tie. "You look delicious in white tie. I can't wait to take it off you later."

"Oh? Is that right?"

Roza leaned forward and whispered, "I've got a surprise for you later. To thank you for coming with me tonight."

"What kind of surprise?"

Roza tapped her nose. "You'll just have to wait and see."

A surprise from Roza could mean anything. She was a wild, free-spirited girl, and that was why she was falling for her.

Major Ravn leaned over from the front seat and said, "It's about to get loud and frantic as we move through the protestors but you'll be perfectly safe, I assure you."

Lex looked out the window and saw the police struggling to hold back protesters as their car went through the palace gates. Roza jumped in fright when a barrage of eggs hit the car windows, and Lex naturally grasped her hand.

"It's just eggs, Princess. Don't worry."

Roza patted her chest. "Oh my, I agree with the protestors' sentiment, but it's a bit scary driving through it."

"How does the Queen feel about this man, President Loka?" Lex asked.

"Bea told me he is the last person they want in their house, but Bo Dixon is immovable on the subject, and George knows it is her duty to follow the government's instructions. I know Bea was furious about the whole visit, and she made me promise that we would be extra gay tonight."

Lex laughed. "We can only try our best."

Their car pulled up outside the palace entrance and after exiting the car they were shown by the footmen to the receiving line.

As they waited in the line, Lex felt every eye in the place on her, and she heard whisperings. This was it, what she was afraid of if they attended a public event together. Their relationship was out, and sooner or later the media would find out about her past.

"Why do you look so serious all of a sudden?" Roza said.

Lex didn't want to spoil their night with negativity. "I'm just nervous. It's a big night."

Roza smoothed her hand down Lex's lapel and said with a cheeky smile, "Don't worry. I'll look after you well."

There was a teasing sexual tinge to Roza's voice that made her shiver with anticipation. "Oh? Is that a promise?"

"Oh yes. Now stop worrying and let's enjoy tonight," Roza ordered.

There was no time left to worry in any case, thought Lex. She looked up at the ornate ceiling and then around the many paintings on the walls. "Buckingham Palace is stunning. I thought it might be a little dated, but no."

Roza smiled. "It is beautiful and well taken care of."

"What's Ximeno Palace like?"

Roza lost her smile. "It's much like this, although more of a European style, but it is different in one respect. It feels empty, like it's lost its happiness, its soul."

"Did you grow up there?"

Roza nodded. "Until I was eighteen and allowed to have my own apartments in one of our smaller royal residences. I couldn't wait to get away from the palace. Gussy said it used to be a happy place before my mother died, but then everything changed."

Lex squeezed Roza's hand in support. "I'm sorry."

"Let's not dwell on my home. I doubt it's ever going to feel happy again, not while father's there."

While they were talking, they moved up to second in line. "Bea looks gorgeous," Roza said.

"She is very beautiful," Lex agreed.

"Don't be nervous. Let's go and face the music."

The Master of the Household called out, "Her Royal Highness, Princess Rozala of Denbourg, and Lennox King."

❖

The banquet had been a tense affair, with the Queen's toast at dinner, which of course was written by the government, met quietly by the assembled guests, who no doubt did not particularly approve of the visit of President Loka. Thankfully for Roza and the other guests, after dinner they retired for coffee and drinks to one of the palace reception rooms where they could mix with others.

Roza was mingling with some of the other guests while Lex talked with Theo and Perri. When she looked across the room and watched Lex, she got that tingly excited feeling and knew she couldn't wait any longer to be at her side. Time to put her plan for tonight into action.

Roza excused herself from the group she was with and walked over to Lex, and said to Theo and Perri, "Could I steal Lex for a while?"

"Of course," Theo said smiling.

She took Lex's hand and guided her over to one of the more spectacular paintings on the wall. As they stood gazing at the picture Roza said, "I missed you."

Lex smiled. "I missed you too."

Roza sidled closer to Lex and rubbed her thumb up and down the back of her hand. "When I looked across the room to you, all I could think about was your fingers inside me."

Lex turned to her with a look of surprise. "Princess, you can't say things like that to me here."

"Why?"

Lex gazed at her with a flicker of the fire she kept hidden down so deep under her control. This is what she wanted—she wanted to drive Lex to distraction but show her that delayed gratification could be a good thing.

"Because we are in a room full of some the most important and influential people in the world and all I want to do is touch you."

Roza whispered, "So it would be wrong to touch me right next to these important people? Bad? Risky? What if we got caught?" Roza could feel she'd hit her mark when Lex gripped her hand tightly, and the fire grew in her eyes. "It would be wrong to be only a few feet away from these people, while you fucked me?"

She saw Lex close her eyes and gulp, trying hard to retain her composure. Roza found it hard too and she knew what was coming.

"Don't say those things."

"Follow me."

Roza led them to a less populated corner of the room. It would have looked to observers as if they were simply admiring a few palace treasures. Roza turned to look at the room of people and checked they were all engaged in conversation.

"When I tell you to move, Lex, move quickly."

Lex looked at her with confusion. "What are you doing, Princess?"

Roza reached her hand to the small table behind her, and once she was satisfied no one was looking, she pressed a hidden button on the table and the corner of the room opened like a small door.

"Move now." Roza darted through the opening and when she was sure Lex had followed, pushed the door shut.

They were in a dark stone corridor, only lit by dim emergency lighting.

"Where in God's name are we?" Lex said.

"Secret corridor. Up to the right is a door to one of the main drawing rooms, and to the left a door leads to a basement area the family used to shelter in during the war. We used to play here when we were children. Come on."

Roza led them just a few feet down the dark corridor, so they weren't next to the door, and walked Lex against the wall.

"Shh, what can you hear?" Roza asked.

Lex listened and said, "Voices from the reception."

Roza grinned and dragged her fingernail down Lex's cheek. "Yes, they're all just a few feet away, not knowing I've got my hands on you."

The fire finally overtook Lex, and Roza quickly found herself turned and pushed forcefully against the wall.

Their lips crashed together and Lex gathered up one side of her flowing gown and grasped her thigh. Her kisses stilled for a minute when they heard the voices get louder as people moved towards that side of the room.

All they could hear was their own heavy breathing as they waited to see if they'd had been caught coming in here, but eventually the louder voices dissipated.

Lex grasped her chin lightly between her thumb and forefinger. "You are a bad, bad girl. You know that?"

Roza was delighted. Lex's passion was freed and she loved it. "Yes, I am. Very much. Do you know what I wish?"

"What?" Lex said with almost a growl.

Roza briefly licked and sucked Lex's fingers. "I would love if you had a strap-on underneath your trousers so you could fuck me against this wall a few feet away from everyone."

"Jesus." Lex closed her eyes.

Roza gathered the other side of her dress, and said breathily, "Show me how you'd fuck me."

Lex lifted her off the ground and Roza wrapped her legs around Lex's waist. "This is what I'd do, Princess. Would you like to be fucked like this?"

This wasn't hard just for Lex. Roza was so turned on that it was as difficult for her to keep control. She dug her fingers into Lex's short hair at the nape of her neck. "I would. Tell me how you'd do it."

"Oh God, yes."

Lex kissed her feverishly, but Roza pulled back. "I want you to promise me something. No matter what, I don't want to come, okay?"

Lex looked at her like she was insane. "What?"

"Please, baby. It's what I want. I want something special for later tonight. Will you trust me? Will you promise me that you'll follow what I say?"

Lex searched her eyes and finally gave a nod, probably thinking that she would change her mind.

"Okay, tell me how you'd fuck me, right here."

Lex rested her forehead against Roza's and with her lips only inches from hers said, "I would unzip my fly and pull out my hard cock, then rub it up and down your wet pussy."

Roza jumped when she felt Lex's fingers on her sex, parting her folds and rubbing slowly up and down.

"You're soaking wet, Princess."

"Because I want you inside me. What would you do next?"

Lex's eyes were closed now as she lost herself in the scene they were creating. "I'd slip the head in just a little to let you get used to it, and then push it in inch by inch."

All the time Lex's fingers mirrored her words, and Roza groaned at the feel of it. "Uh-huh."

"Then when it was in fully, nice and big, stretching and making you want more—I'd start to thrust."

Lex thrust inside her, while thrusting her own hips, and it felt so good, Roza was in danger of losing control of her own game.

Lex continued, "What does it feel like getting fucked just a few feet from everyone, huh? What would they think, Princess? Would they think you're such a bad girl who likes to get fucked?"

Both of their breathing was getting really heavy and Lex appeared to be getting lost in her own headspace. Roza only had a few moments more before she couldn't turn back.

"Lex, stop." She gasped.

Lex couldn't hear her so Roza let her legs fall, and Lex opened her eyes slowly. "Princess?"

"You promised you would follow my lead. I don't want to come yet."

"You can't be serious. I can feel you—"

Roza placed a finger to Lex's lips, and smiled. "I know, but I want tonight to be special. I want you to learn how good waiting can be, and going slow. You told me you didn't do delayed gratification. But I want you to tonight."

Lex took a big deep breath and stepped away from her. "I'll try anything you want to try once, but it's so hard." Lex lifted her hand to show Roza. "Look. I'm shaking, I'm so turned on."

"I know, but it'll be good, I promise. Come with me." Roza led them out the other door into the empty drawing room and out to find the bathroom to freshen up.

Lex was hungry. Hungry like she was desperate for her next fix. And her fix was Roza. Roza had wound her up so tight she was just about ready to explode. After they returned to the reception from their little alone time, the rest of the evening seemed to last for unending hours.

When they finally got back to the hotel where they were staying the night, to have some privacy, Lex felt a kind of madness. They went into the room, and as soon as the door was shut, Lex threw Roza's overnight bag on the bed and made a beeline for her.

Roza put her hand against her chest to stop her advance. "Not yet. You promised."

"That was before." Lex pulled off her bow tie and ripped open her top shirt buttons. "I don't do waiting. You don't understand. It feels like you're everywhere. In my head, in my heart, burning beneath my skin. It's like I can feel every little sensation multiplied a hundred times, and I'm going crazy for you."

Roza stepped towards her and scratched her nails down Lex's neck making her moan. "That's the point. I want you to feel like that. This is all for you. I want to show you what going slowly can feel like, and that it's not a bad thing, and breaking your rules doesn't have to be destructive. I promise letting me have this control is a one-off, unless you want it again, and from now on a princess will be your willing slave."

That image was making her horniness even worse.

Lex kissed her softly and said, "I'll do anything for you. What do you want?"

Roza smiled and hurried over to her overnight case and pulled out a bag. "Take this to the bathroom, and give me ten minutes."

Lex had no clue what this was all about, but if it ended with touching Roza, that's all that mattered.

She went to the bathroom and opened the bag. "Oh yes, that's my princess."

Inside was an Intelliflesh strap-on. A strap-on that responded to the body it was attached to and gave the wearer the full sensory experience. Lex had always loved using these when she had been more sexually active. It mirrored her sexuality and who she was inside.

Since she was to wait ten minutes, she decided to take a quick shower first. The power shower hit her overstimulated skin and made her hand travel down to her sex. She could have relief in a few strokes, but inside she knew the only one who could give her relief was Roza.

Lex got out, dried off, and attached the strap-on. After a few minutes it started to react to her body and bulge in her boxers.

She sat on the toilet seat and held her head in her hands. "Oh God, I want her so much."

When ten minutes had passed, she opened the bathroom door slowly and nearly swallowed her tongue at what she saw. Roza had lit candles around the room and was lying naked on the bed with some sort of chocolate body paint spread at strategic places all down her body.

"Baby?" Roza said.

Lex's feet started to move over to the bed before she even thought about it. Lex went to touch her but Roza said, "Not yet."

Again Lex had to use an iron will to stop herself. Her eyes were riveted as Roza ran her finger through the chocolate liberally spread on her nipples and trail down her stomach. "This isn't any old body paint. This is high quality Belgian chocolate sauce. I know you don't eat chocolate but I want you to break a rule and lick me clean before you make me come. Can you do that?"

Without hesitation Lex said, "I would break all my rules for you."

Roza took her hand and kissed it, before giving the bulge in her boxers a squeeze. "Come and eat me all up, baby."

Lex dispensed with her boxers and T-shirt, climbed on top of

Roza, and lowered her mouth onto one chocolate-covered nipple. The first taste was an explosion of flavour, and she hummed in pleasure.

Underneath her, Roza moaned and her hands went to grasp Lex's head, but Lex clasped a hand over Roza's wrists and held them down over her head. *Time for a little payback.*

She took long, slow swipes with her tongue, making Roza squirm beneath her.

"Is this what you wanted, Princess?"

"Yes, just like that."

Lex bit and gently pulled her nipple, and felt Roza's hips start to move, seeking relief from the strap-on teasingly touching her sex.

Before moving on to sucking the other nipple, she kissed Roza full on the mouth so she could taste the chocolate smeared on her lips.

"You taste so good, baby," Roza said.

"You too, Princess. I can't wait for more."

Roza looked at Lex with a storm of emotion in her eyes. "I want you inside me. I think I've lost my own game."

Lex stroked her brow and shook her head. "We've both won. I've never felt my body more alive, and it's all because of you."

Lex quickly moved to suck her other breast and lick the trail of chocolate down Roza's stomach, and swirled her tongue around her navel.

She felt Roza's hands pushing her down towards her sex, and she couldn't stop herself from increasing her pace. She kissed Roza's thighs, and opened up the lips of her sex to lick and tease the protruding clit she found there.

"Yes. Lex, I need to come."

Lex looked right at Roza. "Do you want me to fuck you?"

"Uh-huh, now, baby. Fuck me."

That's all Lex needed to hear. She got up quickly and slid her cock into her slowly. "Jesus, you feel...I can't describe it." She slid all the way in and started to thrust. All the teasing and waiting had taken its toll on Lex. "Shit, I'm not going to last long." Lex groaned.

Roza wrapped her legs around Lex's hips, pulling her deeper. "Me neither. No more slow, baby. Fast and hard."

"Fuck, yes."

Lex kissed Roza as her hips frantically thrust. The orgasm that was building was nothing like she had experienced before. Better than sex on cocaine, much, much better. It felt almost painful as she neared the edge.

"Ah...I'm going to come, Princess," Lex cried out as her hips slapped into Roza. She could feel Roza's nails dig into her shoulders as the fire that had been slowly burning under her skin exploded all over her body and in her heart. She collapsed into Roza's arms.

She gasped and tried to get her breathing under control. Lex had expelled some of her fears, her fears of losing control and succumbing to her body's needs. Things were different now. They were different—now she had Roza.

"Baby?" she heard Roza say. "Are you okay?"

Lex got her strength back and leaned up so she could look Roza in the eyes, and for the first time in her life said, "I love you, Roza."

Roza cupped her face and tears welled in her eyes. "I love you too."

"I think you nearly killed me though," Lex joked.

Roza giggled and rolled them over so she was on top. "You made me come so hard, Lennox King. I think I might need to kill you some more."

Roza started to move her hips, and unbelievably Lex started to feel her sex come to life again. She wondered how she was going to have the energy to keep up with someone ten years younger than her.

I'll have fun trying.

Roza woke and saw Lex sitting at the end of the bed. She was disappointed that she was dressed, but she crawled over and wrapped her arms around Lex's neck, and kissed her cheek. "Good morning, baby." She immediately felt Lex stiffen. "What's wrong?"

Lex handed her the computer pad she was reading. "What's right?"

All the morning news sites were running with pictures of her and Lex. The picture that was most telling was at the Dreams and Wishes launch event, and the photographer had caught her looking back to Lex for support. It captured an intimacy between them that was far beyond propriety.

Royal Rebel love scandal exposed. Princess Rozala in torrid love affair with former City trader and drug addict.

"I'm sorry your past is spread across the media because of me, but we were always going to have to face this, to be together."

Lex pulled out of her grasp and stood. "We were always going to face the fact we can't be together, and we were doomed to failure. I kept trying to tell you we would both get hurt if we went down this road."

"Don't say that. We can make this work. Apart from some royal duties, my father and brother leave me to live my life pretty much as I please. I'm not the heir, and I don't have the same limits that Gussy has."

"That was before your relationship with Thea Brandt. Look at this." Lex turned to the TV on the hotel room wall and said, "Computer, play BBC News."

Roza watched news reports of a joint operation between Denbourg, British, and US Special Forces to destroy sixty secret weapons caches, where illegal arms and drugs were being stored for her ex's business and criminal business partners.

"Oh my God."

Lex sat beside her and softened her tone. "Do you think after all that, your father is going to risk more bad publicity by giving his blessing to your relationship with a drug addict?"

"I don't care what my father says. I love you, and I want to be with you, Lex," Roza said as tears started to well up in her eyes.

"Sometimes love isn't enough," Lex said sadly.

Roza clasped Lex's hand. "What do you mean? Don't you love me enough to fight for us?"

Lex looked down at Roza's delicate hand in her own. She did love her, but didn't know if she was capable of the fight that she was sure would end in disaster. "Princess, I can't handle a lot of stress in my life. To keep myself well and away from my addictions, I have to live a life of balance. I love you, but I don't know if I'm strong enough to fight."

Watching the tears rolling down Roza's face was killing her inside and it was just going to get worse.

"Lex, please don't leave me."

"I have to go home and think." Before she could change her mind she put on her jacket, lifted her overnight bag, and walked out.

CHAPTER SEVENTEEN

Roza wiped away her tears quickly. She was angry that Lex didn't seem to have the stomach for the fight, but at the same time understood her fear of losing control of her ordered life and losing the battle to her addictions. If Lex was afraid, maybe it was now time for her to take the lead and make her believe in them.

She got dressed and had Major Ravn and her team drive her back to St James's Palace. They struggled through the crowds of press at the front gates and Roza hurried upstairs. When she walked through the door, Perri was there waiting for her.

"Roza, my darling." She hugged Roza tightly. "Did you know about Lennox?"

She nodded. "Yes, but it's not like the media have reported it this morning."

"I never expected it was. The press always get things wrong. Do you need me to do anything?" Perri asked.

"Not at the moment. I'm going to phone Father. I need to fight for what I want and face him for once in my life."

Perri grasped her hands tightly and gave them a squeeze. "Sounds like a plan. I'll get you some breakfast. You must be hungry."

Roza kissed Perri on the cheek. "I don't know what I'd do without you."

She hurried to the privacy of her bedroom and asked the computer to call her father. Roza was nervous as she waited for the call to connect, but this time she kept her outward self upright and confident. She had to show him she was a woman capable of making her own choices, not the rebel who didn't care.

The phone connected and Lord Dahl, her father's private secretary, came on screen. "Good morning, Your Royal Highness. How can I help?"

Roza had never got on well with him. He had been dispatched to deliver the King's displeasure to her on many occasions, and she felt he enjoyed every word.

"I would like to speak with my father please, Lord Dahl."

"I'm sorry, that will not be possible, ma'am. Your father is extremely busy."

Roza was infuriated. Who was he to speak for her father? "I ask that you go and convey my message to the King himself."

"The King is in deep conference with the prime minister and the heads of his defence staff. Last night's military actions have created a lot of business that needs the King's personal attention, and he left instructions not to be disturbed."

"I'm sure that rule doesn't apply to his daughter, My Lord."

"It certainly does, especially considering the catalyst for last night's actions," Lord Dahl said in a condescending voice.

"End call," Roza said. "Pompous little prick."

What to do? She was clearly being kept from the King. "Computer, call Gussy."

Her brother immediately answered. "Roza? Are you okay?"

"I've been better, but I need your help. I take it you've seen the headlines about me this morning."

"Briefly, yes. All hell has broken loose over here with the attacks on Thea Brandt's arms stores. What the news stations haven't reported as yet is as well as bombing, our troops were engaged in a heavy exchange of fire. Her organization is much larger than we thought."

Roza sighed and lowered her head. "I'm sorry I brought her into our lives, Gussy. I live with the guilt every day."

"You were an innocent, and you've really turned things around while you've been in Britain. Cousin George says that you and Bea are great friends and you're doing wonderful things for her charity."

Roza nervously pushed her hair behind her ears. Praise was a strange experience for her, especially praise given by her family, but she liked it. "I've tried hard, Gussy. Timmy's is where I met Lennox King."

Gussy's warm smiling face became serious. "Tell me about her."

"It's not what you would have read in the media. Lex has been clean from drugs for six years, and since then she's dedicated her life to charity and keeping healthy. I've fallen in love with her, Gussy. She makes me a better person."

She watched her brother clasp his hands together as he seemed to consider this carefully. "What do George and Bea think of her?"

"Bea works really closely with her, and likes her. I believe George does too."

"Major Ravn reported to me that she saved you from Brandt's attacker and has gained her respect," Gussy said.

"When did you speak to Ravn about her?"

"This morning when I saw the news reports." Gussy moved closer to the screen. "Ravn is my eyes and ears around you."

In the past that statement would have made her angry, but she knew it was just her brother's protective instincts. She felt safe and secure with Ravn, and the major always tried to accommodate her wishes, so no, Roza was not upset this time.

"I need your approval, Gussy."

"I'll support you, but Father is a different matter. You know what his views are like. Especially with what he's dealing with now."

"Please tell me you'll try. Lex loves me but she's convinced you and Father won't approve and will bring an end to our relationship. She's frightened of getting hurt."

"That's a good sign in itself."

"Gussy, this isn't like what I felt for Thea. I know now that wasn't love. I can't imagine spending the rest of my life without Lex. She makes me stronger, more independent, and, above all, a better person."

"As I said, I'll try for you, Roza. I know how I'd feel if I wasn't allowed to be with Freja. Carry on as you are, but be discreet. You might have to wait for what you want."

All the pent-up stress and emotion came out in the form of tears. "Thank you, Gussy."

Gussy smiled at her. "You're a good girl, Roza. I've always known that. You have everything in you to be anything you want to be. Believe in yourself and remember that I love you."

"Love you too, big brother."

The screen went blank and Roza wiped her tears. *Now I just have to convince you, Lex King.*

❖

When Lex turned the corner of her street and saw the crowds outside her house, she changed her plans quickly. She arrived at Vic's house, and her friend immediately took her downstairs to her office.

"I'm glad you came. When we saw the news this morning...Well, I worried about you, mate. How do you feel?"

Lex took a seat at the front of the desk and gripped her wrist tattoo. If she could just hang on to that, maybe she could steer her way through this. She looked up at Vic and said, seriously, "Like I want a bottle of vodka and a two gram bag of coke."

Vic didn't even bat an eyelid. She went over to her office fridge pulled out two bottles. "Fortunately we're all out of coke and vodka, so you'll have to make do with organic carrot, beet, and ginger juice. A new line we're trying at the supermarkets."

She threw Lex a cold bottle of purple juice. Lex smiled and took a sip. She could always rely on Vic to find humour in any stressful situation.

"Thanks." She ran her fingers through her short hair. "I don't know where to begin or what to do with myself. I can't go home because the press are twelve deep outside, and I can't go to the gym because everyone will recognize me and I'm sure it won't be long till the cameras are there too. You know the gym is my coping method. I need it."

"How did the media get your personal information?" Vic asked.

"I've no idea. I knew after we attended the dinner at the palace last night they would know I was the mystery suitor, but I never expected this." Lex held her head in her hands as she thought of her parents who had tried to call her a few times. "Oh God, what are Mum and Dad going to think? I've embarrassed them enough throughout my life already."

"Stop that. All they'll be concerned with is if you're okay."

Lex nodded. "I know. I walked out on her this morning. I didn't want to, I just had to get away to think."

"Princess Rozala?"

"Yes. Roza's quite innocent in a way, despite appearances, and she thinks we can just walk off into the sunset, but I know life doesn't work like that. Life is not a fairy tale."

"You think her family will bring a stop to it?"

"Vic, her family has already been embarrassed by Roza's ex-girlfriend. I'm not a good bet for being next woman in."

"What does the princess say?"

"That she wants to fight for us. I told her I don't think I have the fight in me."

"Why? You're one of the strongest people I know."

Lex got up and walked over to the window that looked out over Vic's large city garden. "I love her more than anything, Vic, but if I fight and lose, I not only lose her, I'll lose my control and myself."

Vic followed her to the window and joined her in looking out onto the garden, where Vic's two little girls were playing with each other while their mother looked on.

"I felt the same when June told me she loved me. I nearly walked away, Lex. Can you imagine if I did? I would never have had the joy of having her as my wife, and these two beautiful little girls out there. Remember there are no guarantees—when you're an addict, there's always the chance we'll fail. I could go out tomorrow and drink a bottle of whisky. There's always a risk."

Lex shook her head. Vic was her strength, Vic was her example. "You would never do that."

"It's a possibility, Lex. June knows that as well as me, and if it happened we'd have to face it and start again." Vic placed a hand on her shoulder. "Don't close yourself off to happiness because of what might be. Her family might not accept you, and you might struggle with your addictions, but you and Roza might find a way to work it out."

Lex sighed. "What do I do now?"

"You need time to think and somewhere you can work out while you do it. Go home to your mum and dad's. Think, climb rocks, and walk in the countryside."

"I don't even know what I would think about. My brain is a mess."

"It's simple," Vic said. "Can you live with yourself if you don't try to be with the one you love? Can you live a lifetime without touching her again?"

Lex put her arms around Vic and hugged her. "Thank you. You're the best friend anyone could hope to have."

"I know—I'm good, aren't I?" Vic joked. "Now you make a list of what you need and I'll pick it up from your house. Then no one will know where you're going—and remember, just keep breathing."

❖

"I have to speak to her, Ravn," Roza pleaded.

The discussion between Roza and her head of security had been going for a while in the drawing room. After repeated failed attempts by Roza to call Lex, she had no option but to go to her.

"Ma'am, I would be derelict in my duties if I exposed you to that level of media attention. The TV reporters are broadcasting from outside her house. If you are trying to win over your brother and the King, this is not the best way to go about it."

Roza had a frustrated retort on the tip of her tongue, but was silenced by the ringing of her phone. She looked at it quickly. "It's Lex." Roza hurried to her bedroom and answered. "Lex? Thank God. I've been trying to call you, and Ravn wouldn't let me come to your house."

"Good. I'm not there. I'm at my friend Vic's. I couldn't get near mine."

A million thoughts rushed around Roza's head, and she didn't know which to say first. "I spoke to my brother, Lex, and he says he will support us and try to lobby the King on our behalf, but even if he doesn't approve, I'll leave everything behind to be with you. Please give us a chance."

"Calm down, Princess—take a breath. Okay?"

"Okay. I'm sorry. I'm just going out of my mind here," Roza said.

"I was calling you to say I'm taking a few weeks off work and going home to my parents' house. To take stock and think away from the press and—"

Roza's heart sank. "You're leaving me?"

"If you'd let me finish, I was going to ask you to come with me, if Major Ravn approves. It's a quiet little village in the middle of nowhere. If we're careful in travelling there, we could have some time away from the press. Time to be ourselves, and work out what we want and if this can work."

Roza had never felt happier in her life. "Yes, yes. I want that, Lex. I can show you we can work."

"There's another reason. I want to introduce you to my family. They are everything to me, so it's important you meet."

Nerves started to set in. Would Lex's parents resent her for bringing all this adverse publicity into her life? Because of her image, would they disapprove? Inside she knew she would face anything to be with Lex. "I'd love to meet your family."

"I'll call Ravn then, and try and sort out the logistics, and you can start packing, Princess."

"Thank you for wanting to fight, Lex."

❖

Roza's apartment was chaos since Lex's phone call. Between trying to pack quickly for her trip and Ravn frantically organizing security, no one had a minute to think. Roza had called Bea to let her know what her plans were, and both Bea and George thought it was a great idea for her to have some time away. Everything was set apart from packing.

"Do you want to take the blue dress, Roza?" Perri held up the garment for her perusal.

Roza looked up from packing all her hair and make-up products and thought hard for a second. "No, too formal. I'd like to take everything, but I don't want to look like the stereotypical princess and turn up with twenty cases."

Perri laughed softly. "You're nervous, aren't you?"

"A little. I'm worried they'll be expecting the princess from magazines, and wonder why on earth Lex got involved with me."

"Don't be nervous. I'm sure they're good people, if Lennox is anything to go by."

Roza brought her make-up case over to the luggage bags, and said, "Do you like her then?"

"I do. She's a good person and has a very calming influence on you," Perri said.

"Let's just hope Father sees it that way. Oh! I forgot. Lex said I'd need walking shoes," Roza said with a heavy sigh. "She wants to take me hiking. Why she thinks walking long distances is fun, I'll never know."

Perri put the blue dress back into the wardrobe and said, "I'll go and call a few sports shops, and have the boots couriered down to Lex's. Excuse me."

Roza couldn't remember when she had last felt so happy. She was positively giddy and those butterflies were exhausted by the amount of fluttering they had to do in her stomach. She giggled and threw herself back on the bed.

CHAPTER EIGHTEEN

They picked up Lex at her friend Vic's house and made their way from London to the remote rural village of Lower Fieldworth, in the Chiltern Hills in the county of Buckinghamshire.

Roza had been quiet since they left London, and Lex hoped this trip was what she really wanted. "Princess? You okay? You've been quiet."

"I'm just nervous, I suppose. I hope your family likes me."

Lex took Roza's hand. "Are you kidding? My little sister will adore you, and Mum and Dad will love you. You know Poppy follows all your comings and goings on the fashion websites. You're super cool, according to her."

That made Roza smile. "I hope I live up to expectations."

They drove through the front gates to the large farmhouse property, and pulled up outside the front door, where Lex's mum, dad, and sister were waiting for them.

Lex squeezed Roza's hand and said, "Here we are. The King family home. Are you ready?"

"As I'll ever be," Roza said confidently, but inside she was unbelievably nervous.

Lex got out and opened the door for Roza and helped her out. Then she watched Lex hurry over to her family, and to Roza's surprise, they greeted her in one group hug, then they happily exchanged kisses and more hugs.

Roza held back, not quite sure what to do. If she found the domestic family life of the British royal family more relaxed than hers, then the King family were in a different category altogether.

"Roza, come and meet my family," Lex said, beckoning her over to them.

Lex's family had the brightest and warmest smiles and appeared to be genuinely happy to meet her.

"Roza, this is my dad, Jason."

Jason moved to kiss her on the cheek, but stopped himself and held out his hand. "Pleased to meet you, Princess Rozala."

Roza took his hand and kissed him on the cheek, making him smile. "It's Roza, and it's wonderful to meet you."

Lex moved on to her mum. "My mum, Faith."

Faith was a beautiful woman who clearly took care of herself. Apparently taking her cue from Roza's response to Jason, Faith moved to kiss Roza on each cheek. "Welcome, Roza. We're so happy to see you."

Lex put her arm around Poppy and said, "Lastly my baby sister, Poppy."

Poppy was a pretty young woman with long, wavy light brown hair. "Hi, Princess Roza, your outfit is super sweet."

Roza could tell immediately she was going to love Poppy. She gave her a kiss on the cheek, and said, "Thank you. I love your jeans—Gucci, if I'm not mistaken?"

Poppy looked more than delighted she'd noticed. "Yes! Lex bought me them for Christmas."

Roza turned and smiled at Lex. She really was the most kind and loving person she had ever met.

"Lovely to meet you all," Roza said. "I'm sorry about all the security people and equipment descending on you."

She saw Poppy's eyes go wide as she caught a glimpse of Major Ravn behind her. "Oh, sorry, this is my head of security, Major Ravn."

Ravn stepped forward and nodded her head respectfully. "Mr. King? I believe the officers I sent to you this morning have a space ready where we can base our team and equipment."

"Yes, we have the stable block around the side of our property. It's more of a self-contained flat really—we redeveloped it for when our elderly parents are visiting. It has two bedrooms, with kitchen and bathroom facilities. Let me take you there now."

"Thank you, sir."

When Jason walked off with Ravn, Faith offered her arm to Roza. "Let me show you to your room, Roza. Lex and Poppy can get the suitcases."

❖

They had a simple lunch around the table in the kitchen. Roza sat back and listened to the laughter, jokes, and family conversation she wasn't used to, and Poppy excitedly asked all about her favourite fashion designers and the models she had met. She was a lovely bright girl.

Afterwards she took a nap as she felt a headache coming on. It had been a whirlwind of a couple of days, and she was now just starting to feel the after-effects.

She awoke to a wet sensation on her cheek. Her eyes sprang open and she came face-to-face with a large caramel-coloured dog. She started to giggle as he continued to kiss her face and wag his tail incessantly.

"Okay, okay, nice to meet you too." Roza giggled as she stroked behind his head, and the kisses stopped so he could enjoy the ruffling of his ears. "You look like a big overgrown teddy bear. What's your name, I wonder?" She saw a name tag hanging from his collar. "Noodles? Is that your name? How sweet." He gave her an excited bark and ran off out of the bedroom.

Roza heard noises coming from the garden beneath her window. She looked at her watch. "Two hours I've been asleep? God, I must have been tired." She walked over to the window to see Jason, Lex, and Poppy play Frisbee with the aforementioned Noodles, who was now jumping high in the air to catch the disc. *They even have a goofy family dog.* Could the Kings be any more like the classic TV idea of the perfect family?

This kind of family was alien to Roza and quite overwhelming. Were all real families like this? Was this what she had missed out on?

As she watched Lex and Poppy fight over the Frisbee, laughing and play-fighting, she realized Lex was so different around them. So much more light-hearted and easy-going, and less controlled.

She had a desire to be part of it, but was nervous too. She walked downstairs and tentatively stepped into the large farmhouse kitchen. Faith was standing at the range cooking all sorts of delicious-smelling food.

Faith must have sensed her presence because she turned around and said, "Hello, ma'am."

"Hello, and it's Roza. I would like just to be Roza here."

Faith nodded, seemingly understanding. "Did you have a good nap?"

"Yes, lovely. A big teddy bear with a slobbery tongue woke me up," Roza said.

Faith sighed. "Noodles. I'm sorry, Jason was supposed to keep him downstairs so he didn't bother you. He's Poppy's beloved Labradoodle. We had one of our neighbours take him for a walk while you arrived and settled in. He can be a bit boisterous."

"It's no problem. He's a lovely dog." Roza hesitated, not knowing what to say or do next. "Is there anything I can do to help?"

"Everything is bubbling away nicely, but why don't we sit and prepare the strawberries for dessert. I'd like to get to know you without Poppy taking over the conversation."

Roza smiled and went to quickly wash her hands before sitting at the kitchen table. "Poppy is such a sweet girl."

Faith laughed and brought over the large bowl of strawberries and two knives for them to use. "Sweet, but talkative. You know, you're going to have to field a million questions before you leave?"

"That's okay. I think she's great. I only have an older brother, so it's nice to be around a girl closer to my age." They started to slice the fruit. "I hope I'm doing this correctly."

"Perfect. If you don't mind me saying, Roza, you seem tense. I hope it's not us?"

"Oh no, not at all. I suppose I am tense. I don't want you to judge me on my image in the media."

Faith surprised her by covering her hand in a comforting gesture. "Jason and I would never judge anyone on what others say. We want to get to know you for ourselves, and because Lex obviously cares so much about you."

"I care about her. I'm sorry that her private life was invaded because of me, and I'm sorry if you were embarrassed," Roza said shyly.

"We aren't embarrassed by what Lex went through. She had an addiction, an illness, and we helped her. All the people that matter know that," Faith told her.

"I think she's the bravest person I know."

Faith never said anything but her warm smile gave Roza the impression she had passed some sort of test she didn't know she was sitting.

They continued chopping the fruit quietly for a few minutes before Faith said to her, "I hope I'm not overstepping any boundaries, Roza, but you look so much like Queen Maria."

This was the first time someone had said those words that she didn't feel shame inside. The feeling was different altogether.

"Did I upset you saying that?" Faith asked.

"No." She plopped another strawberry into the bowl. "It used to. I used to feel guilty, and angry, when people said that."

"Why?"

Roza let out a breath. "I suppose, I felt guilty that she died because of me, and I felt I could never live up to her. She died for someone she would never know."

Faith listened and then said, "I had a lot of problems during Poppy's birth."

"What happened?"

"Poppy was a very late baby and a complete surprise to Jason and me, although Poppy prefers to say a precious gift rather than surprise." They both chuckled. "We were happy with one child—Jason had little time during his surgery days and I was busy with my business—and when my doctor gave me the news I was more than shocked. Jason hit the floor. I was convinced it was the menopause."

"I bet Lex was surprised," Roza said.

Faith got up and collected the meringue bases that had been cooling on the side and took a large tub of cream from the fridge. "Surprised but very excited. She always wanted a little sister to look after." She placed them on the table and started to whip the cream in a bowl. "The first time I saw Poppy's scan I fell head over heels, and every time she kicked inside me, I managed to find more love for her, even though I thought I already loved her with all my heart."

"What are you trying to say?"

"Your mother knew you and loved you from the first time she saw and felt you inside her. You were her daughter already, even though she couldn't hold you in her arms and, like me, I'm sure, would have willingly given up her life for her child."

Faith's words hit somewhere deep inside her, somewhere she had kept locked away for a long time, and the emotion overcame her.

❖

Lex checked their bedroom and couldn't find Roza. She went downstairs and eventually followed the voices to the kitchen. When she took a step in she found a sight she was not expecting—Roza crying and being comforted in her mother's arms.

She knew she should be doing something but couldn't move her feet. Her mum looked up and indicated for Lex to leave. Lex managed to make herself move and wandered out into the front garden of the house. She took a deep breath and tried to calm her hammering heart. Seeing the two women she loved embrace like that had a profound effect on her.

Roza and Vic were right. She had to try and be with Roza no matter what King Christian would say about it, and no matter the risk to her sobriety. That was her problem to deal with and shouldn't interfere with her love.

No more pulling away from her. Roza deserved the full devotion of her love. Thea had kept her on an emotional rollercoaster and she was doing the same thing. Roza needed security and certainty in her life. She needed to know that someone would be there at the end of every day to love her and take care of her.

She walked around the gravel driveway to the side of the house and saw Poppy sitting on the wall watching Roza's security team. They were busy going in and out of the stable building, setting up security equipment and organizing patrols of the property.

"Hey, baby sister. What are you doing sitting out here on your own?" Lex sat on the wall beside her, put her arm around her shoulder, and gave her a squeeze.

Poppy immediately laid her head on her shoulder. "Watching her."

She said that with almost a purr to her voice. Lex followed her line of vision and was surprised to find Major Ravn at the end of it. She was directing her men, and had dispensed with her tailored suit jacket, showing her crisp white shirt, tie, and shoulder holster.

Lex sat back in surprise. "Major Ravn?"

"Yes, I've never seen anyone like her in my life. She's like ten feet tall and so, so strong, and she's got this scary, sexy thing going on."

"She's also about forty years old with a wife and two kids, Pops—you're sixteen."

"So? I'm allowed to look, aren't I?"

Poppy had grown up so fast. The thought of her lusting after someone did not fill Lex with joy. One day someone would return that look. "I thought boys were your thing?"

Poppy gave her an incredulous look. "You are so old-fashioned, Lex. People under twenty-five don't limit themselves to one gender or another. We are attracted to the person."

"Well whatever, don't be attracted to Ravn, okay?"

Poppy sighed dramatically. "I can dream." She bumped Lex's shoulder. "So, big sister, how did you manage to catch a beautiful princess? Does she know that you drink kale and spinach juice, run at disgusting hours of the morning, hang off mountains, and are generally annoying?"

Lex laughed. "Mostly. She'd probably agree that I'm annoying." As Lex thought back on their time together, she realized she'd tried to resist Roza all along until she had been caught. "I don't think I caught her. She caught me and I've been trying to get away ever since."

"Are you crazy? She's Princess Rozala of Denbourg, one of the most beautiful women in the world, a style icon, and you're trying to get away from her?"

When it was put like that, it seemed so simple. "I'm clearly an idiot."

Poppy took her hand and smiled. "No, not an idiot. You've just been alone so long that you're scared."

"When did you get so wise?"

"Mum teaches me," Poppy said.

Faith King was wise, smart, maternal, and loving, everything a mother should be. Lex couldn't imagine not having that influence in her life, something Roza never had, but maybe this was something she could share with her.

Lex spotted her father coming out of the kitchen carrying a large tray filled with covered dishes.

"Lex can you help me? Your mum's made food for Major Ravn and her team, and there's another couple to come."

That was typical of her mum. Ravn had said her team would go to the local hotel for meals, but obviously Faith had other ideas.

"No problem, Dad."

As she stood Poppy jumped up excitedly and said, "I'll help take food over to Major Sexy."

Lex laughed, and gently pushed her. "No more drooling over Ravn. Go and help Mum."

Poppy stuck out her tongue at her. "You're such a spoilsport."

❖

Dinner with the Kings was like one of those cosy family scenes Roza had seen in cheesy Christmas films, and didn't quite believe actually existed in real life. The family teased each other back and forth, told stories about themselves, and generally laughed their way through the meal.

The whole scene was so different to her own family life, if you could call it that. Their roast chicken dinner was prepared in a warm farmhouse kitchen and served to the family together, in the same room. That never, ever happened in her life. Everyone was served food when they asked for it in separate rooms, and meals were cold and sad compared to this warmth. Roza was basking in it.

"So, Lex," Jason said, "where are you two hiking to tomorrow?"

Roza felt Lex's arm stretch around the back of her chair and hold her. It felt wonderful how open Lex was being since they'd arrived here. She wasn't pulling away any more.

"I thought we'd walk to Foxglove Wood, and stay there overnight, then start hiking up Greenfield Hill the next day and do some climbing."

"Excellent, have you ever done any hiking or climbing, Roza?" Jason asked.

The word *hike* actually sent shivers down her spine. "No, but I'm happy to try anything that Lex enjoys," Roza said.

She was surprised when Lex leaned over and kissed her cheek sweetly, causing her parents to smile warmly at each other. Things were definitely different here. Lex was so relaxed, and she loved it.

When they finished dinner, Lex went to discuss tomorrow's plans with Ravn, and Poppy took the opportunity to get Roza to herself. They went upstairs to Poppy's large bedroom. The room was tastefully decorated with pictures of models, designers, and what looked like hand-drawn fashion designs.

"You have a beautiful room, Poppy," Roza said.

"Thanks. I designed it myself. I love design and fashion. Come and see." Poppy pulled her over to her desk and computer, and they both sat down. "Okay, computer, display King fashion folder."

As Roza looked through the designs, she was really impressed with Poppy's talent. "These are beautiful, Poppy. Are you going to pursue this?"

"Yes, I really want to, but I'm not sure where yet. London would be close to Mum and Dad, but there are great schools in Paris and Denbourg. What's Denbourg like to live in?"

Roza smiled. Despite all her troubles at home she loved her country dearly. "It's a wonderful place to live. There's a good mixture of country, scenery, mountains, and modern cities. Battendorf is very like London or Paris, except more laid-back. People don't like to rush in Denbourg."

"Sounds great. I saw video of you at Matthias Boudet's couture show in Paris. Was it as amazing as it looked?"

"Stunning. Matthias is a good friend of mine, so I got a sneak peek at some of his designs, but it was nothing to seeing them in the flesh."

Poppy's mouth hung open in shock. "Whoa! Matthias Boudet is your friend?"

Roza smiled and nodded. "He designs for me quite often."

"Matthias is my hero. I want to design just like him."

"Next time he is showing in London, Paris, or Denbourg, you'll need to come with me," Roza said.

"Oh, I'd love that. We'd have to leave Lex at home—she'd get bored and annoying."

"Oh would I?" They both jumped in fright as Lex rested against the bedroom door frame. "Having fun, Pops?"

"Yes, Princess Rozala is friends with Matthias Boudet," Poppy said excitedly.

"Who?" Lex asked.

Roza and Poppy shared a look and rolled their eyes. "The world-famous fashion designer?" Poppy got up quickly and lifted her bottle of perfume from her dressing table. "Look, you got me his perfume for my birthday. You are hopeless, Lex."

"Oh, the weird guy?"

"He is not weird, Lex. You're weird," Poppy said.

Roza laughed out loud. The siblings had such a great relationship and Lex clearly adored her little sister.

Lex walked in and took Roza's hand. "Can I steal the princess, Pops?"

Poppy gave her a stern look, and joked, "As long as you don't keep her too long."

❖

Lex and Roza walked hand in hand through the Kings' back garden. "This is a beautiful garden, Lex."

"Thanks, this is Dad's domain now he's retired."

Roza sighed with contentment. She just loved being here with Lex. "I love your family, Lex. You're really lucky to have them."

"Thanks. I feel lucky. I put them through a lot when I was an addict, but they never let me give up. Did you have a nice talk with Mum before dinner?"

"Yes, Faith is wonderful. I hope I'll get the chance to know her much better, and Poppy is just adorable, and so intelligent."

It made Lex so happy that Roza had fitted in perfectly with her family. As ever they hadn't let her down and welcomed Roza with open arms. "I'm glad you get on well with them. My family is everything to me."

Roza smiled and leaned into Lex, clutching her arm with two hands. "I'd love you to meet Gussy. I know he'd love you."

"I don't know about that, but I'd love to meet him," Lex said.

"Of course he will love you, because I love you," Roza said firmly.

Lex didn't want to ruin the moment, so she just nodded, and said, "I hope so."

They walked on down to the edge of the lawn area, and Roza asked, "Where are we going?"

Lex smiled and grasped her hand to take her through the small opening in the trees. "Somewhere from my childhood I'd like to share with you."

After a few minutes they came out to a pretty little glade with a shallow river, a small stone bridge across, and an old stone wishing well.

"This is so pretty." Roza hurried over to the well and looked down into the deep dark cavern, which was covered by an iron grille on top for safety.

"I thought you'd like it." Lex came up behind Roza and slipped her arms around her hips, and rested her head on her shoulder. "Mum used to bring me, then Poppy, down here to play when we were little. She said the fairy folk lived here."

Roza looked up at her smiling. "The fairy folk?"

"Yes, it's a village legend. They live down in the well and come up to hunt for food in the forest, but if you leave them a gift of food or money, then they can make your wish come true."

"That's so sweet."

"There's something else. Come over here." Lex led her over to a giant tree across the stream. Its trunk was covered by countless carved names with hearts. "This is the magic tree."

"Is everything magic around here?" Roza asked.

"Of course, it's an old English village. There were witches here too at one time."

"I've obviously had a sheltered life in Denbourg. So what's magic about it?"

"The legend goes that a young woman called Constance met her lover here, back sometime in the seventeenth century. Their names are carved on the tree. They were going to run away together because her father didn't approve of him."

"What happened?"

"Her father and brother were lying in wait, and they grabbed her true love and stabbed him."

Roza gasped, completely taken in with the story. "Did he die?"

"Yes, he died against this tree. The young woman took the knife from his body and stabbed herself in the heart, so she could join her lover on the other side."

Roza snuggled into Lex's side unable to take her eyes from the tree. "A tragic love story."

"Legend says their blood seeped into the ground and nourished the tree, and because they sacrificed their lives for love, the fairy folk blessed the tree with the magic of love, and whoever carves their name on the magic tree will find their true love."

"How romantic. That's why it's covered in names?"

Lex nodded. "It started to become a tradition that you carved your name in the trunk when you were a teenager, and then when you did meet the one you loved, you added their name later."

"Did Poppy and you do that?"

Lex guided her over to the trunk and pointed out the crudely carved names of *Poppy* and *Lennox*.

"What a beautiful tradition."

Lex took a penknife from her pocket and smiled at Roza. "I've found my true love, and no matter what happens, you will always be the only one I love."

Roza clasped her hand to her mouth as Lex carved her name in the bark and formed a love heart around their names. She could think of nothing more romantic than this.

When Lex finished, Roza threw herself into her arms. "Oh, Lex, this is so romantic."

Lex cupped her face tenderly. "I know I haven't said I love you as much as I should, and I've been wary about what we can be to each other, but I never want you to doubt that I love you."

Roza looked at her in wonder. "You are my dream come true. Kiss me."

Lex turned them both and walked Roza back against the tree, and whispered, "I love you."

They kissed slow, deeply, each kiss reaffirming their love together. Roza pulled back and said, "I'm not going to let you go, Lex. No matter what my family think."

"Let's cross that bridge when we come to it and just enjoy our time together."

CHAPTER NINETEEN

The next morning, after Faith had given them a wonderful country breakfast, Lex and Roza set off on their hike. Lex led the way with a huge backpack filled with everything they'd need, and Roza dragged her heels behind her. They had been walking for an hour and were now deep into Foxglove Wood.

Lex felt calm and happy to be back in her natural element. The sounds of birds chirping and the rustle of wind through the trees were all you could hear, and they were alone—apart from the five security agents twenty feet behind them. That was as far away as Roza could get Ravn to agree to.

Lex took a deep breath and said, "It makes you feel glad to be alive doesn't it?" When she didn't receive an answer, she turned and found Roza more than ten feet behind her, trudging along, with a glum look on her face.

Lex jogged back to her. "Hey, Princess. You don't look as if you're enjoying yourself."

Roza gazed at her with annoyance. "That's because I'm not. This bag is too heavy, it's too hot, my feet hurt, it's dirty everywhere, and these disgusting flies keep hovering around and biting me."

"So other than that, you're having the time of your life?"

Roza dropped her bag and hit Lex in the arm. "How can you even enjoy this? It's torture."

Lex sighed. She thought it might turn out like this, Roza moaning the whole way, but she had been insistent that she wanted to try the things that Lex enjoyed.

She clasped Roza by the shoulders and said, "You have to think about the spirit of the place as you're walking through, not just trudge aimlessly. This is ancient woodland. Imagine all the sights it's seen, the people and animals who have come through it. You need to try and connect with it."

"I'd rather connect with my phone. I don't know why I let you persuade me to leave mine at your house. I can't check my email, my social media. Anything could be happening in the world and I won't know about it."

"I thought this would let us connect and be alone and cut off from the press. Besides, you've got a team of security agents, armed to the teeth and with more gadgets and phones in their backpacks than you would know what to do with. I'm sure if the world is coming to an end, Ravn will let you know." Lex picked up Roza's bag. "Now, no more glum faces. You are going to enjoy this if it kills me. I'll carry your bag, as well as my own, and if you keep walking for another hour or so, we'll make camp, and I might have something chocolatey in my backpack for you for dessert tonight."

The smile was back on Roza's face. "Ooh, is it more chocolate body paint?"

"No, it's a surprise—plus there's one more thing I think you'll enjoy." Lex leaned over and whispered in Roza's ear, "Have you ever made love outdoors in nature, under the stars?"

She saw Roza gulp. "No."

Lex gave her a sly smile. "You have lots of experiences ahead, Princess, if you're a good girl."

Roza giggled. "I can be good."

Lex was delighted to see the spring back in Roza's step. There was a little part of Roza that would always be the spoiled princess, but Lex would never want to change that about her. She was high maintenance, but that kept life interesting.

They started to walk again, hand in hand this time. Roza squeezed her hand and said, "There is one part of hiking I love. You in jeans, boots, and a tight T-shirt. So sexy."

"Just keep walking and I might let you take off my boots for me."

Lex wasn't surprised when she felt another play-hit, this time to her backside.

❖

Roza had to admit that when they reached the camping area, and Lex set everything up, it actually looked really romantic and sweet. The camping area was no more than a large field on the edge of the woods, but it had an outdoor toilet block and power cell points beside each tent pitch. Luckily since it wasn't a very well-known spot, they were the only ones there.

Ravn and her team were on the other side of the camping area so as to give them privacy. When early evening came, Roza and Lex sat on logs beside the open fire, outside their hard-shell tent, having just finished a dinner of sausages and beans.

Roza put down her plate and said, "That was tasty. I didn't think you'd eat something as unhealthy as sausages."

Lex took her plate and put it into the bucket of soapy water she had to the side of the tent. "It's all right when you've been hiking. You need the calories." Lex sat down beside her and took her hand. "So? What do you truthfully think about camping? It's not that bad, is it?"

Roza smiled, rested her head on Lex's shoulder, and pulled her arm around her. "No, I like this part. Just you and me alone and in front of a crackling fire. It's so romantic."

She felt Lex kiss her head and sigh contentedly. "Yes. This is nice."

"What about my chocolate surprise?" Roza suddenly remembered.

"Ah, of course. I did promise. I'll just be a second."

Roza watched as Lex rummaged around in her backpack and brought out a box of one pound blocks of her favourite chocolate, and five bags of big American marshmallows.

"Have you got enough there, baby?"

"Well you eat a lot so—"

"Hey, not funny," Roza said in a huffy voice.

"I'm only joking. I didn't how much it would take to make a big melty bowl of chocolate."

"Hmm." Roza licked her lips. "A big melty bowl of chocolate. Hurry up then, I'm salivating."

Lex got a clean pot to hang over the fire, and broke up the bars to melt. She handed Roza some wooden sticks and told her to prepare the marshmallows. The chocolate started to melt into gooey, glossy deliciousness, and as Roza gazed across the fire to Lex, her heart and her butterflies fluttered.

"I've never been happier than in this moment, Lex. Thank you for making it so special."

Lex smiled. "You're welcome, Princess."

Roza took her spiked marshmallow and dipped it deeply in the chocolate pot. "If there wasn't melted chocolate here, I would be dragging you to bed."

Lex nudged her and joked, "Eat quickly."

Just then they heard raised voices and saw lights snapping on over at Major Ravn's camp.

"I wonder what's wrong?" Roza said.

Lex stood up to get a better look and saw them checking their weapons and talking seriously. "Why don't you finish your mallows and I'll take a walk over to Ravn," Lex said.

"Okay, then bed when you get back. I have some aching shoulders I need you to take care of."

Lex smiled and bowed. "Yes, Your Royal Highness."

She started to walk over towards Ravn's camp, but Ravn must have seen her because she came and met her halfway.

"Is everything all right, Major? It sounded as if you had a lot going on over there."

Ravn looked impassive. "Nothing to worry about. Just checking in with headquarters."

Lex couldn't put her finger on it, but it felt as if Ravn was hiding something. "Are you sure because if you want us—"

"Just some internet threats after the bombings the other night." Ravn put a hand on Lex's shoulder. "Go back to the princess and have a wonderful night. You've got to treasure all these little moments together."

Now that was strange. The normally stoic Major Ravn didn't often use those kinds of words. "If you're sure, Major."

"Yes, we will be doing hourly patrols around the perimeter of the campsite during the night, so don't be alarmed if you see lights in the dark."

"I won't. Thank you, Major."

Lex walked back over to their tent with a slightly uneasy feeling. She looked up at the sky as night fell and the stars started to shine. "Treasure all these moments together."

She noticed Roza wasn't at the fire and the chocolate pot was off the heat. Thinking she had gone to use the bathroom facilities, Lex damped down the fire and cleared the plates and disposed of the litter in the bin.

Lex went into the tent and jumped when she saw Roza in their double sleeping bag, beckoning her in.

"Oh, baby, I'm waiting for you."

Lex wanted to jump in beside her that second. "I'm coming for you, Princess."

As she took off her clothes, something of Ravn's words echoed inside her. She wanted this to be special.

Roza leaned on her side, never taking her eyes off Lex. She could look at Lex's body for hours. She wasn't just sculpted and well-honed in the gym—there was an indefinable something that drew her to Lex, a certain swagger that she had, the way she held herself with confidence, which made Roza want to do bad things with her.

"Lex, hurry up and take those jeans off or I'll start without you."

Lex kicked off her shoes and jeans and was in the sleeping bag in seconds. She grasped Roza's hand and held it to the ground beneath her.

"You don't ever need to do that yourself when I'm here." Lex gazed at her with emotion in her eyes. "There has never been any woman who has made my heart feel like this."

Roza felt Lex stroke her fingers through Roza's soft hair and across her cheeks and lips.

"You are so beautiful, and I want to remember this night forever. Keep your eyes on mine."

"What—"

Roza's words died when Lex gently grasped her breast. "I want to see every moment of love and pleasure in your eyes."

Roza groaned in pleasure as Lex's hand went straight to her sex and grasped it.

"Touch me, Lex. I need you."

Lex slipped her fingers straight into the wetness she knew she would find. "If you stop looking in my eyes, I'll stop, okay?"

Roza nodded and put her hand on top of Lex's encouraging her to continue.

"Uh-uh. I don't need your help, Princess. Just keep looking." Lex rubbed around Roza's clit, teasing her but not giving her the direct contact she wanted. "I remember I used to sit in the office and just stare at you. You were so beautiful, and when you were angry, you were so passionate, that all I wanted to do was kiss you."

Roza's hips moved rhythmically along with Lex's fingers. "And when I flirted with you, and teased you?" Roza gasped.

Lex let her fingers slip down and only slightly dip inside. Roza closed her eyes and breathed, "Lex…"

As soon as she saw Roza's eyes close, Lex immediately stilled her fingers.

"Don't stop, baby. Please don't tease."

"What did I tell you, Princess. Keep your eyes open. I want to see every second of your pleasure and love in your eyes."

Roza opened her eyes and pleaded, "Make me come, Lex. Make me feel you love me."

She pushed her fingers back inside Roza and hastened her pace. "You're so wet."

Roza desperately grasped her own breast and squeezed it in her palm.

"Yes, squeeze it, Princess. Show me how much you want it."

Lex loved the way Roza's eyes softened the more her excitement grew, and her skin flushed red.

"Tell me about when I teased you."

"I wanted to bend you over my desk and fuck you until you begged to come."

Roza started to buck her hips, and Lex could feel Roza start to pulse around her fingers. "Yes, baby."

"Keep your eyes on mine and come for me, Princess."

Roza's hips met every hard thrust from Lex and demanded more until she clutched onto her neck.

Lex watched every moment of her orgasm on Roza's face, in her eyes, and in the loud scream she gave. As her breathing calmed, Lex peppered kisses all over her face and lips. "Thank you for giving me that, my darling princess. I love you."

"I love you, baby, but I think I might have broken something, I came so hard."

Lex laughed softly before Roza caressed her cheek and said with a sly smile, "I want my King to do bad things to me out here in the wild."

Lex's sex clenched in response. "I'm your King?"

"Oh yes, and I'm your pillow princess. You can do anything you want to me," Roza said with a coquettish grin.

Lex groaned as she realized she could assuage her craving and hunger for Roza now, without fear. Roza had given herself to her in both body and heart, and nothing that Lex could imagine could keep them apart now.

❖

By six o'clock the next morning, Lex had the fire going and tea brewing. When she had gotten up at five thirty, she'd noticed Major Ravn's camp was bustling with activity. The uneasy feeling she had gotten the night before returned.

She heard a big yawn from behind her, and a pair of arms snaked around her neck. "Morning, baby."

"Good morning, Princess. You're up early. Is it the country air?"

Roza kissed her sweetly. "No, it's Lennox King. I just want to be with you. Thank you for last night. You made it something I'll remember for the rest of my life and—"

Lex noticed bright car lights illuminating the early morning gloom, pulling into the car park.

"Early morning dog walkers?" Roza asked.

A quick glance to the side and she saw Major Ravn and her team making their way over to the camp. "I don't think so." This was the source of the bad feeling, she was sure. Lex stood and pulled Roza into her arms.

Roza's security team started to encircle the camp and Ravn approached with a serious look on her face.

"Ravn, what's wrong?" Roza asked.

"We are expecting company from Denbourg. I'll let them explain, ma'am." Ravn stood off to the side.

"Are they going to arrest me, Princess?" Lex joked.

"Don't be silly." Roza laughed. "It's more likely to be me."

The cars came to a halt and security officers got out to open the passenger doors.

"Denbourg officials? Wait a minute, that's Father's head of security. What is going on?" Roza walked forward a few steps.

Lex's bad mood was getting worse by the second. The atmosphere was what she could only describe as sombre.

Everyone stood back and two of the officials stepped forward.

"What? Am I in trouble again?" Roza said.

The female official said, "No, ma'am. My name is Lund, and I am Chief Privy Counsellor of Denbourg. We bring some bad news."

The other took out a red velvet bag with the Denbourg crest on the front. Roza immediately gasped and held her hand to her mouth.

"What's going on?" Lex said.

Everyone in the clearing, including Major Ravn, dropped to their knees, and all the blood drained from Roza's face as she began to weep.

Lex held Roza tightly, trying to calm her. "Princess? Tell me what's going on."

Lund took a large gold and jewelled sovereign ring from the bag and presented it to Roza.

"It is with a heavy heart that I must tell you that His Majesty King Christian and His Royal Highness Crown Prince Augustus were killed yesterday afternoon in a terrorist assassination. It falls on me to bring you your father's ring. The King is dead, long live the Queen."

The bodyguards and officials repeated the phrase, while Lund pushed the ring onto Roza's finger, and then Roza collapsed. Lex caught her and cradled her in her arms.

"They can't be gone. Tell me it's not real, Lex. Please, please, please."

Lex met Ravn's eyes who nodded and her stomach dropped to her toes. "Shh, darling. I'm here. I'm here for you."

The sound of a whirling helicopter came from above, and a man came forward and introduced himself as Roza's head of security, Colonel Voltz.

"Excuse me, Your Majesty? We have to get you to a secure location. The helicopter will take us to London."

Roza clutched Lex's T-shirt even tighter. "No, I don't want to leave her. Lex, don't let them take me."

Lex moved into full protection mode. She wasn't handing Roza over to anyone. "Colonel, I would like to take her back to my family home. She'll be safe there."

"Impossible. It isn't safe. Denbourg has been subject to an attack at the heart of our constitution. We have to protect our Queen. Your Majesty, please follow me."

"Major Ravn," Lex shouted.

Ravn hurried over and saluted the colonel. "Sir, I have Lennox King's home fully secure. I think it would be a good base until the Queen has come to terms with this."

He was silent for a time and eventually said, "Very well but only for tonight. Major, I'll let you handle this."

When he walked off, Lex lifted Roza and carried her over to the car to take her home. As she did, all she could think was, *I've lost her.*

❖

Lex sat in the living room with her family while the village doctor attended to Roza. The news played in the background as they waited. It showed military and police on the streets of Denbourg, as they hunted down terrorist snipers.

Lex wasn't allowed to stay in the bedroom with Roza and every minute away from her felt like an hour. She walked over to the TV. They were showing the military commemoration event both the King and Prince Augustus had attended earlier in the day. The camera panned out and the cracks of shots rang out, before the two men fell where they stood and chaos broke out.

"Roza can't see this. Shut off all the TVs when she comes down."

Jason stood and patted her shoulder. "Of course we will. Try and stay calm—she's going to need you to be."

"What can be taking so long? I need to see she's okay," Lex said.

Just then the family doctor, Dr. Kray, walked down the stairs with Lund.

"How is she, Doctor?" Lex asked quickly.

"Settled now. I've given her something to make her sleep," Dr. Kray said.

Lund rounded on the doctor. "Doctor, do not give out any of the Queen's medical or personal details. I thought the confidentiality document we had you sign made that clear?"

"But she's been staying with the Kings. Lennox is her—"

Dr. Kray struggled for words, but Lex finished for him with confidence. "I'm her girlfriend, and I want to see her now."

Lund looked her up and down, and clearly didn't appreciate what she saw. "Queen Rozala may have been dating you, but that gives you no rights or official position."

"I don't want a position. I want to see the woman I love." Lex closed her eyes for a second. Had she actually said that out loud? She looked at her mother and Poppy who were smiling proudly. Yes, she had said it, and she was glad she had.

"The Queen is sleeping now. You may see her if she calls for you later," Lund said, and then she turned to her father. "Mr. King, we may need to use your home until we move the Queen tomorrow. The majority of our staff will get rooms at the local pub, but we will need to leave a large presence here."

There was no question there, simply a statement of fact. Lex couldn't stand this any further. She walked out of the house and slammed the door behind her. There were new faces everywhere, armed guards at the front gates and all around the perimeter.

Lex spotted Ravn coming out of the stable block, and she hurried over to her. "Major? Can I talk to you?"

"Of course, Lex," Ravn said.

They walked over to sit in her mother's summer house, where Lex hoped they might have privacy.

"How is the Queen?" Ravn asked.

Every time someone used Roza's new title, she felt her slipping away from her just a little bit more. "I know she's settled and sleeping, that's all. The pompous Lund didn't even want me to know that. You knew this happened last night, didn't you?"

Ravn nodded sombrely. "I hope you will forgive me, but I wanted Her Majesty to have one last normal night. It's not something that she will be able to do again."

"You were right to keep it from us. I'll always remember our night together." Lex rubbed her face in her hands. "There's a guard she doesn't know on her bedroom door, and I'm not allowed in till she calls for me. What is going on?"

"That's the Denbourg court in action, and that's only a few of them. Wait till she gets back home. She'll be surrounded by people like Lund, telling her what's best and making her so very isolated, and dependent only on them. The late King's court was full of old men and women set in their ways, just like him. She'll need a strong Consort."

Lex couldn't imagine Roza coping with that pressure on her own, but the one thing she was certain of, after the way Lund had looked at her, was she would not be entertained as a partner for the Queen.

"If I can't be there, you need to be at her side, Ravn. She trusts you with her life, and I trust you to protect her."

Ravn sighed. "That's where I want to be. She's like my little sister, but there's a chain of command. The late King's security staff are now the Queen's, until she requests otherwise."

"You mean she can request you, Johann, and your team to stay in charge?" Lex asked.

"Of course. She is the Queen. Her word is law," Ravn said.

"I think Roza needs to know that. With people like the Colonel and Lund, she may get pushed into things that are not in her best interest."

As soon as she was able to speak to Roza, she would make sure she was able to make her own decisions.

"What happened in Battendorf? Surely when the King and the heir to the throne are attending an event, it's the safest place in Denbourg."

Ravn nodded her head in agreement. "It should have been. Usually we have agents spread out through the neighbouring tall buildings, all eyes trained on the royal family. One of our men was killed at his vantage point and the terrorists took their shots from there. They are still looking for the culprits, but they left a weapon that was linked to Thea Brandt."

"I wish I could get my hands on that woman," Lex said angrily.

"You're not the only one. Denbourg is reeling. I've never experienced anything like this in my career or my life. The country needs calm leadership, and we need to hunt down the person or persons responsible."

"Voltz wants Roza to leave tomorrow. What do you think?" Lex asked.

"I think she should stay here for a few days. She's safe and more comfortable. Denbourg needs her as head of state, but a few days here would be sensible."

"That's what I think. She needs to be around a loving family, until she's strong enough to leave—" *Me.*

Bea put on her ivory silk dressing gown and walked through their living quarters to George's office. She had been waiting for George to join her in bed and when she hadn't arrived went in search of her. George had an enormous number of red boxes arrive this evening, because of the terror attack in Denbourg, and they had missed dinner together.

She knocked lightly on the door and walked in. George was on the telephone, but waved her in. Bea noticed straight away that the sandwich she had asked to be served to George while she worked was left untouched.

"I appreciate that, Prime Minister, but I don't want to let the terrorists win. Our presence amongst the public is an important—"

She could see the tension and strain written all over her partner's face, and she wasn't surprised. It felt like the whole world was in chaos and George's family and everything she believed in was under attack.

"Of course. Thank you, Prime Minister. End call."

George held out her hand and beckoned Bea over. "I thought you'd be sleeping. It's half-past twelve."

"I was worried, and I can't sleep well without you there."

Bea was pulled down into George's lap and George automatically untied Bea's dressing gown so she could place her hand on her stomach.

"You have to take care of yourself now. Let me do all the worrying."

Bea caressed George's cheek. "I want to share your worry. Did you speak to Roza?"

"Only briefly. She found it difficult to talk but I spoke to Lex and Major Ravn. Ravn tells me Lex and her family are being a tower of strength for Roza. You were right about her—she's really proven herself an excellent partner for Roza, and she's going to need it. The Denbourg officials are trying to take control and manoeuvre her for their own ends."

Bea was shocked. "But her father and brother have just died."

"I know, but you can understand them in a way. They are jumpy and uneasy. The King and his heir have been taken out in one day, the people are on the streets protesting and demanding stability, and you never want a nervous population."

"But she's just a young woman."

"Her court and government don't see her as a young woman, they see a head of state, a symbol, a person who embodies the Denbourg constitution, and they want her back, safe and sound in Ximeno Palace. Bo Dixon informed me that the Denbourg prime minister is extremely worried that Roza will break under the pressure. Her second cousin, Prince Bernard, is next in the line of succession and is watching eagerly for her to fail and abdicate."

"He should be more worried about helping her. Where is he from?"

"He was brought up in Denbourg but now lives in Monaco. The worrying thing is he is heavily involved with a European right wing organization. If he was to get his hands on the crown it could cause problems for Denbourg, as well as all of Europe."

Bea sighed and leaned her head on George's shoulder. "We all need to make sure Roza feels supported. You sounded annoyed with Bo when I came in."

George wrapped her arms around Bea. "She and the intelligence services took part in a Cobra security meeting, and raised the terror threat to the UK to *extremely likely*."

"Why?"

"Our armed forces took part in the bombing of Thea Brandt's organization. We could be in the firing line, and to that end the prime minister wants to cancel our upcoming engagements."

The thought that she could lose George was terrifying. They'd come close enough when George was shot, and now they had a child to consider.

"We can't let the terrorists win."

"Exactly what I said. As monarchs we have to be seen to be believed. I said as much to the PM and she has reluctantly agreed for the moment, but we will have to put up with increased intrusive security."

"If I ever lost you, George..."

"You won't lose me, but if anything happened to me, I have an heir to replace me. So I had to inform the prime minister of our news. Security around you will be increased dramatically—no one will get near you or our child."

Bea felt immediately angry. "Don't talk about yourself as if you're replaceable. You are irreplaceable to me."

"I know that, my darling. I'm simply being pragmatic. We would have had to have this talk in any case. I have drafted a new will, now we are expecting a child. A copy of my wishes will also be held in Number Ten. If anything happens to me, both you and Theo will be joint regents until our child turns eighteen, at which point he or she will inherit the throne."

Bea could see why George brought it up, but she didn't want to even consider it. "Okay, I understand. Now it's been said, don't ever say it again."

George nodded and kissed her tenderly. "I love you."

CHAPTER TWENTY

Roza sat on the end of the bed and stared at the TV news. Every ten minutes they would repeat the shooting of her father and her brother. She couldn't tear herself away from it. She was scared and not because of everything that was happening, but that she felt numb inside, since waking up. She hoped that if she kept watching, she would feel something, anything.

When Roza woke she was surprised to find herself alone. She thought Lex would be at her side, and so she sent for her straight away.

There was a knock at the door and one of the new security agents opened the door slightly. "Your Majesty, Lennox King is here to see you."

"Why are you announcing her? Just let her in. She's my girlfriend."

Lex pushed past him and shut the door. "I'm sorry I wasn't here. Lund wouldn't let me see you unless you called for me." Lex pulled her into her arms, and squeezed her tightly.

For the first time since this happened, Roza felt some sort of safety and protection. "Don't leave me. I need you."

Roza felt Lex kiss her head and whisper, "I won't leave your side while you're here. But what are you watching that for? Computer, switch off TV."

Roza pushed Lex away in anger. "No, I want it on."

"Why?"

"Because I want to feel something and I can't. I'm watching my father and brother shot, and I feel numb." Roza banged her fist against her chest. "Why can't I feel anything? Am I bad? Am I evil?"

Lex approached her slowly. "Of course you aren't. It's just part of your grieving process. It won't last forever."

"Everything's in chaos, my world's turned upside down. I've got strangers around me, protecting me, telling me what to do."

"I know, but you can take some of that control back. I was speaking to Ravn and you can have her team in command. You just need to take control and use your new authority."

"I can't do it alone. Will you help me?"

"Of course. I'll support you in whatever you want to do."

Roza rested her head on Lex's chest. At least in the midst of all the chaos, she had Lex, her anchor.

"Let's get you some sleep."

The next morning, when Roza's new orders were issued, there were more than a few disgruntled faces among the assembled group. Lex felt the accusatory stares as she stood by Roza's side holding her hand.

Apart from that brief meeting, Lex couldn't get Roza to leave the bedroom. Lex came downstairs to get some food for Roza, and found her mum and dad in the kitchen eating lunch.

When Faith saw her she immediately got up and hugged Lex. "How is she, sweetheart?"

"Not good, I don't think. She's lying on the bed holding a picture of her mother, staring at the news. She won't put it off, and won't cry or show any kind of emotion."

"Why don't I take her some soup and have a chat with her. She opened up to me before."

"Thanks, Mum. That might just work. She really misses a maternal figure in her life."

Faith kissed her on the cheek and said, "Leave it to me."

"Johann is on the door. He'll let you in."

Her mum got some soup and bread and went upstairs to see Roza. Jason told Lex to sit and got her some food too.

"How are you holding up, Lex?" Jason asked.

Lex lifted her spoon and stirred through her soup, not feeling hungry for food in the slightest. "I don't matter, Dad. It's Roza that matters."

"Lex, you have to take care of yourself too, or you'll be no use to anyone. You know what stress does to you."

She knew exactly what he meant. As she lay holding Roza last night, she could feel the cravings build in her stomach. One drink or hit would take the horrible feeling away. The feeling like she wasn't good enough. The pain of knowing she was going to lose the love of her life.

"I know, Dad, but I need to focus on Roza just now. I need to get her through these few days, and protect her from those Denbourg officials who want to treat her like their possession."

Major Ravn knocked on the kitchen door. "I'm not interrupting, am I?"

"Of course not, Major," Jason said. "Come in and I'll get you something to eat. Faith made a huge pot of soup for everyone."

"That's very kind, sir." Ravn sat beside Lex and asked, "How is she?"

"In shock, I think. My mum's gone to spend some time with her and try to get her to open up."

"That's a good idea. I'm glad she has your family."

They were interrupted by Colonel Voltz. "Ravn, the MI6 agents have arrived to help protect the Queen. I want you to give them a briefing on the security situation."

"As you wish, sir."

The colonel looked at Ravn with disdain and said, "I don't know what kind of advantageous game you've got going on here, Ravn, but once we get back to Denbourg and the Queen is free from certain influences"—Voltz looked at Lex when he said that—"the chain of command will be returned to what it was."

Lex jumped up angrily, and was about to tell Voltz exactly what she thought of him, when Ravn stood and said, "It's all right, Lex. I am Her Majesty's servant and I will serve wherever she sees fit."

Colonel Voltz stared her out for a few minutes and left the room.

❖

That night Lex held Roza in her arms, stroking her body, head, and neck until she fell asleep. The talk with her mum had drained Roza until she was exhausted, and now she held on to Lex like she was her only anchor in a storm.

Lex eventually fell asleep herself, but when she stirred later that night, she found her arms empty. Roza was gone. She was fully awake in seconds, and pulled on some jeans before going to the door.

"Major, is Roza downstairs?"

Ravn looked surprised at the question. "No, I thought she was in bed—she never passed me."

"Fuck. She's done a disappearing act." Lex smacked her palm against her forehead.

"Christ. I'll need to raise the alarm," Ravn said.

Ravn was about to speak into her radio when Lex had a thought. "Could you give me half an hour before you raise the alarm? I think I might know where she went."

"No," Ravn said. "If I lose her again, I could be disciplined."

"Give me a chance, please?" Lex begged.

Ravn sighed. "Thirty minutes and that's it."

"Forty just to be comfortable," Lex said as she gathered Roza's sovereign ring from the pillow.

She went out onto the bedroom balcony and shimmied down the drainpipe as Roza had done, and as she had done many times in her youth.

All had been quiet inside the house but outside it was still a hive of activity as agents protected the house and gardens from intruders, but they hadn't anticipated that their Queen would want to escape.

Lex clambered over the garden wall and hurried down the road as she heard the guard dogs start to bark, noticing someone's scent. She jogged down the road and walked down the little worn path to the wishing well and magic tree. Lex pushed her way through the branches and foliage until she saw Roza staring into the wishing well.

"Roza? It's me." She announced herself so as not to give her a fright. But Roza never jumped in fright or jumped an inch, so she walked forward and wrapped her arms around her from behind. "Why did you run, darling? I was so worried when I woke up."

Roza leaned her head back against her. "I was going to run and keep running, but then I realized wherever I go they'll find me, and lock me in my cage again."

"You forgot this." Lex held up the state ring.

Roza turned around and said to her desperately, "I won't come back. I can't do this, Lex. I'm a spoilt party girl. I'm the last person who should ever be Queen, lead the nation. My father—"

"Your father was wrong. He never took the time to get to know the girl I know. You can do it. I know you can. You care about people and you're the most loving person I have ever met. You will make a fantastic Queen."

Roza wiped away tears, and said, "I don't feel like a Queen."

"Remember what I told you yesterday. You are the royal authority now. It has passed from your father and the generations before him to you, symbolized by this ring. You are Queen Rozala and you can do anything you want to do."

Roza gazed at the ring in Lex's hand. "Except run away. This is it, Lex. The rest of my life isn't my own. I'll be trapped in this cage forever. I'll be ferried from one place to another like a precious ornament, with people expecting someone like my mother or my father."

Lex took out her phone and showed her the live video from Denbourg. The crowds were gathered in the thousands outside the palace. "Look, Roza, your people are desperately looking for a figurehead to lead them in their grief. Their democratic constitution has been attacked and they are frightened."

Roza pushed away from her. "I can't help them. I'm just a girl with no talents, and no good sense."

"Stop trying to live up to your father's expectation. Think of Summer and her friends. Think of the responsibility you took organizing everything for Dreams and Wishes, making connections, playing with the children, and listening to their parents' concerns. That is a Queen, not a party girl. Step out from King Christian's shadow. It's now the reign of Queen Rozala. What happened in the past doesn't matter any more."

Lex watched Roza physically pull herself together, and stand taller. Her words had obviously gotten through.

"You're right," Roza said. "For once in my life I can do something right, something my mother and brother might have been proud of."

"That's my princess." Lex stopped herself. "Excuse me, that's my Queen." Lex dropped to her knees and slipped the ring onto her finger and kissed it. "I love you and pledge myself to your service, Your Majesty."

"Don't call me Your Majesty." Roza smiled shyly.

Lex stood. "That's who you are now."

Roza leaned her head on her chest. "I love you, Lex. You and your family made me become a better person. I am a better person with you. Will you come with me? Will you come to be with me and become my Consort?"

This was the moment Lex had been dreading. "No, I can't. Not *now*. I'm not the right one for you. I'm an ex drug and alcohol addict. I can't be the person you need."

Roza gasped. "Now? So before, if all of this hadn't have happened, you would have been with me?"

"I don't know if your family would have allowed it, but I would have tried to be the person you needed with everything I had."

"I'll give it up, renounce the throne. I just want to be with you, Lex."

"You can't do that. Your country needs you. There would be a constitutional crisis if you didn't take the throne, and at a time like this that's the last thing your country needs. I love you so much, Roza—that's why I'm letting you go."

"Please, don't give up on us, baby," Roza begged. "Look at Bea, she and George bridged the gap."

"The Queen Consort was not a cocaine addict."

"You are not a cocaine addict any more. It's all behind you."

"I will always be an addict, Roza. There's always a chance I'll fail," she said angrily. Over the last few days, with all the emotional turmoil, her cravings had been creeping up on her.

Roza's face went stony. "If you loved me enough to be with me as a princess but not now I am Queen, you obviously didn't truly love me, and carving my name on that tree meant nothing to you."

She set off walking at a fast pace, leaving Lex to try and catch up. Roza looked furious and hurt, and Lex knew letting her go was going to kill her.

As they approached the gates to the Kings' home, Roza said coldly, "I'll sleep in my own room tonight, and I'll be leaving first thing."

Lex stood still as Roza walked up to the surprised guards at the gate. As they escorted her back to the house, Lex could barely contain her emotions. The love of her life was walking away, and she wasn't brave enough to follow her.

The next morning Roza was up and dressed by six o'clock, not that she had slept at all. To say her heart was broken was an understatement, but as she'd stared at the ceiling in the small hours of the morning, she realized the only way she was going to cope with losing Lex, and the enormity of her new life, was to shut down her emotions or she would drown in them.

By the morning her deep-seated numbness had returned, and with it an acceptance of what her life was to become. She had a duty to her ancestors and her people to do the best job she could do. Roza dressed in the soberest outfit she had brought with her, a grey skirt with matching jacket, and cream blouse. Until she got back to St James's Palace it would have to do.

There was a knock at the door, and Major Ravn said, "The car is waiting for you, Your Majesty."

"I'm ready."

Roza couldn't wait to get out of here and as far away from Lex and the warmth of her family as quickly as she could, before that warmth could seep back into her heart. She walked downstairs and found Faith, Jason, Poppy, and Noodles waiting to say goodbye next to her car. They were unsure of how to react to her now, going by how nervous they looked.

Jason bowed and held out his hand to shake hers, but she wrapped her arms around his reassuring broad shoulders, so much like Lex's.

"Thank you for a wonderful few days, Jason. I'll always remember them."

"You're welcome, Your Majesty. I know you have a lot of difficult times ahead. We'll be thinking of you."

Roza let him go and kissed his cheek. "Thank you."

Next, Poppy gave her a grand curtsy. "I've been practising. Is that okay?"

"Perfect." Roza hugged her tightly. "I'll call you—email me your designs, and look after Noodles, okay?"

"Yes, that would be amazing. You're going to need lots of fashion advice with all the Queen stuff you're going to be doing."

"I will." Roza smiled.

Faith curtsied and opened her arms without hesitation. "If you need to talk, or just a friendly ear to listen, I'm always here."

Roza drank in every last drop of maternal warmth from Faith, and knew she was going to never have this type of connection again. "Thank you. You've all been so kind."

Faith released her and said in a low voice, "Lex loves you, she's just scared. Don't give up on her."

Roza felt the urge to look up to Lex's bedroom window, and there she was, staring back at her. Without taking her eyes from Lex's she replied to Faith, "I'm scared too but I'm facing it, Lex isn't. Goodbye."

She got into her state car, and when the door slammed shut, the last bit of hope that Lex might come to her died.

❖

Lex stuffed all of her belongings in her bags as quickly as she could. All she could think about was getting back to London, back to her structured, controlled life. Only in the safety of her controlled life could she try and survive this pain in her heart.

She had just finished packing her last bag when her mother walked in, and she didn't look happy.

"Lex, why are you doing this to yourself? You just watched Roza walk out of your life without a fight."

Lex piled her bags on the floor. "I'm protecting her, from me. Now she can go back to Denbourg, find a nice woman with no problems to be her Consort, and the Denbourg court doesn't have to worry about whether the coke-head is going to embarrass the monarchy."

"I saw the way you were together. This was real—it was something special you had together."

"I don't deserve her, okay?" Lex nearly shouted at her mum and instantly regretted it. "I'm sorry, Mum. I'm sorry." Faith tried to hug her, but Lex shrugged out of it. "Don't comfort me, Mum. I don't deserve it."

"Lex, you're scaring me. Don't go back to London like this. You're not coping well," Faith said in a worried tone.

Lex forced a smile on her face. "Don't worry, Mum. I just need some time to myself. Once I get myself back into work and my daily routine, I'll feel better."

"But the woman you love won't be by your side. You need love, Lex," Faith said.

"I can't have love."

CHAPTER TWENTY-ONE

Ever reliable, Perri had a black dress, hat, and jacket ready for Roza when she returned to London. As soon as she was changed into her new uniform, she was driven over to the Denbourg embassy. She sat in the back of the state car with Perri and Lund, who was filling the role of private secretary until Roza could appoint one permanently.

Lund handed her a computer pad and said, "We will enter the ambassador's office where you will have a few minutes to greet Queen Georgina and the Queen Consort in private, before you will be taken to the meeting room. You will be met by the Denbourg prime minister and various Denbourg courtiers and officials. They will be your witnesses as you make your royal pledge of service, and then we will escort you to the embassy entrance hall where you will give a speech live to the world's media and the people of Denbourg. This is your speech."

Roza's heart thudded as she read over the first few paragraphs, and she remembered the last time she gave a speech. Lex had been the tower of strength behind her to get her through. Now she would be on her own. She quickly shut those thoughts out of her brain, and looked up to Perri who gave her a smile of support, but it wasn't the same.

They drove past the front of the embassy and she was touched to see people had laid hundreds of bouquets of flowers at the front entrance, and a long line of people stood in a line that stretched out of sight down the road.

"They are so kind," Roza said.

"There is a book of condolence in the embassy for the public to sign, ma'am. We have stopped anyone from entering until Your Majesty has completed the formalities."

Roza saw the drizzle of rain on the car window, and thought of the discomfort the people would be standing in until she had finished.

"Lund, I wish you to organize an overhead covering to protect the people from the elements. Have it run down to the end of the street."

Perri smiled at her thoughtfulness. "That's a wonderful idea, ma'am."

Lund looked less than impressed. "Ma'am, is that really necessary?"

Roza touched the sovereign ring that gave her connection to all those members of her family who came before and felt a strange feeling of self-assurance and confidence. "Yes, it is. I also want tea, coffee, and bottles of water taken to the line as they wait. Is that clear?"

"Abundantly, Your Majesty." Chief Lund activated her phone, and started to make the necessary arrangements.

The car stopped around the back of the building for security. Ravn opened her door and she and four other agents circled Roza as she walked inside the embassy. Everyone was so frightened there could be a sniper anywhere at any moment.

When she was shown into the ambassador's office, she felt calmer at seeing George and Bea. They both were over to her in seconds, and out of habit Roza started to curtsy, but George stopped her.

"No, you are Queen now, Roza. You bow to no one." George engulfed her in a hug, and Roza drew from her strength. "Sorry doesn't seem like an adequate word, but we are truly sorry for your loss. Remember, Bea, Theo, and I will always be your family and be there for you."

Roza struggled but succeeded to keep the impassive composure she had been wearing like armour since last night. "Thank you, George, and thank you for coming."

George pulled back, apparently surprised at her impassive composure.

"I've cried myself out, and I need to keep myself calm or I'll go under," Roza explained.

"We understand," Bea said and gave her a warm hug of her own. "Where's Lex?"

That was something she didn't want to talk about, the other gaping wound on her soul. "At her family's house. She didn't come with me." Roza walked over to the desk and gazed at the painting of her father on the wall behind.

"Is she meeting up with you later?" Bea asked.

"No. We are no longer together," Roza said flatly.

"But you seemed so happy," Bea said.

"We were, but apparently, she doesn't care enough to walk into royal life with me." Roza walked to the door, and said, "I have a pledge to take. Will you come with me?"

George and Bea shared an unreadable look, and then George walked forward to the door. "Of course. Lead on."

They were led into the meeting room and everyone apart from George and Bea went down on their knees. Lund lifted the Denbourg Book of Prayer from the table, and as she had rehearsed, Roza placed her hand on the book.

"I, Rozala Maria Ximeno-Bogdana-de Albert, being King Christian's one and true heir, pledge to uphold the laws, democratic rights, and privileges of the people of Denbourg."

Everyone repeated with one voice, "Long live the Queen."

Later that evening, Lex sat on her couch watching the news reports over and over. Watching Rozala, the woman she loved and could never have, was a form of torture, but in some perverse way she believed she deserved that torture. She had turned her back on Roza and broken her heart, all because she was scared.

I'm pathetic.

Since Lex had returned to London, she had nothing to do but think, and she realized that as much as she tried to pretend that she left Roza because it was best for Roza, for Roza's future, that was only an excuse. Lex had let her go because she was scared, and now it was too late. She'd lost the one woman in the world who loved and understood her.

Lex felt her hunger for a hit and a drink grow to match the pain in her heart. It would be so easy to have a drink and numb this misery in her heart. Her phone started to ring and she saw it was Vic calling. No doubt she thought she was going to do something stupid—and she was. She was going to hide in oblivion.

"Computer, switch off phone."

She looked up at the lonely figure of Roza giving her speech inside the Denbourg embassy. The strain was evident on her face.

"I dedicate my life to your service, and I give my word that my prime minister and my government will find those responsible for striking at the heart of our way of life, our freedom, and everything we hold dear—"

Lex felt such a sense of pride. "You're doing so well, darling. It might be hard but you'll do so much better without me in the long run."

Lex lifted her glass of apple juice to her lips, and said, "To you, Queen Rozala, the love of my life." Her voice broke at the last word and her gaze fell to the tattoo on her wrist. She remembered Roza's finger tracing over it and saying, *I'm so proud of you, Lex. You are the strongest person I know.*

The emotion and shame crashed like a wave upon her, and she began to weep for the first time in years. She smashed the glass down on the coffee table, furiously wiped away her tears. "I'm sorry, Princess. I let you down. I'm not strong enough to be what you need."

Lex became aware of an incessant ringing as she woke. "God, how long have I been sleeping?" The clock on the TV news said nine o'clock. "Fuck, I must have dozed off."

The doorbell kept ringing repeatedly. "Okay, okay, I'm coming."

Lex stood and ran her hands through her hair. As she was about to walk out of the living room, new footage of Roza caught her eye. Queen Georgina was escorting her to her private plane at the airport. Roza and George walked up the red carpet, with ceremonial troops lining the way.

Roza was walking out of her life for good. *I love you.* Lex forced herself to look away.

She opened the front door to find Captain Cameron there.

"Good morning, Lennox. The Queen Consort has sent me to ask if you would join her for morning coffee."

"I'm not quite in the best condition to meet with Her Majesty. I—"

Captain Cameron was undeterred. "We can wait while you freshen up. Her Majesty was quite insistent."

Lex looked down at her jeans and T-shirt that looked as if they had been slept in and knew she'd have to change. "Could you wait in the living room while I have a quick shower and change of clothes?"

"Of course."

Lex hurriedly cleared up the mess on the coffee table and the couch. "Make yourself comfortable, Captain. Just give me fifteen minutes, and I'll be with you."

❖

Captain Cameron led Lex through ornate palace corridors until they reached the Queen's private quarters. She was shown in and found Bea was waiting for her. Lex bowed immediately.

"Thank you for coming, Lex. Please sit down."

On the table between them were pots of tea and coffee. "Can I get you tea or coffee? They're both decaf. I remembered you don't take caffeine."

"Coffee, please, Your Majesty."

Bea poured the coffee, and handed her a cup. "I'll be blunt and straight to the point, Lex. I know it's none of my business, but I hate to see anyone I care about in pain, so humour me. Roza loves you and is distraught about leaving you. If you feel the same—"

Lex sighed. "I do. I love her with all of my heart, and it's killing me to let her go, but I'm doing the right thing for her. I could never be what she needs, a steady, supportive Consort. I would only bring her shame. I've told you what I was, what I am."

"I knew you were a cocaine addict and went through rehab before you even got the interview at Timmy's."

Lex was taken aback. "How did you know?"

"All the applicants for your job were given the secret service once-over before the interview, and I was given the reports. Apparently it's standing practice if you are going to be working with a member of the royal family. I remember I was furious when I found out that George had one done on me." Bea smiled.

"You knew this and gave me a job?" Lex said.

Bea took a sip of her coffee and said, "Of course, you are exactly the sort of person who can relate to the people we work with. You've been at your lowest and pulled through, and that's why you would be the perfect Consort for Roza."

"But I would be an embarrassment, her people would think—"

"Roza's people would know you are no different to them. You can look them in the eye and say you've faced your demons and won. Roza has blossomed with your friendship, and then your love. You've shown her she doesn't have to live down to her father's expectations. I can't tell you how happy George and I have been to see her so relaxed, so happy."

Was it possible that she could have Roza? Could it work if she just tried?

Lex's silence obviously spoke volumes to Bea. "The simple fact is Roza needs you, Lex. She doesn't have a close family and now with the death of her father and brother, she has no one. She's going to be lonely and isolated—a young woman who hasn't been trained for the role of being sovereign. George tells me each side of the political elite are gearing up to influence her for their own ends. Political marriages are being talked of already. She needs you, but if you don't love her enough to give up your life here, I won't judge you. I know from experience what a terrifying choice that is. The choice is yours, but I just wanted to let you know that the Queen and her family will fully support you if you decide to go to her."

"I do love her, ma'am. The thought of royal life is daunting, especially given the way I handle stress. It's been so difficult with the press and everything, and we were only dating."

The public scrutiny had been overwhelming, but now she had no secrets to keep. She had no more skeletons in her closet, no more scandals.

Bea sat forward in her seat. "The crown changes you, Lex. I would never have believed it even after George and I married, but when we had our coronation…it changed me. I felt responsible to something much greater than myself or even my community. Roza will feel that too, but she is alone."

Could she do it? Not for herself, but could she do it for Roza?

Lex rubbed her face with her hands in frustration. "I can't bear the thought of her being alone." Or being with someone else.

"But remember, Lex," Bea said with caution. "You will have to walk one step behind her for the rest of your life. Can you do that?"

CHAPTER TWENTY-TWO

Queen Rozala's plane came to a halt at Battendorf airport. Roza looked out the window and saw the rows and rows of Denbourg ceremonial guard ready to meet her, and dozens of men and women in sober suits ready to shake her hand. She felt nervous and just a little bit panicked. How different it had been the last time she'd walked through this airport in her dress meant to shock.

Everything had come full circle. This was her life now, and as much as it wasn't her own choosing, she was going to make sure she did her brother Gussy proud. He'd been born for this job, but she would carry it out in his honour.

Perri shook her from her contemplation. "Your Majesty? You look to be thinking very hard."

"I was just thinking about the last time I was in this airport. I was the royal rebel, desperate to cause a stir." She looked down at her black outfit with matching black hat and veil. "Now I'm—"

Roza still struggled to say the words so Perri finished for her. "The elegant and dignified Queen of Denbourg."

"Do you think my people will agree? Will they give me a chance?" Roza asked.

"Of course they will," Perri said. "They saw what a fine job you did in the UK, and the grace and dignity with which you handled your father's and brother's deaths."

Roza reached across to take Perri's hand. "I couldn't have done it without you. You won't leave me, will you?" If she couldn't have Lex by her side, the last thing she would need was for Perri to leave. It might be the thing that broke her.

Perri lifted Roza's hand and kissed it. "Never, ma'am."

Major Ravn approached. "Your Majesty? If you're ready, everything is in place for your journey to the memorial site."

Rozala wanted to go and see the place where her father and Gussy had been killed at the Battendorf war memorial. The people had created their own memorial at the site, with flowers, candles, and cards. Huge crowds were holding vigil there, and Roza felt she had to be part of it.

Ravn continued, "We are informed that people are lining up along the route. Are you sure you want to do this? You will be exposed to great risk."

Roza had been given the latest in bulletproof armour to wear under her clothes, but that couldn't protect her from the head shots that killed her father and brother.

Roza felt a deep sense of surety and determination rise within her. "Yes, I'm sure. I want to show Thea Brandt that the House of Ximeno-Bogdana-de Albert will not be frightened by acts of terror. Not while I am Queen."

Both Perri and Ravn smiled at her with obvious pride on their faces. Ravn bowed her head with reverence. "As you wish, Your Majesty."

❖

Roza was determined and calm, but the visit to the memorial did take an emotional toll on her. As she stood in front of the spot where her family were gunned down, emotion overcame her and tears rolled down her face. There were countless TV cameras trained on her and she was surrounded by thousands of the capital's inhabitants. Everyone seemed to appreciate her open emotion, and as she made her way through the crowds of people, thanking them for coming, and receiving flowers and words of support, the crowd broke out into the Denbourg national anthem.

The sentiment and her people's acceptance of her touched Roza beyond words. She made an internal vow to always put these people and her country first. She would live as an embodiment of Queen Maria's legacy.

Roza waved to the people who were gathered outside the palace as her car drove through the large gates. She took a breath as her eyes took in the grand building that was now hers. Perri must have noticed her trepidation, because she said, "This is your home now. I know it must be daunting."

"It is. I was so lonely here as I was growing up, and I moved out to my own apartments as soon as I was able at eighteen, and now I'm back in *his* house."

"It's not his house, it's yours, and you can make it whatever you want it to be."

"I might be able to make changes to the décor and such, but I will still be lonely, with no one to share my life."

Perri gave her an enigmatic smile and said, "Oh, I don't know about that."

Roza ignored the comment and got out of the car. She was met by Lund and the Master of the Household. Neither looked very happy. She had thought they would be delighted to get her back to Denbourg and under their influence.

"Lund, is everything in order?"

"Yes, Your Majesty. Your belongings from your old apartments are in the process of being moved to the late King's apartment. It should be completed by this evening."

"Thank you." Roza walked up the grand entrance to the palace and through its doors. *I'm in my cage now, with no going back.*

Lund struggled to keep up with her fast pace, and spluttered, "Ma'am, if I may? The speech for your first TV broadcast to the nation has been sent to your email. The live broadcast goes out at five p.m."

"Thank you, Lund. I'm going to my private quarters now. You are dismissed."

Perri who was by her side said, "With your permission, ma'am, I'll stay and make sure your luggage is safely delivered in one piece from the airport."

"Of course." Roza kissed her and walked up the large staircase that led to the private quarters.

She slowed as she walked by the rooms that housed her childhood nursery. Never in a million years did that little girl who yearned for her father's attention ever think she would follow in his footsteps. A gun and a ruthless killer had stolen Gussy's destiny to rule, but now she had to make sure their legacy remained alive.

Roza arrived at the door to her father's—now her—apartments, and hesitated with her hand on the door handle. Roza remembered Lex's words of encouragement and her belief in her abilities. *You can do this. You can be everything he thought you couldn't.*

She opened the door gingerly, walked in, and gasped. Lennox King was sitting quite nonchalantly by the marble fireplace.

Roza couldn't breathe and couldn't speak. Could this be real? Lex was here, but was she here to stay? The dread, sadness, and worry that settled in the pit of her stomach turned to hope, and those butterflies that had deserted her suddenly flapped their wings.

"Are you—" Roza spluttered. She could barely speak from the unexpected rush of emotions swirling around her body.

Lex stood and bowed. "I understand there's an opening for a Consort in Denbourg, but I'm told that royal protocol prohibits me from asking you what I would like to. I can only hope the question is something you will be ready to ask me someday."

Roza took a deep breath and the question burst from her heart immediately. "Marry me?"

Lex sighed jokingly and said, "Oh, all right then."

Roza had never felt happiness like it in her life. She ran, jumped into her arms, and kissed her all over her face, ending in a deep butterfly-inducing kiss on the lips. "Oh God, I thought I'd lost you. I love you so much."

Lex caressed her face tenderly. "I'm so sorry for hurting you, but I was scared because I love you. I never wanted to do anything that would damage you or your image, but someone pointed out that it was hurting you more not to take my place beside you, and that's where I want to be, by your side in marriage, and as your Consort to give you strength."

"Thank you for giving us a chance. Wait—how did you get here so quickly?"

Lex kissed her nose, and then whispered in her ear, "Your favourite cousins let me borrow their plane."

In reality Lex would have swum the English Channel and walked the rest of the way if she'd had to.

Everything hit Roza at once—the strain of the day, her grief, and the thought that she had lost Lex—and she sobbed on Lex's shoulder.

Lex stroked her hair in an effort to soothe her, and knew she should have come with her from the start. "Shh, it's okay. I'm here now. Look at me?"

Roza pulled back and Lex wiped away her tears with her thumb. "I'm so sorry I didn't come with you straight away. I've caused you so much pain simply because of fear, but in the end I had no choice but to follow you."

"Why?" Roza sniffed.

"Our names are carved on the magic tree, and that binds our souls together. There's nothing that can keep us apart now. I love you."

"I love you too."

❖

Lex and Roza walked hand in hand to the room next to her father's study. Here she would meet with some courtiers and palace officials before she addressed the nation.

Lex could feel the tension come off Roza like flashes of electricity, and when they entered, Roza grasped her hand tightly. The room was full of officials waiting on her to perform this historic moment, and they could hear the chants of the crowd from outside.

Lund spotted her and shouted, "Her Majesty the Queen."

Those in the room all stood and bowed or curtsied to Roza, but Lex could feel every one of them look her up and down and wonder why she was holding their Queen so intimately. She could see how hard it would be to become accepted here, but she chose this, she chose it because Roza and her love for her were more important than her discomfort at being judged.

Lund approached them and bowed. "Your Majesty, I understand Lord Dahl is not to continue his service?"

"Yes, that's correct. I would like someone who isn't averse to new ways of doing things, and perhaps closer to my age. Draw up a list of those who would be suitable."

"Of course, ma'am." Lund looked at Lex and said, "If you'll excuse me, Ms. King, I need to talk to the Queen in private about her speech."

"You can talk freely in front of Lennox. I have proposed marriage to her and she has graciously consented to be my partner and Consort. I trust she will be treated accordingly."

There were a few gasps from the assembled courtiers, and Lex raised a questioning eyebrow at Roza. She wasn't expecting it to be made public as yet.

Lund struggled to speak. "Well…of course, ma'am. Congratulations to you both."

Lex gave Lund the most gracious smile she could. "Thank you, Lund. I'm so delighted you are here to share in our joy."

She felt an elbow to the ribs from Roza, and saw her smile as she whispered, "Behave."

"Is there anything else, Lund?" Roza asked.

"There is a new addition to your speech. I received information from the secret service and thought it helpful to add."

Roza took the computer pad and gazed over the words, and clasped her hand to her mouth.

"What is it?" Lex asked.

"They got her. Denbourg special forces captured Thea alive last night and are bringing her back to Denbourg for trial."

Lex pulled her into a hug. "That's wonderful." A trial and subsequent punishment would be a way for Roza to get some kind of closure.

A courtier came over and said, "Three minutes until the Queen goes live."

Lund took the pad back. "Your speech will appear on a screen in front of you, ma'am."

Lex could feel the tension in Roza's body. "Come on, let's walk over to the major."

Major Ravn and Johann were on either side of the study doors. Ravn smiled broadly when they approached. "Congratulations on your engagement, ma'am, Ms. King. You'll both be very happy, I'm sure."

Roza blushed. "Thank you. I couldn't have gotten here without you, Ravn. You've been such a tower of strength."

"It is an honour to serve."

When Roza entered the study, Ravn leaned over and whispered to Lex, "I know what you're giving up to be with her, and I thank you for it."

"She needed me, and I love her. I'd give up everything and do anything just to be allowed to love her."

She followed Roza into the office.

"I can't do this Lex, I can't." Roza froze when she touched the desk, and started to panic. "I can't sit at his desk. The last time I was here, he was disciplining me and sending me to Britain."

Lex held her softly. "For that I am forever grateful to him, because if he hadn't, I would never have met the love of my life."

"I'm the love of your life?" Roza grinned and pulled her towards her by her tie, thankful that Lex had broken the tension.

"Of course. There will only ever be you." Lex walked over and pulled out the chair behind the desk. "Sit, Your Majesty."

Roza sat down gingerly, and ran her hands along the top of the old oak desk. "Okay, I'm fine now." The clock beside the small hovering camera was counting down till it went live. It read thirty seconds. She took a sip of water and put it aside.

Lex stood behind the camera and smiled. "Say the speech to me. I'll be right here, and I always will be. No matter what happens, where life takes us, or where in the world we go, you can be certain that I will always be right behind you, giving you strength."

"You don't know how much that means. I love you."

"I love you too—now do your Queen thing."

Roza looked at the paintings of her ancestors on the wall staring at her, daring her to fail. Her heart hammered as the clock counted down.

Lex nodded and mouthed, "You can do it."

Roza smiled back at Lex and knew she could do anything with her by her side. The clock counted down to zero and she was on air.

Outside the study the gathered officials watched her speech on screens, and those gathered outside listened to every word uttered by their new Queen.

They watched the feisty royal rebel turn into a dignified monarch.

Maybe this was meant to be?

EPILOGUE

Six months later

The grand ballroom of Ximeno Palace was alive with the sounds of music, laughter, and, for the first time in a long, long time, happiness and hope.

The day had started with Queen Rozala being driven through the streets of the capital in the royal carriage, and led down the aisle of Battendorf Cathedral by Queen Georgina, to be given in marriage to Lennox King. The ceremony was watched live by millions of Denbourg citizens and people all around the world.

Afterwards the Queen and her new Consort passed through the streets in their carriage, waving to the thousands who had turned out to cheer and wave.

The Master of the Household brought the room to order by banging his wooden staff on the floor of the palace ballroom. "Your Majesties, your Royal Highnesses, lords, ladies, and gentlemen. I ask you now to stand for the cutting of the cake."

Roza took Lex's hand and was led out onto the middle of the dance floor. "Have I told you how beautiful you look in that dress?" Lex said.

"Just the one hundred times, but you can keep telling me," Roza joked.

Roza's long flowing dress with embroidered train had made the crowds gasp as she left her carriage.

While they waited on the cake being brought out, Roza straightened the diamond Order of Honour badge on Lex's chest, signifying her new authority and role as Consort. "You look so handsome in your white tie and tails, and I can't wait until I get you alone."

Lex whispered in her ear, "I'm going to tire you out so much, you're going to beg for sleep, my pillow princess."

Roza felt a fluttering in her stomach. "Oh God, they're still here."

Lex looked at her strangely. "What's still there?"

"The butterflies. From the first moment I saw you, I've had this colony of butterflies constantly flapping their wings inside, and they're still here now we're married."

Lex laughed and gently tickled Roza's stomach. "I hope that feeling never leaves you."

Roza wrapped her arms around Lex's neck. "Oh, I've got a feeling that they'll still be there when we're old and grey and surrounded by our grandchildren. They might flap a little slower though."

"Maybe," Lex said and kissed her. "I can't wait. I also can't wait till you see your cake. I think you're going to love it."

During the wedding preparations Lex had asked if she could take on the organizing of the cake as a surprise for Roza, and she'd agreed.

"It's not a spinach and kale cake, is it?"

"Would I do that to you?" Lex winked at her.

The Master of the Household interrupted them to announce, "The cake will now be brought in. Will the Guard of Honour assemble on the floor."

This was an old Denbourg tradition that a group chosen from the newly married couple's family and friends surrounded the cake while the happy couple cut into it.

In order of precedence the Master called their names. "Their Majesties Queen Georgina and Queen Beatrice of the United Kingdom."

George held Bea's hand as they walked onto the dance floor. Bea, now six months pregnant, kept a hand on her baby bump and rubbed it soothingly.

"Bea is just glowing, isn't she?" Roza said.

Lex slipped her arm around her waist. "She is, and George looks so proud holding her. Just as I will be."

Roza sighed happily. "I can't wait to have babies with you, but first we've got to shake up the Denbourg establishment and bring them out of the last century. I've still got some royal rebel in me."

"Oh, I know that. I sleep with her every night. She's wild," Lex said in a low voice.

Soon Prince Theodore and the rest of the British side of her family joined them on the floor, followed by Lex's family and Perri, Major Ravn and her wife, and Conrad, who had been such a good friend.

They all started to clap as the ballroom doors began to open. Lex stood behind Roza and wrapped her arms around her waist. The doors opened wide and five footmen wheeled in the enormous wedding cake.

Roza bounced on her toes with excitement when she saw the fifteen-tier wedding cake. "A chocolate cake!"

This wasn't any normal cake—the chocolate covering the cake was styled to look as if it was melting down the sides, and on the top sat a white chocolate tree bearing both their names.

"The magic tree." Roza kissed Lex excitedly. "That is so romantic, baby. Thank you."

"I can't take all the credit. Poppy helped me come up with the concept."

Roza looked over to her head bridesmaid, Poppy, and smiled. "I'm so lucky."

The Master handed them the cake knife and their friends clapped steadily faster until they cut into the cake—and then the whole room broke out in applause.

Roza dipped her finger into the chocolate frosting and painted some on Lex's lips before kissing it off them. "Can I take that cake on our honeymoon?" Roza said.

"Not a chance. If we do that you'll spend more time with the cake than with me," Lex joked.

There was one final formality to attend to before they left to enjoy their first night together.

Roza nodded to the Master of the Household, and he struck his staff against the floor. A footman brought over a scroll.

"What are you up to, Roza?" Lex asked.

"Wait and see."

The Master held out the scroll and announced to the room, "Her High and Mighty Majesty Queen Rozala has issued a proclamation to the Privy Council of Denbourg, and it reads as follows. The Queen decrees that from this day forward, the old and noble house of Ximeno-Bogdana-de Albert, shall henceforth be named Ximeno-Bogdana-de Albert-King. This proclamation is now law."

Clapping and cheering rose from the assembled guests, and Lex just stood silently trying to take in what had happened.

"What do you think? I wanted to show you that you have an

important place here with me. Your family was instrumental in keeping this royal house alive, and I wanted all those generations who follow us to bear your name."

Lex gulped and pulled her into a tight hug. "Thank you. I love you so much, my Queen."

Roza whispered in Lex's ear, "And I love you, my King."

About the Author

Jenny Frame is from the small town of Motherwell in Scotland, where she lives with her partner, Lou, and their well-loved and very spoiled dog.

She has a diverse range of qualifications, including a BA in public management and a diploma in acting and performance. Nowadays, she likes to put her creative energies into writing rather than treading the boards.

When not writing or reading, Jenny loves cheering on her local football team, which is not always an easy task!

Jenny can be contacted at jennyframe91@yahoo.com. Visit her website at http://www.jennyframe.com.

Books Available From Bold Strokes Books

Forsaken Trust by Meredith Doench. When four women are murdered, Agent Luce Hansen must regain trust in her most valuable investigative tool—herself—to catch the killer. (978-1-62639-737-8)

Letter of the Law by Carsen Taite. Will federal prosecutor Bianca Cruz take a chance at love with horse breeder Jade Vargas, whose dark family ties threaten everything Bianca has worked to protect—including her child? (978-1-62639-750-7)

New Life by Jan Gayle. Trigena and Karrie are having a baby, but the stress of becoming a mother and the impact on their relationship might be too much for Trigena. (978-1-62639-878-8)

Royal Rebel by Jenny Frame. Charity director Lennox King sees through the party-girl image Princess Roza has cultivated, but will Lennox's past indiscretions and Roza's responsibilities make their love impossible? (978-1-62639-893-1)

Unbroken by Donna K. Ford. When Kayla and Jackie, two women with every reason to reject Happily Ever After, fall in love, will they have the courage to overcome their pasts and rewrite their stories? (978-1-62639-921-1)

Where the Light Glows by Dena Blake. Mel Thomas doesn't realize just how unhappy she is in her marriage until she meets Izzy Calabrese. Will she have the courage to overcome her insecurities and follow her heart? (978-1-62639-958-7)

Her Best Friend's Sister by Meghan O'Brien. For fifteen years, Claire Barker has nursed a massive crush on her best friend's older sister. What happens when all her wildest fantasies come true? (978-1-62639-861-0)

Escape in Time by Robyn Nyx. Working in the past is hell on your future. (978-1-62639-855-9)

Forget-Me-Not by Kris Bryant. Is love worth walking away from the only life you've ever dreamed of? (978-1-62639-865-8)

Highland Fling by Anna Larner. On vacation in the Scottish Highlands, Eve Eddison falls for the enigmatic forestry officer Moira Burns despite Eve's best friend's campaign to convince her that Moira will break her heart. (978-1-62639-853-5)

Phoenix Rising by Rebecca Harwell. As Storm's Quarry faces invasion from a powerful neighbor, a mysterious newcomer with powers equal to Nadya's challenges everything she believes about herself and her future. (978-1-62639-913-6)

Soul Survivor by I. Beacham. Sam and Joey have given up on hope, but when fate brings them together it gives them a chance to change each other's life and make dreams come true. (978-1-62639-882-5)

Strawberry Summer by Melissa Brayden. When Margaret Beringer's first love Courtney Carrington returns to their small town, she must grapple with their troubled past and fight the temptation for a very delicious future. (978-1-62639-867-2)

The Girl on the Edge of Summer by J.M. Redmann. Micky Knight accepts two cases, but neither is the easy investigation it appears. The past is never past—and young girls lead complicated, even dangerous lives. (978-1-62639-687-6)

Unknown Horizons by CJ Birch. The moment Lieutenant Alison Ash steps aboard the *Persephone*, she knows her life will never be the same. (978-1-62639-938-9)

The Sniper's Kiss by Justine Saracen. The power of a kiss: it can swell your heart with splendor, declare abject submission, and sometimes blow your brains out. (978-1-62639-839-9)

Divided Nation, United Hearts by Yolanda Wallace. In a nation torn in two by a most uncivil war, can love conquer the divide? (978-1-62639-847-4)

Fury's Bridge by Brey Willows. What if your life depended on someone who didn't believe in your existence? (978-1-62639-841-2)

Lightning Strikes by Cass Sellars. When Parker Duncan and Sydney Hyatt's one-night stand turns to more, both women must fight demons past and present to cling to the relationship neither of them thought she wanted. (978-1-62639-956-3)

Love in Disaster by Charlotte Greene. A professor and a celebrity chef are drawn together by chance, but can their attraction survive a natural disaster? (978-1-62639-885-6)

Secret Hearts by Radclyffe. Can two women from different worlds find common ground while fighting their secret desires? (978-1-62639-932-7)

Sins of Our Fathers by A. Rose Mathieu. Solving gruesome murder cases is only one of Elizabeth Campbell's challenges; another is her growing attraction to the female detective who is hell-bent on keeping her client in prison. (978-1-62639-873-3)

Troop 18 by Jessica L. Webb. Charged with uncovering the destructive secret that a troop of RCMP cadets has been hiding, Andy must put aside her worries about Kate and uncover the conspiracy before it's too late. (978-1-62639-934-1)

Worthy of Trust and Confidence by Kara A. McLeod. Special Agent Ryan O'Connor is about to discover the hard way that when you can only handle one type of answer to a question, it really is better not to ask. (978-1-62639-889-4)

Amounting to Nothing by Karis Walsh. When mounted police officer Billie Mitchell steps in to save beautiful murder witness Merissa Karr, worlds collide on the rough city streets of Tacoma, Washington. (978-1-62639-728-6)

Crescent City Confidential by Aurora Rey. When romance and danger are in the air, writer Sam Torres learns the Big Easy is anything but. (978-1-62639-764-4)